midnight sky

a McKenna chronicle

midnight sky

a McKenna chronicle

elizabeth miller

This book is a work of fiction. Names, characters, places and incidents are the product of the author's imagination or are used fictitiously. Any resemblance to actual events, locals or persons, living or dead, is coincidental.

Synopsis: Confused and upset by dark revelations, Charlise "Charlie" Carter ended her relationship with the beautiful yet damaged presidential hopeful, Colin McKenna.

But Charlie learns all is not lost, nor was her love given in vain. With a new understanding of how she came into Colin's life, and his true feelings, their sensual affair continues.

Holding on to hope, Charlie gives him her heart and he's promised to protect it *and her*. Yet real danger lurks at every corner, in every city and behind each door. Colin must find a way to keep her safe and by his side, all the while remaining committed to his bid on the White House.

While Colin wrestles with Charlie's security and the campaign, she struggles with new-found fame. Washington demands perfection and she is far from pure. Can Charlie remain true to herself and help Colin realize his dream? Or will outside forces tear them apart for good? Midnight Sky is a story of sacrifice and a love so true, it transcends public persecution and deep-seated insecurities.

acknowledgements

To Bryan, Jackson and Sean who sacrificed their wife and mother to allow me time to live my dream and see it to fruition—thank you. It means more to me than you will ever know. Lauren McKellar, editor extraordinaire. I will be forever grateful for your support, direction and encouragement. No words can express my gratitude. To those who have taken this journey with me – Thank you, thank you, thank you! Your enthusiasm and encouragement keep me going!!!

Xoxo –EM

CONTENTS

PREFACE 10
ONE 17
TWO 30
THREE 42
FOUR 55
FIVE 69
SIX 82
SEVEN 101
EIGHT 113
NINE 129
TEN 146
ELEVEN 158
TWELVE 171
THIRTEEN 181
FOURTEEN 192
FIFTEEN 201
SIXTEEN 216
SEVENTEEN 228
EIGHTEEN 243
NINETEEN 257
TWENTY 267
TWENTY-ONE 279
TWENTY-TWO 298

TWENTY-THREE......308
TWENTY-FOUR......324
TWENTY-FIVE......334

PREFACE

FIVE YEARS AGO – COLIN

THE WORLD STANDS STILL when yours is falling apart. It's something I can't ignore when seconds stretch into minutes and my wife has no explanation for the empty wine bottle next to the bed. The two glasses that go along with it sit in silent condemnation of what just happened here. And it wasn't with me.

My lip curls into a snarl as I take her in. A sheet, snatched up in haste when my early arrival caught her off-guard, is pressed against her breasts. The rise and fall of her chest in rapid succession matches her shifting eyes. I've studied her face and the flush of her body after I made her come—the symptoms are obvious. "Who is he?"

She recoils. Licking her lips, she says, "I . . . it's not what it seems."

I bark out a laugh. "Really? Because it appears as if you just fucked someone in my bed." Walking to the side table, I pick up the bottle and tip it toward her. "Do I know him?"

"Colin, I . . ."

The bottle explodes against the far wall after I hurl it with the force I want to use on the man who took my place. "How long, Abby? Tell me that at least." I study her widened eyes and her shaking head. "Don't lie to me. I'll know and it'll make it worse for you."

"What do you mean?"

I stuff down the growing resentment and straighten my shoulders, as if my game face will tamper the pain of finding out of her infidelity. In one minute I was whole with a wife and daughter, a family, and now? Now, what's left? "Let me be clear, so there's no misunderstanding between us. I want the truth. You're going to tell me who you've been fucking and we'll discuss the freedom you need to keep doing it. Do you understand?"

Slipping from the bed, she takes a step forward and says, "Please. I can explain . . ."

Her approach is met by my retreat into the closet. "Put some clothes on when you do because I can't stand to look at you." I throw her robe into her stomach, and she's forced to let go of the sheet to catch it. She wraps it around her shoulders, and rage rolls through me at the ruddy marks left on her hips.

I snatch clothes from random hangers and stalk toward her. "Better, yet. Put this on." I yank away the terrycloth, and her surprised cry is muffled as I force a sweater over her head and then toss her on the bed. From somewhere deep in my mind the need to calm down presents itself, but I can't. Not with the evidence of her deceit surrounding the flaming curls I've loved for so long.

"Stop, please," Abby says, while trying to push me away with her feet. As she struggles to get her arms into the shirtsleeves I force jeans onto her legs, and then scramble for her hands to press them into the mattress.

Wild eyes meet mine. Our breath crashes together as I look down into her flushed face. Days turned to weeks, and months and then years flash before me, always with Abby in them. I love this woman. I've loved her for so long I don't know how to send her away. She's the mother of my child.

Sara.

"How long?" I grind the words between my teeth and squeeze her wrists.

Her gaze flicks toward the door to the nursery and back to me. "I . . ."

The unspoken answer boils in my stomach. "Is she mine?" At only three months old, it's a fair question.

"I don't know . . ."

Hatred, so much I never knew existed, coils around my spine like a snake ready to strike. And I want to. I want to strangle the answer out of her until it's the one I want to hear. My stomach heaves, and I stare while Abby begins to sob.

"I trusted you," I squeeze the words past my teeth as my fingers sink in to her flesh. "How could you do this?"

She cries out. In seconds I'm on the other side of the room, pacing. What the fuck just happened here? My life is crumbling around me. The anger gives way and I double over as it's forced from my body in a howl. I grip my hair, the pain an anchor holding me in place. When I turn to find her, Abby's watching me and rubbing her wrists.

I fall against the wall and slide down. Staring at my hands, I twist my wedding band around and around. Her "I'm sorry" reaches me too late to mean anything.

"I didn't want to hurt you. It just happened."

Minutes pass before I can answer. I'm stuck in a rerun, watching her scramble, naked, from the tangled sheets. It's like a knife in my heart every time. "And you thought what? That this wouldn't kill me? Is that it?" Her gray eyes are filled with torment, yet I'm numb to it. Yesterday I would have done anything to alleviate her pain. Now she's the cause of all of it: hers and mine. "Why?"

A small bleating cry escapes from her mouth as she slides off the bed to sit in mimicry of me on the other side of the room. "Does it matter?"

"It does to me."

Glancing at the ceiling, she chews on her lip before answering. "Because he was there and you weren't."

"So it's my fault you're a whore?"

Flinching, she swipes tears from her face with her sleeves. "You're gone all the time. If it's not for travel or to campaign, you're at the office . . ."

"So naturally, instead of sharing your needs with your husband, you turned to someone else? Don't make this my issue. I gave you everything."

"It's not enough; you're not enough . . ."

"Excuse me?" I'm up so fast she scrambles to get to her knees before she's yanked to her feet.

“You want the perfect family waiting for you on Sunday afternoons? Well guess what?” Fisting her hand in my shirt, she pulls me closer. “I didn’t wait to fit into your schedule. I want more.”

More? I’ve given Abby years, she’s my world, and she gave herself to someone else. “I thought you were different.” I sigh, and some of my fight goes with it.

Her lip pulls up on a derisive laugh. “Different how? That I wouldn’t find someone else to fulfill the needs you couldn’t meet? Don’t fool yourself. Women want control as much as men; it sometimes comes out in a different way. When you couldn’t give me what I needed, I went and found it myself. And you had no idea. That is my power over you.”

“Secrets and lies? That’s not power—it’s cowardice. You’ve made your choice.”

“Colin, listen . . . we can work on us. I need you . . .”

It’s my turn to recoil. “You need my wallet.” I pry her fingers loose and throw them off.

“That's not fair.”

“Why else did you stay?” The anger streaming through me doesn't alleviate the pain that’s slowly turning into an emptiness I've never felt before. “You hate my job because it takes me away, but you love the lifestyle it offers? Is that it? If not, why are you still here if you've been with someone else for over a year?” The hardest question is yet to come. I've never been afraid of the future because I've been sure of it, where I'm going and whom I'm with. Yet my stomach tugs into a tight knot when I think about what I'm about to ask. "Do you love me?"

Seconds turn into a minute and I have my answer in her quivering chin and downcast eyes. The silence is thick and I choke on it while stumbling away. "Christ, Abby. How did this happen?" Infidelity had never crossed my mind; losing her love is altogether unfathomable.

"You want your career more than me." The nonchalance in her shrug is a twisting of the knife. "It wrecks everything, and the fact you couldn't see it and still don't want to is all I need to know. You don't deserve us."

Something in my chest bristles in acknowledgement. Maybe I don't. Maybe, with the life I lead, it's impossible to have trust, a truth and fidelity I'd thought we shared.

Pushing past me, she says, "I'll stay with my mother. She was expecting me this weekend for a visit. Have your things out when I get back on Sunday." It takes minutes to pack a bag and then tuck a sleepy baby under her chin. Sara's honey-brown eyes gaze back at me and I reach for the chunky fingers waving between us. My gut clenches and something screams to keep her by my side. Instead, I step away and cross my arms. I'll fight for her in court. It's the only way.

I look around the room: the bed that no longer belongs to me, a photo of my family next to the wine glasses, the shattered bottle that feels like my life, and then Abby, wide eyed and breathless.

“This is over,” I say and turn, heading down the stairs for the door.

I let her go. I let them both go.

Standing and staring, I do nothing but watch Abby throw the bag into the trunk and strap my daughter into the car seat. A light mist coats the air and quickly sharpens, the rumbling sky opening its floodgates. The cold rain pelts my skin, yet my heart blisters as I watch Sara cry. Through the deluge her tiny arms appear to reach for me, but that’s not possible—is it?

An overwhelming need to tear her from the car wraps around every muscle in my body, but I don’t move. The tires spin, slipping on the slick street. Lunging forward, the car gains traction and it speeds off, taillights a blurred red in the waning evening light. Gripping my hair, I double over and scream as Abby pulls away, taking my world with her.

A crushing weight settles on my chest and suddenly I can’t breathe.

ONE

PRESENT DAY - CHARLIE

MAY

I GAVE COLIN MCKENNA everything: my past, my present and the hope for a future with him in it. What he returned was a lie. Every word, every touch, every feeling, all of it was to reincarnate what he's missing: Abby.

Charging through the hotel lobby, I race to the door and onto the sidewalk. The rain halts my progress. Tipping my head back, I take in the sting of each drop. It mimics his parting words in a staccato rap. "*Don't do this. I need you to breathe.*"

I study the rolling clouds and the torrent pelting the earth from the greenish, gray sky. It all becomes a blur. Colin and I warmed a blizzard in New York as we came together. It's only fitting that on the day we fall apart the sky does the same.

A soaking chill takes over. I wrap my arms around myself for protection against the weather and the devastation creeping into my heart. How do I move on from this moment? Not just in the physical sense, but more so, how do I let go of what became of my life?

How do I let go of Colin?

I'm caught in this thought as my situation sharpens into focus. There is little movement around me. A few people run for the cover of a nearby awning and into the safety of the bar, pulsing to a heavy beat. When the taxi pulls away from the hotel drive, I'm alone. Abandoned again. It sticks in my throat and I choke on the feeling. Fearing the tears will come, I start across the street to find refuge with the many in a place where I can blend into the background to form a plan.

My first step is met by the progress of a man advancing from the shadows of the alley next to the bar. The second is made into a puddle. *Crap*. I lose my footing as the tenderness surrounding my injured ankle gives way to the slick pavement below. The jarring force to my hip breaking my fall is only overcome by growing anxiety.

The dark figure draws near. His face swallowed by a hood, the waning evening light doing little to convey if he is friend or foe. Colin's duplicity seems simple compared to the fear clawing up my spine. Without him I'm vulnerable, and I feel it more now than ever before.

Bright lights draw my attention when they round the corner. *Double crap*. Scrambling to find my footing, I barely make any progress before being yanked out of harm's way. The car barrels by, horn blaring as reality sets in with the frantic beat of my heart and the panting breath warming my ear. I close my eyes and sink into a calming musk.

Colin.

Every emotion held at bay searches for release. Allowing my chin to fall to my chest, I let them come: shock, distrust, anger, and relief. Tears too. Rolling with the clouds overhead, my shoulders shake with the force and weight they bring.

Tightening his hands around my midsection, he whispers "Charlie" and drags me into the protection of the lobby. "I'm so sorry."

For one minute, I relax into his heat. All of the courage I carried for fifteen years seeps into the carpet, along with the water dripping from my clothes. Since meeting him I've laughed and loved harder than I ever dreamed possible. His gentle kindness and silent strength empowered my new beginning. The pain of our ending is too much to bear.

"Baby." The endearment sparks something inside and I struggle against the whispered word and his grip. As I squirm away from his embrace, he clamps down harder. "Don't. Not here. I'm taking you upstairs."

Anger rips through me, along with what I learned not an hour ago—the look a-like-wife, the folder, his deceit. *He knew everything.* "I'm not going anywhere with you."

"Like hell you're not." In another second, I'm turned and pinned by his eyes: midnight blue and storming with the sky outside. Face to face with the only man I've ever loved, my resolve crumbles and my rage goes with it.

"I don't know how to do this," I say, my fingers twisting into his shirt. "It hurts, Colin, so much."

Pain slices across his features, and his lips tremble with it. He licks them and they fall open as if he wants to say something, but no words come. After another moment and a deep breath, he says, "Let me explain."

When I nod, he takes my bag from around my shoulder and guides me to the elevator with a hand to my lower back. The ride is quiet, as is the walk to the suite. Parting from me when we're just inside the door, he sets my bag down and retrieves a towel and a robe from the bathroom. Careful to keep his gaze anywhere but on mine, he takes off my cardigan, leaving me to stand before him in a silk tank and jeans. His touch is tender as he draws the soft cotton along every inch of exposed flesh and then through my hair.

Without any protest from me, he continues. I don't know why I allow him this intimacy, to remove my clothes one piece at a time, to caress my body with the tips of his fingers and his eyes. He strips me bare emotionally and literally, until I'm naked beneath the robe he wraps around my shoulders and belts across my waist.

The silence stretching between us is broken when he finally looks into my eyes and then says, "I've never felt this way, Charlie. Only you—it's always only been you."

Tears pool in my eyes and I bite my bottom lip to hold back a bigger cry. When I have it under control, I ask, "How can I believe that?"

Cradling my face, he tips my head back and brushes a kiss over my forehead and cheeks, my nose and chin. Hovering over my mouth, he takes a deep breath and then another. His fingers reach into my hair and dig in, holding me in place. "I've never lied to you. I promised to tell you the truth and to that I hold true. I will always protect you. Baby . . ." He brings us nose to nose and then touches my mouth with his. "This is real."

My stomach does a somersault. I want to believe him, I do. But there's so much between us. Entwining my fingers with his, I study him: the earnest weight of his stare, the parted length of his lips and the tongue that glances over the bottom one, and his eyes that widen when mine connect with his. "I need to know."

He breathes out on a sigh. "I'll tell you everything," he says, and then he tugs me over to the sectional. Standing, he waits for me to sit before he does the same, leaving two feet between us.

This is it. What comes next will decide our fate and if there's a possibility of a future. Taking a deep breath, I lay my heart on the line and my voice cracks with the fear it'll never be the same again. "I'm afraid."

Tears that threatened moments ago well and fall over the brink. Sliding down my cheek, the sweet saltiness mixes with the bitterness of a deceit I wish we didn't have to confront. I close my eyes to the pain I see in his, as if he fears what I'll say next. Maybe he should. A part of me, the part afraid to feel and live that seeks the protection of simple days, is screaming for home. The newer, more engaged part, is hanging on the edge of belief. *He would never hurt me*. "I'm so afraid what you're about to say will destroy me. Please . . ."

"Charlie." My whispered name is enough to dislodge the breath stuck in my throat. "I love you."

My face crumbles and a whimper sticks in the space that was just cleared. I've longed to hear those words from him for so long, and now I don't know if I can believe them.

Does he love Abby, or me?

In a heartbeat he's next to me, pressing my face into his chest as I cry, really cry. At once, my hands that were limp in my lap rage against him, fisting in his shirt and wailing against the hard muscle beneath, all the while he whispers in my ear *I'm sorry, don't be afraid, we're good and I love you. I love you. I love you Charlie.*

In time the well runs dry and we just stay pressed together, my sniffles the only thing interrupting the serenity between us. With fingers in my hair, he pulls until my head is tipped back and I'm forced into eye contact. "I love you. I should have said it a long time ago. I'm sorry I didn't and I'm sorry these misunderstandings hurt you."

I tense, as does the hand holding me in place. "Misunderstanding?" I push against his chest, but his arm snakes around my waist and clamps down. "How is a folder depicting my entire life a misunderstanding, Colin? Ella knows about . . . about everything. How is that a misunderstanding? Am I a distraction? Tell me because I need to know."

"Yes, all of them misunderstandings. It's not as complicated as you may believe. Are you ready to listen?"

I nod, but he doesn't let me go. In fact, he pulls me onto his lap and cinches both arms around me. "I sought you out prior to the conference because I wanted to meet you. For no other reason than your style—I was intrigued by it. That and because I thought it'd be a good fit to engage the thirty-and-under crowd in my campaign." He purses his lips at the roll of my eyes. "It's true. If you don't believe even this simple truth, the mountain we're about to climb is going to be exhausting."

I roll my eyes again, but for some reason a wobbly smile comes along with it. "Okay. I believe you, but call me silly for thinking it could have been because I look like your wife."

He growls, a real growl rumbling in his chest, and draws me closer. "That was my deal breaker. I had to make sure the similarities ended there."

My brow tightens down. "What does that mean?"

He smoothes out my forehead, while his falls into three lines. "Charlie," he sighs. "My marriage wasn't as it appeared to be. I didn't even realize it until it was over. I came home early from a trip to Indiana, arrived minutes after Abby's lover left." He continues talking over my gasp. Holy shit—the perfect marriage was not so perfect. "I placed a lot of faith in Abby and our wedding vows. I loved her, and maybe even more than that, I trusted her. As it turns out, she lied. The truth between us, whatever honesty I thought we shared, didn't exist. I was devastated; it was something I'd never do to you." He tips my chin until his intent gaze captures mine. "What you've done is open me up to love again. Abby's infidelity and the consequences of it twisted my perspective on relationships. I didn't believe I deserved one. I gave myself to physical needs only, never emotional."

"Just a 'good fuck'?"

Closing his eyes, his shoulders sag as if a weight has been added to them. “I don’t know how to say this without hurting you.”

“You’ve already hurt me . . .”

He nods. “I said things to John to get him off my back. As I had done before, when we first got together, I thought we’d only have a physical relationship, that you . . .” He shakes his head. “*We* were a distraction from the campaign. But very quickly you became so much more than a casual lover. Almost immediately I didn’t want to be without you, *couldn’t* be without you. That was cemented when you left to visit your family. It was as if you ripped my heart from my chest. I couldn’t breathe without you.” He draws in a deep breath now, as if the memory is suffocating. A small smile pulls on the side of his mouth. “I was under your spell from the very beginning.”

“You liked my leopard print?”

He laughs and the vibration reaches me, pulling out my own tiny smirk. “Yes, and your leather too. But it’s more than that. I tried to stay away from you those first few weeks. The similarities in your appearance to Abby were disturbing. I left to separate you from her. But Charlie, you beguiled me from the moment we met—your impromptu outburst at the press conference, your confidence—everything. I fell for you because you’re all of those things, and nothing like the women I’m surrounded by every day.”

“So why wear the watch from Abby?”

“To do exactly what she asked of me—to remember who she was and that the women I knew didn’t want me, but what I could give them. I gave Abby everything I had, and it wasn't enough. I never want to experience that devastation again."

"I'm sorry."

"You didn't do anything wrong. There's nothing to be sorry for. In fact, you're everything right in my world."

I swallow a sudden lump in my throat. "How . . . why do you have . . . you knew everything about me."

"The folder and all of the contents are from a background check. Everyone, including my closest advisors, is thoroughly investigated prior to working for me. I'm sorry yours included medical information; actually, I was surprised it did. That information should be private."

"It was supposed to be," I whisper, my lip quivering when I do.

Tilting my chin up, he says, "Phil's team is thorough, they have to be. Campaigns are fragile. Because of that they dig so there aren't any surprises. The State kept online records of your time in foster care, and the subsequent investigation into Shane Roberts when your parents reported his actions. It was too easy to find." He sighs when I try to pull away from his grip. "I meant what I said. I wish I could erase the past that haunts you. I can't. What happened to you didn't change my opinion of you when I hired you. I'd be a selfish coward if I let it affect how I feel about you now."

"Why does Ella know?"

He cringes. "John, Ella and Evan review all background checks with me."

I'm on the verge of something and I don't know what it is. Anger that he knew and made me tell him; relief that he did and still wanted to get to know more about me; maybe in part because he didn't hold my past against me. It's so confusing. I feel as if I should strangle him, and at the same time I want to throw my arms around him and never let go. "Why didn't you tell me you knew?"

"How could I? That information is extremely personal. It's yours to tell only when you're ready to share it, not if it's demanded of you."

"Oh." Tears blur my vision. I tuck my head into the crook of his neck, and he rubs my back. Everything he's told me swims around my mind. Abby and the affair, the background check—misunderstandings. All of them? Can it be that simple?

"Why was my picture next to hers on your computer?"

"Ella asked to use my laptop earlier in the day. I had downloaded the picture I took of you this weekend and she saw it. She was infuriated and added a picture of Abby. We argued about it then, and again after the meeting when you were here."

"Why does she care you may have moved on?"

"It's a long story."

"I have time."

"Basically she's been pissed since I started dating her sister and not her. When it turned out I was completely wrong about Abby's character, she learned to torture me with it."

Stretching over to the side table, he grabs the leopard bracelet he gave me not too long ago. "This belongs to you."

"No." I try to scramble away, but he captures my arm.

"Look at me," he says, and I blink him into focus. His tongue sweeps out to lick his bottom lip.

"For generations the men in my family have been silent with their deepest emotions. My grandfather started what became a tradition with the McKenna men, by giving my grandmother something similar to this when he knew he loved her. My mother has one, and yes, I gave one to Abby too. It's buried with Sara where a part of my heart will always remain."

I stare wide-eyed as he slips it on my wrist.

"You captured my heart from the very beginning. It will belong to you for all of time. Charlie." His chest rises on a deep inhale. "Baby . . . would you give me the greatest honor by holding it in safe keeping?"

"Colin . . ." I breathe his name on a whisper. The something I was verging on crashes around me.

It is this simple. Everything he's told me had been there all along. From the beginning I knew he'd run a background check prior to my employment, as he had for all staff members. I hadn't known it was complete, or that it was shared with his team. But in hindsight, that's not surprising. John, Ella and Evan are his closest confidants. On the other hand, our relationship was founded on a physical connection. Colin had made that clear. It morphed into something entirely different when real feelings became entwined and changed the direction in which we were headed.

The truth only seems crude when wound into a ball of hatred meant to injure. I've no doubt Ella knew I was here. Just as my bag gave me away to Colin, she must have seen it too.

I study his face. The beautiful, sculpted edges of his jaw are drawn tight with anxiety. I know this man. He's the one who introduced me to passion and love. I see him when I close my eyes to dream of a future I never thought I'd have.

"There's more to truth than words. Don't hide anything from me again."

He nods. "Never."

"Okay."

"Okay?"

My smile is fragile, pieced together from what was a broken heart. "I love you."

Relief flashes across his features in an instant, and in the next his whispered "Thank God" is lost against my mouth. Anger, fear, and love combine into a savage connection. I can't help but wrap my hands into the soft curl of his hair, pulling as I have done so many times before and for a moment, feared I never would again. He drags me closer, my knees sinking down on either side to straddle him.

A low growl moves through his chest and then somehow I'm on my back, pinned beneath him. God, he feels good between my thighs, rotating his hardening length . . . yes . . . right . . . there. I gasp. Our lips part, and he watches as he does it again.

"Mine," he says, as the perfect pitch of his hips sends every nerve into a tingling sense of awareness. "No more running."

I shake my head, completely distracted by the swivel of his hips. "I promise."

"I'm giving you my truth. I lost trust in a woman I loved long ago. I'm out on a limb here, Charlie, and I'm asking for you to believe in me—for my word to be enough."

I nod and draw his face to mine, nose to nose. "It is. I believe in you." And I do. When his mouth claims mine this time, he's hungry for it, for me. His touch is everywhere: my hair, along my neck and arms, my breasts and stomach.

A never-ending, shrill siren fills the room but I'm not distracted. "No," I beg, when Colin is and begins to pull away.

"Charlie, something's wrong . . ." His warning is overpowered by the loud banging on the door.

"Colin," Evan shouts.

Jumping up, Colin rushes over, and Evan springs in as soon as the latch is released.

He glances at me and then does a double take. "We have to get out of here."

The lights flicker on and off. My pulse is pounding; I can't understand what's going on.

"Tornado," he says, just as guests run down the hall.

TWO

***OH MY GOD.* COLIN** is next to me in the blink of an eye, pulling me to my feet, his arm around my waist guiding me out the door. We're running for the stairs with at least twenty other people when the ringing is overcome by an overbearing thundering, pummeling like a train.

"Colin?" My scream is lost amongst the others as we sink into darkness. An eerie illumination sprouts up from the emergency lights peppered along the floor.

"I'm here." His arm tightens around my waist. "Get into the stair well," he grounds out. Pushing me into the corner, he tucks me under the rise of the steel casing, away from the wall. We're buffeted by a mass of strangers and Evan, all held hostage by the unbelievable reality that's taking place outside. Colin's body hovers over mine as the deafening noise closes in and drowns out the fear-filled cries echoing off the walls. His arm tightens and I grip it, as he clenches us against the railing.

There isn't time to be scared. The hotel shakes, groaning under Mother Nature's power, yet it bears the weight of the storm. Seconds become minutes as it passes. Close but not on top of us, the force reverberates through every breath.

As suddenly as it began, it ends. The electric current of the wind passes by and the air stills; the only sound is the rising chatter of guests as they process what just happened.

Turning, I grab Colin's neck, holding him in a fierce hug. His nose presses into my hair and we remain clenched together for another minute until he rises, with me held to his side. Gripping hands, we follow Evan and the remaining crowd down the hall. The door to the suite was left ajar in our haste to leave. It's dark, but untouched—everything as it was when we rushed out only minutes ago. A surreal fog lies heavy among us and we remain silent knowing there must be devastation outside of our protective walls.

I jump and catch my gasp before it's out when a singular lamp pops on in the corner. Sinking onto the sectional, I wait for Colin to join me, but he begins to pace instead, his forefinger and thumb pulling at his bottom lip while he contemplates our circumstances. I catch Evan's eye when he takes a seat at the far end and winks.

"It's official."

"What is?"

"You," he says with deadpan seriousness. "You're officially back on the campaign trail; vacation's over. Only you could induce tornados to hit at the exact spot we're scheduled to tour."

My mouth falls open. "You can't possibly blame the weather on my luck."

Chuckling, he replies, "Sure I can. Without you and your luck, life is not nearly as interesting. If there's an earthquake when we're in California, you'll need to turn yourself into the authorities . . ."

"That's enough, Evan." Colin's stern reprimand has both our eyes snapping to find his.

"Just saying it like I see it."

Colin's look silences any further retort, his phone already up to his ear. Miraculously, he finds a signal and calls for a damage assessment while heading to the bedroom. With a brief glance to Evan, who is now on his cell, I head to the window for my own evaluation. I'm shocked by what I see.

The midnight sky is crying; thick bountiful tears pour and pound into the earth. Wind howls and the trees lining the city streets bend with it, bowing under the pressure.

Emergency lights flicker against the rain-slicked pavement, and the distant wail of sirens reach into the protection of the hotel. The bar that at one time was alive with the pulse of music lost its awning, and the front windows are blown out. Patrons hover inside, some being treated by EMT.

It could have been me. I shiver, and push away from the violent weather to find Colin in the bedroom. My eyes flash from his pacing form to the computer on the desk, still humming in silent censure of what I found there just hours ago. I'd acted as judge and jury, convicting him without allowing him to speak so I could understand his truth.

My eyes sink closed and my shoulders go with them. I'm new to this. A relationship is novel and unknown. A common thread woven within my parents' and grandparents' marriages is trust. For Colin and

I to have any chance at all we need to have faith and believe in each other.

I'm irritated I took Ella's venom at face value, yet I didn't give Colin an opportunity to explain. I won't make the same mistake again.

Colin's constant monologue draws me from my stupor. I watch the man who will one day be the commander in chief. There's no doubt in my mind. He asks the right questions, listens and directs, quick to formulate a plan of action to assist neighboring communities. He unabashedly calls in favors and pushes others to do the same. In less than thirty minutes, he has a full-blown army coming in to provide aide.

After the last call to an acquaintance who is the mayor of a town close by, he tosses the phone onto the bed and unzips his pants. Slipping thick muscled legs from the fine cotton, he's left in tight black boxer briefs and a white button-up. It's not the right moment, but my body doesn't care. My stomach flutters. Colin catches my gawk and the corner of his mouth lifts. He reaches for me, and tucks my head into the crook of his neck. I hold on tight, snuggling into his heat.

"I love breathing you in," he murmurs, nose buried in my drying hair.

"Hmmm, I was just thinking the same thing."

Tipping my chin, he leans in and brushes a kiss against my forehead, and nose and then my mouth.

"We're okay?" His eyes sweep over my face and settle on my eyes.

I nod, because we are. "I trust you."

He lets out a breath and presses his lips to mine once more. But that's it. A brief touch and he moves over to his suitcase for a pair of jeans. "I need to go. From what I just learned, entire towns are destroyed. I'll do whatever I can to help."

"I'm going with you." I turn to find my bag. My progress is halted at the door when he spins me so we're face to face.

"No, you stay here. I'll be back as soon as I can."

My brow falls. "I can help too."

"It's dangerous, Charlie. The weather is too unpredictable; there could be more storms rolling through. I won't put you in harms way."

Raising my hand to his cheek I hold him, caressing his skin and the new growth of his dark beard. He nuzzles into me and I smile. "I understand your need to protect me"—he turns and kisses my palm—"but I'm going with you. We're together and it means I support you with everything you do, including tornados and helping in the recovery."

His eyes fire at my response, but I'm more surprised by his reaction. Crushing his mouth to mine, he possesses me. Protect, cherish, love—I clearly understand everything he communicates with his body. It's been here all along, the true meaning of us. I'm breathless and dumbfounded when he pulls away.

Smiling at my stunned expression, he turns me toward the door, swatting my butt and nudging me into the main room. "Hurry up and change. We'll leave when you're done." He laughs when I stumble and roll my eyes. Easier said than done after Mr. McPerfect manages to jumble every one of my coherent thoughts, causing my brain synapses to fire irregularly.

ooo

An hour later, the devastation is real. May in Arkansas is a nightmare, and heartbreak inescapable. The unexpected weather pattern rolled through this state and several others, wreaking havoc in a path of destruction. Eight tornados passed through various counties over the course of two hours. It's too soon to understand the extent of the turmoil, but early reports indicate it's widespread and severe. Too much lies in ruin to believe otherwise.

Drake drove us a short distance to meet Jillian Browning, Arkansas's governor. She's come to a town just outside of Little Rock that took the brunt of the storm. Rescue vehicles arrive to brighten the scene and spotlight just how devastated the city is. Nothing is whole. By now, the media and police are everywhere. We find Governor Browning coordinating relief efforts in a makeshift tent. Colin greets her with a friendly but stressed hello, before turning to me.

"It's nice to meet you, Governor. I'm so sorry we're here under these circumstances," I say.

"Please, call me Jillian, and what matters now is that you're here. We're happy to have the help." As the two of them begin a conversation about the path of the tornado and what needs exist within the town, I slip from Colin's grip and wander away. My attention is drawn to a woman hovering over the mud, tears streaming down her face.

Kneeling next to her, I ask, "Can I help you?"

“It . . . it’s all gone.” She pulls a photo from the mud. “All the memories gone,” she whispers.

“Let’s keep looking; we’ll find them together.” I swallow my emotion, thankful for everything I have.

Mementos from so many families are strewn around, torn, buried in dirt, some salvageable, others destroyed. We work to dig through the rubble and save as much as we can. I lose track of time and Colin, lost in the search for anything that means something to someone. Pictures, books, birth certificates, cell phones, everything at one time found in a home now lies in the mud. While digging out a jewelry-box I hear what I think is a cat mewling. Following the weak sound, I start to climb a mound of debris.

With each step I take, the cries grow louder, and the hill steeper. I glance around for Colin, knowing he won’t be happy with my precarious perch, but continue on when he’s not in sight. Convincing myself I’ll be done before he looks for me, I take two final steps before dropping to my knees. Sweat beads on my brow while I struggle to pull away wood fragments, pink painted drywall, shingles and clothing, and dig beyond what was someone’s bedroom. Through so much destruction I focus on the one thing I may be able to save. A large beam lies over the arms of a chair, providing just enough protection for a brown and white kitty that remains cradled in the cushion, maybe where she was sleeping when the tornado hit. She appears uninjured, but scared. I scoop her up and she claws her way into the crook of my neck, shaking.

"Shh," I whisper, soothing her with a stroke down her back. "It's okay. Let's get you down and we'll find your people."

Turning slowly, my head spins when faced with ten feet of jagged wood and siding. I'm not much for heights and I've gone higher than I thought. I take my time, as it's much harder to balance with my new friend clutched to my chest. The end is almost near, just a little over four feet to go, when the voice of a little girl reaches me.

"Murphy!"

Ah, she is a he. "You should have told me," I scold him while my hand runs along his fur. Lost in mumbled conversation with the cat, I fail to study my next step. Placing my weight down on a wet board, it snaps. A small, surprised cry escapes my lips, warning others of my impending tumble. One arm, stretched to the side, rounding like a windmill, is not enough to find my balance and I pitch forward.

The landing is hard but familiar, saving me from the sharp pierce of pain I was expecting. It seems he's never far away. A familiar scent washes over me and I relax into him before it hits me. *I'm going to be in trouble for this*. Confirming the thought, his low growl rumbles against my chest. I can't help my smile and decide to enjoy the hard press of his body against mine, even with Murphy squeezed between us. Sweeping my legs up, he takes the final few steps to the ground. I savor the flight, tucking my head into his neck.

Content to stay in his arms, it's a long moment before I open my eyes, prepared to face his anger. Instead I'm met by a somewhat amused expression; the blues I love so much are alight with mischief. *I need to use this to my advantage.*

"Thank you for saving me, and Murphy too," I whisper, batting my lashes to avoid trouble.

Colin actually rolls his eyes and my smile broadens when his nose dips into my hair. His voice is a sweet vibration against my ear. "Saving you is becoming a full-time job, or at least a fulfilling hobby I could use to extend my resume." He squeezes before lowering me to the ground. "No. More. Climbing."

His tone leaves little room for negotiation, and had we been alone it may have come with a swift crack to my ass. *Hmmm, now there's something.*

"Yes, sir." I would add my mock salute, but we have an audience so I smile again and lower the kitty from my shoulder.

By now, Murphy's people are surrounding us, along with a small crowd. *Lovely.* What I hoped would be a quick trip has turned into a media event with Colin at the center.

"This little guy must belong to you," I say, kneeling in front of the small girl. Tears rush to my eyes at the joy I find in hers.

"Thank you," she sobs into his fur after I hand him over.

"You're so welcome." I rub her shoulder and with one last touch to Murphy's fur, I stand to greet her parents who are now hovering behind the reunited pair.

ooo

The sun has long since risen. Heat and humidity slowly enveloped the rescue and recovery efforts. Volunteers and residents powered through clean up, and worked to confirm everyone has a place to sleep. Evan left a few hours ago with Drake to adjust Colin's schedule and make sure the hotel was stable for a continued stay. When Drake returned for us, we'd visited a few more communities where Colin was interviewed by various media stations before heading back ourselves. I've already reviewed the pictures I took for his social media sites. It was a careful balance to find the right shot—never wanting to exploit those who are suffering, yet needing to capture Colin doing what he does best: connecting with people and helping them find their way.

Now I'm barely conscious in the back of the SUV, snuggled into his side with an arm draped around me. Exhaustion sets in and I drift between sleep and the draw of his voice. He's forever on the phone, ensuring everything that can be done is being done. The continuous monologue of his conversation with a fellow state representative is a lullaby. Burrowing down, a small moan escapes when I stretch my well-worn muscles.

"Hey, you okay?"

I love the weight of his hand on my arm as he draws me even closer.

"Mmm, I am now." My fingers find their way around his waist, digging below the loop of his jeans in search of skin. I snuggle deeper, breathing in his familiar musk. He smells too good, stirring emotions that have no place visiting this desolation.

"I need to get you to the hotel so you can sleep." His lips brush into my hair.

"I'm fine. I'll follow you anywhere."

"Mmm, I like that, but it doesn't change my mind. You need to rest, so we're going back to the hotel. Evan called; it didn't sustain any structural damage."

"You're coming to bed too?" I ask while stifling a yawn. "I'm hoping you're not too tired to teach me a lesson."

His laugh jostles my head and makes me smile. "Yes, baby. I'm coming to bed too."

We remain glued together through the remainder of the ride and up to our room. His arms are wrapped around my waist and his nose pressed into my hair as we stand together in the hallway, while he swipes us in.

"Let's get a shower and go to bed," I whisper.

"Best idea I've heard all day."

We stumble into the suite. Just as I step up to kiss him, his damn phone rings.

"You're going to have to turn that thing off if you want to get any rest today."

"This will be the last call. Go get the water warmed up and I'll be with you in just a minute. I promise." His smile settles nicely in my lower abdomen. Colin's promises are always executed with perfection and have me begging for more.

My smile must say it all as he laughs, welcoming my kiss on the cheek, just as I appreciate the smack on the ass I was missing from earlier. *Nice.*

Heading first to the couch for my bag, I pause and look around. It's not here. *That's odd.* Thinking back, I'm sure this is where I placed it. I grabbed my clothes and took them into the bedroom to change, just after Colin finished dressing. One last glance around the sofa confirms it's definitely not here. I must have taken my bag into the room with me and forgotten I did. It's been a completely surreal twenty-four hours—surely no one would hold a small memory lapse against me.

Pulling open the doors to the bedroom, both of them at the same time, I expect the giant bed I saw yesterday, but all I see is red.

THREE

WHEN SHANE ROBERTS BEGAN visiting my room, I found a place to go and it wasn't a happy one. At the time nothing in my life invoked happiness and what he did to me so horrible I had to find an escape. The place I would go was somewhere in my mind; it safely sequestered what was left of my sanity and insulated it from the horror of the physical act of rape. I learned to call upon it and find it instantly. It was the only way I made it through—that is, until Ali saved me.

With little thought, I search and find that lonely place now. I need it to see through all of the red. It's like looking through someone else's eyes, not my own. A looking glass fogs the outer corners so everything resembles an old movie.

The once white room is splashed in deep red. It appears to be blood, but this is a movie so it can't possibly be true. Nailed to the walls by hands and feet are baby dolls, some with heads and some without. Those with them have lifeless, crazy eyes staring straight ahead. I bet they'd follow me if I moved, but I can't. I'm rooted to the spot. Unable to step away—unable to speak, just staring. Red covers the lifeless bodies, so many of them I can't count.

Amongst the dolls are pictures of me, some with Colin, and others solitary visions of Charlie Carter. They're precious, really, a chronicle of our time together, beginning with my days at campaign headquarters last February and then from each stop of the tour. There are many of Colin and me in New York, the first as we walked hand in hand down the steps of the plane, my hair flying manically in the wind. Oh, and a gorgeous one of us in the newly falling snow, Colin kissing me as the flakes fall around us. And so it goes, picture after picture, ending at the hotel pool in Florida with Colin protecting me because my suit slipped and I was exposed—caught on camera, all of it.

The piece de résistance hangs centered above the bed. A blown-up shot of me, babies pinned all around, the photo torn at the neck with red oozing from the now jagged space. Above it, in red of course, is a message.

An eye for an eye

An eye for an eye—the punishment must exactly fit the crime. I killed my baby, and now someone wants to kill me? Through the camera lens I'm drawn to the bed where my clothes have been dumped, some ripped, all destroyed by red. Bile rises, my hand flying up to my mouth to hold it in at the sight of a solitary rose placed on the pillow where my head would lie.

Fear takes over and my heart races. Red, so much red I'm drowning in it. When my knees give out, I grab the doorframe to catch myself, and choke on a cry. The wood is wet to the touch. Warm, thick blood paints my fingers, so heavy it oozes between them and drips down my arm. The weight pressing in on my chest is suffocating. Short, jagged breaths are lodged in my throat, pumping to the same beat of the babies crying. I can hear them dying and looking to me for life. *Save me, save me* . . . but it's not their voice. It's mine.

"Charlie? What's wrong?" Colin is a small hint of sound, barely recognizable while I'm in my faraway space. I try to respond, I do, but words won't form. The best I can offer is a mournful whimper, which sounds dejected as it echoes against the walls.

His hands reach me first before the harsh and much louder expletive. "Holy fuck."

From red to black my vision is cleared when I'm wrapped tight into his chest. I suspect we're moving, but I don't actually feel anything. This is the beauty of the faraway place—sticks and stones *won't* break my bones and words will never hurt me. Words, grunts, tearing pain, nothing. I *feel* nothing. I can make as if it never happened.

Only Shane Roberts did happen, and the red room does too. For now it's all very far away, tucked nice and neat in a pile I won't unfold until I'm forced to.

His voice once again becomes a soothing monologue. I'm snug and protected, burrowed into his side, his grip on my shoulder powerful. Colin is my happy, secure place. For him I would come out of my safety zone, but he hasn't asked me to so I'll stay happily tucked in. I don't know how much time passes before there are more voices than people I know—Evan for sure, Drake and John Montgomery, too. Hotel security and the manager arrive shortly after the others. I vaguely hear a call to the local police department and then it's all a blur—the many shocked curses, a rehash of the red room with details I don't want to hear.

All too soon I'm asked to come out and play. Join, what is very reminiscent of Our Gang, to dissect what occurred and when. The only player missing is Alfalfa, but I'm sure he'll be here soon. I laugh out loud thinking of the old show characters and crack up again as everyone's eyes round with worry. Spanky, that's it. The chubby security guard is for sure Spanky, and the giggles continue. Absolutely they must think I've gone into hysterics.

Maybe I have. An unearthly need to jump out of my skin clamps down, yet I'm paralyzed, stuck in a nightmare covered in red. Sweat dews on my forehead and the slow drip down my temple is enough to drive out a cry. But I swallow it down before it can escape. Deeper, I dive into myself so the pain of my tense muscles will ease, along with the metallic tang I can't seem to wipe from my tongue.

Colin whispers comforting words in my ear. *Don't be afraid. Answer a few questions. Can you do this for me*? Others are stating the obvious. *Not injured. Shock. Get her out of here*. They're all asking the unknown—*who hates Charlie Carter? Why would someone do this?* My answers are the same as everyone else's. I don't know, I don't know—I DON'T KNOW! I lose my mind or my temper, or maybe both when four different people ask the same question.

Deal with it Carter, you're a big girl. Clarity returns. I say goodbye to the faraway place and stop to think who's stalking me.

I stand and move away from Colin. His startled expression barely registers in my peripheral vision. Hours ago, I committed to fight for my relationship with him and I will. No one, not Ella, not John Montgomery or a crazy stalker will separate us. I will not fall victim to fear. Pacing as Colin does so often, I peer now and again at the red room. It's gross, but I see it for what it is: paint, pictures and dolls. Colin's hovering close, but I wave him off as I think about who did this.

There's the obvious—Ella. But it's too obvious, and she wasn't the person taking pictures of me at the schoolhouse. No, it's not her. It's a man. A stranger, maybe, but how would he know about my past? Colin's background check pulled it up, but I doubt the everyday person would know to look for my records. John Montgomery? He would never hurt Colin's chances at the presidency, and this could. Any distraction could pull him away from the campaign. Alex Miller? Maybe, but what would stalking me accomplish for him? Shane Roberts? The blood drains from my face and my gait falters. Has he found me? The shear possibility of that has the hair on my neck standing on end, and then it hits me out of nowhere. "Sara Abbott."

"What did you say?" Colin's voice is unusually terse and much too loud. He very rarely takes this tone with me. Evan, who is behind him, lays a hand on his shoulder. Colin closes his eyes and pauses before asking. "Charlie, repeat what you said? Please . . ."

"I think I may know who's doing this. Well, not really, but it's something to think about anyway." I look around and everyone; the police officer, Evan, Drake, hotel security, the hotel manager—Our

Gang—all nod their heads with encouragement. Everyone except Colin. He's standing rigid with his fists clenched by his side.

"Who?"

"Sara Abbott," I rush, at the same time looking for my laptop. "She sent me an e-mail message in New York via the campaign Facebook page. It said *'I know who you are and I know what you did'.*" Returning to Colin's side I close out the rest of the *Little Rascals* to concentrate on him.

Horror.

Tendons are standing taut in his neck, his pulse visibly pounding in rhythm with my own frantic heart. He's not just worried as he was minutes ago—now fear grips him.

I forge on. "Look, I'll show you. When the site first went live I received a message. I erased it because it was inappropriate for your page, and frankly hurtful for me, but I took a screen shot of it. I don't know why. For some reason, I thought I should. Whoever sent this message created the red room; I'm sure of it. Maybe if we backtrack through an online history we can pinpoint the sender. Look . . ." I've pulled out my laptop, holding it at his eye level with the opened e-mail at the forefront.

He's staring, unfocused at my face.

"What?" I'd thought this might be a breakthrough. I didn't think it would have this effect on him. "Do you know who this is?"

His eyes finally find mine—they're light, drained of color, like the rest of his face. I drop the computer on a nearby chair and reach for him. Holding his cheeks between my hands, I run my thumbs over his lips.

"Talk to me. Do you know who Sara Abbott is?"

He moans and shakes with a violent shiver. "Yes . . ." It feels like a lifetime before he finally croaks out, "She's my daughter."

ooo

Hours pass, and finally it's the three of us. Drake and Evan stayed behind after the others left, helping to move Colin's things into a new suite. Most of my belongings are held as evidence or they were destroyed, including all of the clothes packed in my bag. Bye, bye magenta pants. I wouldn't let Colin cut them from my body when he was treating my burned ankle, but the red room took care of them instead. Drake drove over to the plane to pick up my larger suitcase and he dropped it off moments ago. Now the poor guy and another security guard from Phil's team are camped outside of our door for the night.

We've been surviving these last few hours on adrenaline alone. Colin hasn't slept in almost forty-eight hours. Couple that with the stress of the last twenty-four, and it's taking a toll. He's exhausted and I'm worried about him. A haunting look set in on his face when I'd mentioned the name Sara Abbott—now it's a permanent fixture. Thankfully he's regained some color, but it includes dark smudges beneath his eyes and he's gaunt. He's become more and more distant as the night progressed. I can feel it. Our eyes connect rarely, and he hasn't touched me in hours. My hand on his elicits a flinch.

The day was so busy we haven't eaten a proper meal, partaking in snacks when they were available. Colin insisted on ordering dinner before bed, providing an opportunity for him to dissect what we've learned about the incident with Evan. I'm along for the ride at this point, listening rather than contributing to the conversation. Evan's eating vigorously—nothing seems to stop him from that task—and Colin's more robotic approach to his meal is telling. It's for sustenance, not enjoyment. He glances at me while I push my food around my plate. His mouth opens as if to speak at the same time his brow crumbles, but he turns away, engaging Evan instead of me.

"I want the security video sent to the FBI."

"Let the investigators take care of this. You have enough on your plate as is. The detective will get the surveillance tapes to them and they'll follow up with information."

"You know I can't just let it go. There's a psycho waiting at every goddamn city for us." He throws his napkin on his plate and leans back in his chair. Gripping the bridge of his nose, he exhales. "I want this bastard off the streets and away from Charlie."

"They'll get him. Whoever this is, he was stupid enough to be caught on camera outside of your room. He's getting sloppy. Detective Sloan's men found the cart he used to get his shit up here. They're dusting for fingerprints now. Give it time."

"I don't have time. Everywhere we go she's a lamb waiting for slaughter."

I cringe, but neither of them acknowledges me.

"Phil's men will watch her."

Colin growls. "I'm not impressed with Phil or the protection provided thus far."

"He's the best in the country. They've intervened in every way up until now. We couldn't have planned any different."

"The bastard walked right into our room and stole her key card."

"He did, you're right. But could you or Phil have anticipated a tornado rolling through the area? No. He got lucky. Your door was open and he walked in and got it. That's not going to happen again."

"You're overlooking one important factor. He was watching so closely he knew when we ran from the room. How in the hell? Where is this fucker hiding that's he's on top of us, and how's he getting the information?"

"Sloan is looking at the hotel guest list. He'll pull names and cross reference to the different cities we've been in."

"I want a list of campaign staff members that have access to my schedule—the hotels, the stops, the exact travel schedule—everything." Colin slams his fist on the table and I jump, startled.

"What are you saying?"

"I'm saying," he grounds out and leans in, "that this is too close to home. He knows everything about my schedule. He knows too much for this to be random." Some silent message passes between the two and there's a possibility I'll get whiplash from looking back and forth to both of them to decipher the meaning.

Evan counters with, "You have to let the investigators do their job so you can do yours."

Colin slumps in his seat, eyes flicking toward mine and back to Evan. "I can't wait for them to figure this out. I won't have her in danger."

"Hey, right here, remember?" Their heads turn at the same time, staring. "*She* is just fine."

Colin's eyes close and he takes a deep breath. "For now."

"I agree with Evan on this one." I lay my hand over his, which is clenched on the table. He tenses beneath my touch. "I'm fine. Nothing is going to happen to either one of us." I hope my tone is convincing, for him and for me. This is scary shit.

Video surveillance from a hallway camera caught a man dressed in janitorial gear enter our room just after six this morning. He pushed a large cart housing all of the items needed for his creation. As it was when he took pictures of me at the school, a baseball hat was pulled tight to hide his face. An oversized uniform protected his build. Mystery man remains a mystery.

He's watching us closely. A long, drawn-out chill travels down my spine at the thought. *He's out there*. He's always one step behind us, or maybe in step with us. The connection to Sara Abbott is disturbing and references Colin's past, not mine, but the babies in the red room feel connected directly to me, not Colin. Could it be about both of us? It's so confusing, and something I can't figure out tonight.

When Colin drops his head into his hands, I know it's time to intervene. "Sorry Evan. As much as I love you, you're not invited to stay for the night." My attempt to lighten the conversation is met by a smirk from Evan and a hint of thanks in the depth of Colin's eyes. He needs sleep, and hopefully me.

"I'll call you tomorrow. With rest, this will all look better in the morning." Evan places a hand on Colin's shoulder and then he's out the door. As soon as it latches behind him, I pounce. We need to talk.

"Are you going to tell me what's going on?" I ask. Colin's blank stare is concerning and so unlike him. It continues for long moments. His eyes are tense, and it's not just with worry. "Talk to me," I whisper.

Swiveling away to stare out the window into the dark night, he sighs. "Sara Abbott McKenna—she was named after my grandmother and Abby's. Abbott is her grandmother's family name."

"Go on," I prompt when he pauses for too long.

He pulls at his bottom lip, rolling it between forefinger and thumb. "The last time I saw Sara, Abby and I'd had a fight. She . . . she was having an affair and confessed she wasn't sure if the baby was mine. I was devastated, but it didn't change my feelings for Sara."

Colin's face hardens, his jaw clenching while his top lip curls. "She was mine," he growls. In the span of a minute, what started as possessive anger fades into utter devastation. He pales and takes a deep, shaking breath.

"I planned on fighting for her in court, so instead of arguing with Abby I let them go . . . I watched Abby drive away." He looks over, blinking rapidly as if he's just now seeing me. "She had my whole world in that car and I didn't do a goddamn thing to stop her. I did nothing."

His eyes connect with mine and they change from clear to clearly tormented. This is a man in pain. I move to sit in front of him, grabbing both of his hands, but his remain listless.

"Minutes after they left, Abby ran a red light. It was pouring rain and she was on the phone; she didn't stop. A truck sideswiped the car . . . I didn't fight for Sara, I let Abby take her and she died."

I feel his pain acutely—it washes over me and lodges as a lump in my throat. "It's not your fault."

He's standing in an instant, pacing, his voice gaining momentum. "The hell it's not. I watched Abby strap her in the car seat and I knew it was wrong. It . . . was . . . wrong. I didn't fight for her. I didn't do it, Charlie. I let my feelings take over and I gave up." His hands are buried in his hair and he doubles over, breathing heavy. I stand and wrap my arms around his waist, pressing into his back so he'll feel the comfort I so desperately want to pass from me to him. My fingers clasp together in front of him, holding tight as he shakes.

"I loved her so much, with everything I had. I would have given my life for hers but instead I did nothing," he says, and then groans.

"You didn't do anything wrong."

"That's just not true. I bear the responsibility of her death," he whispers, his hands seeking and clutching mine. For a brief moment he squeezes, but then he unlocks my grip and pushes away, moving to stand on the opposite side of the room. He's become void, loosening his features into an expressionless expression. All but his eyes—they always give him away. They're determined and distraught at the same time. Fear begins to grip my heart, restricting blood and oxygen. This can't happen again. He's done this before, pushed me away because of the past, withdrawing completely. But this is different. Something has changed.

Something is very wrong.

"Sara was mine to love, to care for and protect. I failed her."

"The burden you carry is too heavy, Colin. There's no way you could've predicted what would happen that day. It's tragic, but not your fault," I plead with him to see the truth.

"Every instinct told me to get Sara out of the car, but I ignored it and let her go." His chest rises and falls with deep breaths.

"It's happening again," he says in a slow monotone.

"What is?" My heart decides in this moment to thrum, pushing the once stilted blood so quickly all my senses are heightened.

"I don't deserve you," he whispers.

"What are you talking about?"

"I'm going to lose the only thing I love."

"No," I cry. "Why would you say that? You're not going to lose me. Not ever."

Unable to contain his emotions any longer, his face slowly crumbles. He's a man burning on the stake. "Oh God, Charlie." His hands are in his hair again, eyes darkening to depths I don't understand. A painful moan prefaces words I never thought I'd hear him say.

"I have to let you go."

FOUR

"WHAT? NO!" I'M ON him in a second, grabbing onto the front of his shirt and catching eye contact. "No, you can't say that."

"Don't you see what this is about? Someone hates me, and he's using you to get to me. I knew it, just as I knew I shouldn't let Sara leave with Abby. Now it's happening again. I can't let him hurt you. I would rather die."

His pained stare reaches into me, twisting my stomach in knots. I'm alone in this fight. He's a statue, white, chilled and hollow. Unmoving. Our singular contact is from my grip, and I'm not letting go. Not ever.

"The only way I can really protect you is to let you go. If you're not with me, you'll be safe. The campaign, my life . . . all I do is hurt you."

With my head shaking, I plead with him. "Stop this. You're not making any sense. We have no idea who's doing this or why. It has as much to do with me as it does you. The babies on the wall—that could be about my past, not yours."

He presses the palms of his hands against his eyes and rocks on his feet. "This is about me; I feel it. It doesn't matter where you are, if you're with me, you're in danger. It's not safe. I will not disregard my instincts as I did with Sara, and let someone hurt you. That leaves few options, and only one will truly protect you. I won't do nothing again."

My fingers leave his shirt to cradle his cheeks. Leaning into him, our faces only inches apart, I whisper, "Don't say it."

His breath is coming fast, pushing hard into my parted lips and drawing in shared air. I'm not sure if his groan is from my touch or my tone or what he's about to say, but it's heart breaking. "We can't be together."

"No," I breathe out. "You're wrong. Stop saying that. Please stop saying that." Tears slide down my cheeks and I can see his determination slip when his eyes soften. Pouncing on the vulnerability, I push him to see reason. "Don't let whoever's doing this win, Colin. If you let us go, you've given in to his demands. Whoever this is wants to hurt us—not just you, but us. Letting me go is his victory. Don't let fear drive you to a decision bound to break us both." Squeezing my fingers to force his gaze back to mine when he drifts, I say, "Don't do this."

"It's not about winning, it's about your safety."

"I won't let you push me away because you think it will save me." I take a deep breath as my knees shake. "Do you love me, Colin?"

He groans again and closes his eyes, but I hold tight. I won't let go of him or his heart. It's mine and I intend to keep it forever. "So much," he says, and my anxiety calms a fraction. "I love you so much it hurts."

"I love you too." *Oh God, with all my heart I do.* "We'll get through this together. We've both felt the pain of what losing each other would be like—it's a devastation I'm not willing to contemplate again, and it was only for minutes. Are you seriously considering a lifetime?"

"I would do it for you, to keep you safe from my insane world. You don't deserve this, baby. You're the best person I know, and the only thing I offer you is pain. You deserve so much more than I can give you."

"Would you stop fucking saying that?" I scream louder than intended and my hands leave his face for the confines of his hair, pulling none too gently to get my point across. The corner of his mouth lifts in response. "Just stop saying it. I chose my life and what I deserve, and I chose you. I could give a shit about some freaking stalker who wants to scare me. For the love of God, we have a ton of security, and in a month you'll have the Secret Service for protection. He is not going to scare me away with some goddamn baby dolls hanging from a wall." My breath comes fast and heavy after my tirade.

"I only want to make your life better than it's ever been."

"It is. Oh, Colin, can't you see that it is? I'm so happy; every day with you is a miracle, one I wouldn't wish away for anything. I've never had this freedom before. Not when Ali and the Carters saved me—never. You've given me the ultimate gift. Your unconditional love has freed me from my past. Nothing is holding me back anymore. I'm really living for the first time in my life and it's so, so good."

Taking his hand I place it between my breasts. A frantic, beating rhythm greets his fingers. "Feel this?" When he nods, I continue. "It belongs to you—forever. No other man could ever own it the way you do."

Minutes pass, his hand on my heart and my heart in my throat. I'm not sure anything's been decided, but we've said all we can for tonight. Exhaustion is about to overtake both of us.

"Come, let's get the shower we missed earlier." I pull him into the bathroom. His eyes are distant and barely connect with mine. I've never seen him this way before, distraught over the red room and its implications for me, the mention of his daughter and no sleep. The combination has pushed him beyond coping.

With the shower running to hot, I turn and strip him a button at a time until his broad, muscular chest is bare. My hands trail over heated skin as I push it from his shoulders, and it's my heartbeat that accelerates from the view. He needs a shower and bed. I know this, but I can't help my reaction. With my pulse racing and need rising from each touch, I drop to my knees to slip his feet from his pants and socks. I look up and into his cloudy eyes when I grab the waistband of his briefs. He looks away, refusing to acknowledge what I'm silently asking for. I want to reaffirm our connection. The last day has turned into a million, and the distance between us is growing with each passing minute.

I refuse to accept his quiet rejection. When he stands naked in front of me, I remove the remaining barriers between us. It's apparent he's trying not to stare at my breasts when they're exposed, but heat flares within his eyes, proving he can't remain completely passive. It spurs my hope he's not totally lost to me.

With my panties removed, I wrap my arms around his waist, squeezing into him, relishing his strength and the energy we share. His hands, although I sense reluctance, round to my back and we move under the hot water. It begins to wash some of the stress away and finally, finally, he relaxes and pulls me in tighter. Dropping his head into the crook of my neck he inhales and picks me up until my feet dangle in the air.

As our hearts beat together, my hands grip his hair and my legs round his back. I know inherently he just needs me to hold him and I do, tight, with my whole body. When his shoulders shake it's my only indication he may be crying. *Oh, Colin, my sweet man.* He's so strong, yet passionate and sensitive too. It shouldn't be possible, but I hold him closer and I love him more.

"I'm not strong enough to let you go," he says, so low I can hardly hear him above the water. "I'm so sorry, baby. I'm so sorry."

"Shh," I soothe in his ear and we just hold on, finding comfort in each other. "I need you too, more than anything." His arms acknowledge my statement, tightening and keeping us flush. After long minutes, I pull his hair to lift his head. Our eyes connect, needing and scared. "Together?" I ask simply.

He searches my face for a long time, contemplating, deciding our fate. “Together,” he finally whispers, and I lean into his forehead, relieved. Tucking my head back onto his shoulder, he holds me as the water erases my fear of separation. “Together,” he says once more with perfect conviction and I cling on, legs and arms surrounding him just as my heart does.

Eventually he loosens his grip just enough to grab shampoo. Massaging it into my scalp, he cleans away the day. He turns, so I’m under the water and I tilt back to let the suds run clear. Our eyes connect when I lift my head. His have cleared, the storm passing, and relief surges, releasing the remaining worry from my limbs. It’s his turn and for now I concentrate on just this, just us. Slipping from his grip, I stand before him and use the same method to wash his hair. My fingers work at tense muscles in his neck and shoulders along with his scalp until he moans in appreciation. Taking our time, we bathe each other in silent, synchronized movements, enjoying a comforting touch and reassuring closeness.

Reaching behind me, he turns the water off and I take advantage of his lowered elevation. Finding his mouth with mine I kiss him, slow and thorough, exploring until I find myself in him and he’s panting into me. Our hands wander, running along sensitive skin, mimicking the soft caress of my tongue against his. Somehow, we’ve silently agreed this is enough—a sweet kiss, a light touch, skin against skin—our connection affirmed. We’re okay, scared maybe, but together we can move beyond the obstacles in our path.

Never far apart, always touching, we dry off and make our way to bed. We curl up in the center with my back to his chest, legs and arms entwined. Warm kisses on my shoulder smooth into the steady rhythm of his breath as he falls asleep in seconds. I'm not far behind to sink into a dream.

My thoughts swirl from the reality of the day into the darkness of night. His sweet breath on my skin turns into a labored struggle to draw in air. The light steam of our shower becomes deep red, thick and choking. Crying out for Colin over and over again, my voice goes unheard amidst the chaos. Surrounded by commotion I become lost to him, left alone to suffer in silent stillness. Enveloped by red, it covers me, covers everything around me, and all I see is suffocating red.

"Baby." He's calling me; I can hear him in the distance as I try to rise from the nightmare. I feel the earth shake, but it's a deep, heavy burden I can't move beyond.

"Colin, please," I cry out again, reaching for him as he disappears farther in the distance.

"Charlie, baby, wake up." He shakes me harder and light finally pierces the red. I gasp, just as I recognize the early morning sun shimmering around the window curtains and it becomes my focus. It was so real yet not at all reality. Working to slow my breathing, I wiggle my way back into Colin's chest. It's his turn to provide comfort. He pulls me even closer, and we find peace once more, my breathing matching his pattern. Reaching around, his hand moves between my breasts, pressing to hold my heart and pulse steady. My fingers find and wind into his. "It was just a dream. I'm right here, not going anywhere," he murmurs next to my ear.

"Promise me." I hear myself say, even though I don't remember prompting the thought to be said out loud.

"I'll never leave you. Now get some rest, baby. I'll be here when you wake."

"Better be," I mumble, just before sleep takes me a second time.

ooo

The light is brighter the next time I wake, an indicator the day has begun. I know without looking that Colin is most decidedly not in bed. Panic rises, and I throw the covers off to lunge for the living room. Just as my foot falls on the plush carpet, I hear muffled one-sided dialogue through the door. He's on the phone. Air exits my lungs in a huff and I fall unceremoniously back onto the mattress.

The red room is there, waiting to confiscate my thoughts. I push it away, something I've become an expert at doing. Not just of late, but when I first came to the Carters, too. I'd shelve items that were too hurtful to work through until there was time for contemplation. Now is not that time. Colin and where we are today must remain my focus.

I roll over to his pillow and breathe in his scent, always calming and always creating a low fluttering in my belly. Damn. I was hoping for a lazy, morning snuggle, but he was probably already dressed, impeccable in a white button-up and dress slacks. In my mind I play Let's Make a Deal. Behind door number one, we have navy; door number two is black. Host Wayne Brady excitedly interjects 'Pick the winner and you get what's behind that very door.' I smile into the pillow, hoping I've imagined the right color—my bet's on navy.

Sliding out of bed, I'm still grinning until I see my hair in the bathroom mirror. Holy hell, talk about a train wreck. It'll take days to tame this, but I do my best to make myself presentable in a minute, weaving it in a knot at the base of my neck. Slipping into a robe, I find my way to the living room just as Colin's winding down his conversation. He's facing the window, and I get my first glance of the day at his broad shoulders and fine ass. *Mmm.* I find myself licking my lips like he's breakfast. All of a sudden I'm a sex-crazed animal and I want to attack my prey. *Here kitty, kitty* . . . I giggle because he's more like a tiger, and it alerts him to my presence.

"Yes, deliver it all to the same address in Georgetown."

He turns and drinks me in. Slow and painstakingly thorough, his gaze wanders from the tip of my bare toes to the curls flying around my head. I follow suit, enjoying the view. And the winner is . . . drum roll please . . . door number one. Navy pants it is, and I can't wait to collect my prize. My grin triples in size at the thought, and his voice dips as he watches me. *Maybe I should just slip out of the robe?*

His mouth takes on a predatory curve. "I appreciate your help on such short notice. I'll be in touch," he says, and then tosses the phone to the couch. Stalking forward, when he reaches me he wraps his hands around my neck, thumbs under my chin. He holds me in place and lifts my face to his. The tip of his nose glances against mine, the sexy smirk remains, and his eyes? Damn, his eyes darken in a taunting warning. *Oh God, I do hope I'm in trouble.*

“Good morning, baby.”

Before I can respond, his mouth is on mine. Careful and sure, this kiss is at first a gentle caress. He savors me, slow and sinful. A tilt of his head, a brush of his mouth, a tug from his teeth, the slightest hint of his tongue and repeat until I’m breathless. This is the kind of kiss that could last for days, and just when I settle in, he becomes reckless. From careful to careless, he licks into my mouth. Asserting his power, his fingers tug the knot from my hair and dive in.

I moan when his teeth pierce my bottom lip. The color of my voice paints the room in vibrant color, giving life to the still air. One of my hands lands in his hair and I pull myself up and into him. The other grips the front of his shirt. Twisting a handful of the expensive cotton in my fist, I hold nothing back, molding my body into his. I circle my hips, until his groan mirrors my own. We’re getting somewhere when he matches my rhythm and I get hungrier, pulling open buttons to get down to my prize.

It’s been forever since I’ve felt him in me, forever equating to three days, the longest we’ve been apart since we came together. I want him, and I make it known, matching his fervor and taking it a step further. My tongue pushes into his mouth, my teeth grip his lip—my need eclipses his. He started this and I want to finish it.

“Don’t,” I whimper when he pushes against my shoulders. He grins at my plea. The stretch of his smile makes it hard to find his lips for a kiss, so I begin a scavenger hunt to find them. My mouth seeks and discovers the beautiful steel plains of his cheekbones, both of them, moving to sweep along his jaw, nipping on the soft dimple of his chin, running my tongue along the rough texture of his newly grown stubble and the soft skin underneath.

"Come back to bed," I whisper into his ear just as I take hold of his lobe, nipping hard enough to elicit a rush of his breath. The grip of his hands on my ass and his deep moan connect directly to my groin. Leaning back, I catch his eyes with my own. I've gotten to him—the need is evident, and with just a little persuasion I'm sure I can get him into bed. Walking backward, my hand re-fisted in his shirt, I say, "Don't be easy on me."

"God," he groans and then kisses me, a long, deep, dueling kiss that is altogether mind-boggling, and over much too quickly. "We don't have time; they'll be here . . ."

I glare at the door and whoever is on the other side of it, his or her knock seriously pissing me off.

"Ignore it," I say, running my tongue along his bottom lip before sucking it into my mouth and stumbling with him to the bedroom door. Just as we fall into each other, the knock resounds through the room a second time, louder than the first. I swear, if it's Ella I will not control myself. She has some sixth sense when it comes to Colin and me. I've had it with her interruptions and meddling.

Once again I'm left breathless and wanting when he pulls away too quickly, his nose and forehead pressing against mine. I find a moment of satisfaction when he has trouble catching his breath.

"Charlie, get off of him. He's got work to do," Evan calls from the hallway, laughing.

Closing my eyes, I shake my head in defeat. "I'm mad at you." I swat his butt and appreciate the feel of it under my hand. I want to get into those navy pants and he's making it hard. *Speaking of hard . . .* I swivel my hips against him. Damn it all to hell, I let my forehead rest against his while opening my eyes.

"Me?" His innocent façade is too much and too cute at the same time.

"You better be prepared to finish what you start next time, Mr. McKenna."

"Or what?" he teases with a brush of his lips against mine.

"Or I will tie you down and take what I want." I laugh when his nostrils flare and he growls.

"Easy tiger," I say and push him away. Heading into the bedroom, I exaggerate the sway of my hips and giggle at his telling groan. Good. *Suffer away, Mr. President.*

Giving up on my hair, I decide on a quick shower and take extra time to smooth out the wild curls with the blow-dryer. Without knowing our plans for the day, I choose a comfortable hunter-green wrap dress that can transition from casual to professional with a change of shoes and jewelry. Searching for a pair of earrings in my bag, heated voices travel through the door.

"This is not the time to flaunt it. You should have been more careful." John Montgomery's stern lecture is easily heard with no other sound in the room than my quickened breath.

Colin's voice is clear when it follows. "There's never a perfect time. I'm not hiding Charlie. I won't do it, so don't ask again. Ease up. Look at this for what it is. She's a beautiful, intelligent, strong woman in love with a single man. There's no problem here; stop trying to create one."

"Colin's right, John." It's Evan's turn to interject. "There's no reason to keep her on the sidelines. Charlie will only help him. America wants their president in a happy, solid relationship. The fact that he is will solidify Colin as the leader going into the primary."

"You both know there's a reason to keep this relationship from public scrutiny. If her past is found out . . ."

I cringe, just as Colin grinds out a response. "It will not be found."

"You don't know that. If it does the press will eat you alive and take her down with your sinking ship."

"Charlie was a child, John. A decision she made as a teenager will not crumble my campaign."

He sighs. "It may not, but the fact that you're hiding it might. You're a pro-life candidate; it's been a solid foundation of your campaign from the beginning. We've played it up when we needed to. You'll be perceived as indecisive. It doesn't take much to sway the vote. Look at what happened to Rogers, his wavering standpoint cost him the last election."

Sucking in my gasp, I press against the door as much to hold me up as it is to hear what follows. "It's your job to make sure none of that happens, so do it."

"I'll do my best, but you have to face reality." It sounds as if he slaps something down on the table. "She's not trained to be in the public eye; she'll fold under the pressure."

Colin chuckles. "You don't know Charlie very well if you believe that. There's a psycho terrorizing her and she's comforting me because I'm terrified for her. She's stronger than you give her credit for. Hell, I don't give her enough credit. I'm not worried about the press and how she'll react to it. Just look at this." He pauses, and I can't tell what he's referring to. "Look at this headline and these pictures. America's already in love."

My knees shake. *In love with me?* Heart pounding a mile a minute I can't contain my rising anxiety and barge into the room.

FIVE

JOHN PACES BY THE window, Evan lounges on the couch and Colin stands next to him, holding a newspaper. He appears as relaxed as Evan, maybe even more so, a small smile lifting the corners of his mouth. All three jerk their heads up at my appearance as I ask, "Who is America in love with?"

Colin arches his brow, his grin growing while he drops the paper to Evan's lap and reaches for my hand. "You look beautiful, baby," he says, while pulling me forward until he's close enough for his arm to round my waist. His smile is breathtaking, really stunning, and for a minute I get lost in it, loving that it's meant for me.

"Don't try to distract me with your brilliance." I bump my hip into his. "What are you boys talking about?"

His smile falters. "Would you like some coffee? I ordered breakfast, too—blueberry pancakes." He sweeps a hand over to the small breakfast table in the corner and now I know he's going for distraction. Blueberry pancakes are my weakness. *What's he up to?*

"I'd love some coffee and the newspaper," I say, looking up through my lashes. *Two can play at this game.* "I'm sorry to have interrupted your business; carry on, please. Pretend I'm not here." Walking over to the breakfast nook I grab a cup, adding sweetener and cream to the rich brew. All three of them are staring, watching as

I set the coffee down and pull out the chair. Darting to the sofa, I snatch the paper from Evan's hand before he has time to hide it.

"Charlie." Colin reaches for my arm, but I'm too quick.

Shaking out the front of the paper I read the headline out loud. "Tornados Ravage Eight States." Nothing's new there, but it's the next one that prompts a gasp and my heart to gallop. "Love Amongst the Ruin." Oh shit. A picture of us is blown up, huge, spread out along the length of the paper. Colin's holding me with Murphy cradled against my neck. His smile is sweet and I'm gazing up at him as if he's the best thing since sliced bread. It was taken just after I fell and he saved me, *again*. "Oh shit, oh shit, oh shit."

"Well, I'd love to stick around for this," Evan says, standing, "but I have a call to make before we leave. I'll see you in thirty minutes." Smiling at Colin and then me, he winks and walks to the door. "John, we need to discuss the media release set to go out this afternoon."

Glancing to Colin, John's glare screams disapproval. "We're not done with this conversation; be prepared to finish it later." I'm prepared for him to wag his finger at Colin as if he's scolding a child but he just huffs and follows Evan out, leaving the two of us alone.

I stare at the closed door, stunned. We're on the front page of the paper, which translates to we're on the front page of every paper in the United States. I fall into the chair tucked behind my legs and read on. "The Herald was able to confirm presidential candidate, Senator Colin McKenna, is in a relationship with campaign staffer Charlise Carter. According to sources close to the couple, they met earlier this year and quietly began dating. Our sources indicate Carter continues to work as the social media coordinator on McKenna's campaign, with no plans to resign from her position, despite the transition from a professional to a personal relationship. Although there is no official word from McKenna's team at this time, a formal statement is expected sometime today. With the highly anticipated primary one month away, a change to McKenna's personal status could either bolster his standings as the one to beat or hinder his chances at claiming the nomination. Only time will decide his fate.

"Other than being raised in Michigan, little is known about Carter. More details will no doubt come to the surface in the coming days."

More details?

Just below this article lies another picture. I'm kneeling, handing Murphy over to the little girl, Colin behind me with a hand on my shoulder. The short article next to it recounts the rescue and recovery of Sydney's cat. She's quoted as saying, "Charlie's super nice. I'm so happy she saved my kitty."

I groan and roll my head back on the chair. Colin stands next to me, looking down with an amused expression, his light blue eyes twinkling. The sliver of brandy peeking out of the left one shimmers, and he's smiling. The bastard is smiling. Kneeling, he removes the paper from my death grip and takes my hand, holding it between both of his. My skin heats immediately from the circular strokes of his thumb. He knows exactly what he's doing. Well, his distraction techniques are not working—not the smile, not the coffee, not the pancakes and not his touch. Well, maybe his touch. *No, no, no, get your head in the game, Carter.*

"Hhmm," he murmurs.

"I'm sorry."

"Why are you sorry?" His thumb keeps rolling and my stomach flutters.

"Because I know you didn't want this to happen, because I know you wanted to get ahead of the media and you couldn't because I had to go looking for a cat."

His laughter fills the room. "I love you because you went to look for a cat."

Tears fill my eyes, threatening to flow. "I'm sorry I could hurt your campaign," I whisper, the words hitching as they come out. It's been my worst nightmare. What if John's right? Will they crucify him for hiding my past? Will it appear as if he's not as strong as his campaign platform promises? Any vacillation on his beliefs could wreak havoc with voters who look for truth and determination.

"Don't do this to yourself. I'm not worried about it and you shouldn't either."

I stare silently, thoughts muddling and crowding together until I can't think clearly.

"Listen to me," he says, drawing my attention back to his shining eyes. "Would you agree I've been successful up to this point in my career?"

"Yes."

"I've relied on many things to get where I am today—hard work, knowledge, connecting with people—I told you all of this before. There's one other thing I rely on: instinct. My gut is always right." He smiles again, broad and disarming. "I've thought about it a lot this morning; after last night I needed to really make sure I was making the right decision. I want you, Charlie, in every way, but I have to consider what's right for you."

My throat tightens. Last night he wanted to send me home, but he said we'd get through it together. Did he change his mind? The bright smile on his face is reassuring and calms my now rolling stomach.

"Do you know what my gut's telling me about you, baby?"

"That you want my pancakes?"

"Well, there is that," he says, while reaching up to pull my face toward his. He brushes his lips against mine. Warm and soft, the connection sings through every heartbeat and calms my nerves. "I know without a doubt you're right for me. I may have suppressed the feelings when we first met . . ."

"It probably felt like you had the stomach flu."

"Let me finish," he says, shaking his head. "Since you have flat out refused to make your safety a priority . . ."

"You're damn right about that . . ."

His fingers cut me off mid-sentence, pressing against my lips. "You're stuck with me."

"You're damn right about that," I mumble and his grin grows wider.

"Together?" he asks, and drops his hand so my answer is clear.

"Together." I draw him in until he's an inch from my mouth.

"No matter what the future brings, we work through it together."

"Yes, always." I smile, sure of him, and sure of the path ahead of me. We're strong enough to walk through the gates of hell and survive, as long as we're together.

"I promise to love you like no one ever has before."

"Colin," I exhale his name.

"It won't be perfect, I won't be perfect, but I'll love you through it all. I'll never stop."

"How did I get so lucky?" My hand runs through his hair and then down to the smooth plain of his forehead. I cup his cheek and just as I'm about to claim my prize he interrupts my plan.

"Lucky? You?" A wicked glint sparkles in his eyes. "I'm not so sure those two words belong together in a sentence."

"Hey." I grab his chin so his blues connect with my green. "I am too lucky. Fate brought me to you and that's the best kinda luck a girl can have."

"If you say so, baby. Whether it was fate or chance that brought you to me, I thank God every day you're mine."

Closing my eyes, I take a deep breath, allowing his words to work all of the tension from my muscles. When they open, I'm met with his intense gaze. "Would you kiss me already?"

"My pleasure, Ms. Carter." Holding my head in his hands, he tangles his fingers into my hair, hovering close, not moving, just taking long, concentrated breaths. Once, twice, inhaling and breathing into me while our eyes remain locked. I part my mouth in anticipation of his actually touching mine. The tip of his tongue runs along his bottom lip. It shines in the morning sun, begging to be bitten, and I want to. I want my teeth on him, on his neck, his chest. Oh God, I want to bite and suck on the sweet line of muscle navigating a very happy trail to the soft skin below his stomach. He smiles and I'm beyond tempted. I need him and yet he continues to taunt with his proximity. So close, yet so far away.

Pressing his lips against mine, he lingers for the shortest moment and then rambles, "We need to talk about a statement to the press and you should call your parents. The media has no boundaries, baby. Now that they know you're with me they'll do anything to learn more about you, including harass your family."

My head reels from the latest turn in conversation. I hadn't thought about my parents or siblings or grandparents, and the ramifications my relationship with Colin will have for them.

I'm drawn back to his voice with the light squeeze of his hands. "Evan and John are working on the release now and it'll go out this afternoon. I expect a lot of media attention, especially over the next few days. Do not speak directly to the press. Smile, nod, wave, but no comments. Understand?"

"Okay?"

"Charlie, the media will take anything you say and twist it. For now, it's better to remain silent. Let John's team feed them information. The world will get to know you from afar and we'll work in your first formal introduction at a rally."

"You'll prep me for it?" I ask, worried if he doesn't I'll fumble on his policy for some bizarre niche topic and embarrass him with the press.

"Yes." Our gaze remains locked as he brushes aside a piece of hair from my eyes. "Everything's fine. We've got this."

"If you say so."

"I do. Now I've got to meet Evan and John. Have breakfast and finish packing. I'll be back for you in an hour." His mouth meets my forehead and then he's standing, rolling his sleeves into place at his wrists.

"Where are we off to next?"

"Washington."

"As in D.C.?"

He smiles. "Yes. We have a cocktail party tonight, but we're open tomorrow evening if you would like to visit with Ali."

Now he's a mind reader along with everything else. "I will. What should we do?"

"Invite her over to the house. I'll ask Evan too."

I lift my brow.

"What? I can't invite my best friend over for dinner with my girlfriend and her sister?"

"You're up to something, Senator. I can see it in your eyes."

The blues I love so much take on a devilish tint. "Baby, there's only one thing I'm thinking about, and trust me, it has nothing to do with Evan or Ali."

Hmm, I may get into those navy pants after all. "Something sinful?"

"Perhaps."

I clap my hands under my chin like a giddy schoolgirl. "Perhaps now?"

He places a hand on either side of my chair, leaning in so close the sweet heat of his breath mingles with mine. The tiger found his prey and I'm okay with that. I want him to bite me.

"Is there something you want, baby?"

"Yes . . ." My voice is all breathy and doesn't quite sound like me. His nose grazes and follows my cheekbone, a slow approach to my ear.

"Tell me." I'd say his tone was soft, but the command in the words hardened them into a demand. One I wouldn't think of refusing.

"You . . . I want you."

"Do you now?"

I gasp with the sting of pleasure when his teeth pick at the sensitive skin of my neck. Blood begins to pulse in my groin as his tongue, teeth and lips make their way to my collarbone.

"Yes. Right now . . ." I issue my own demand and it's met with another nip of his teeth on the curve of my breast. *Yes.*

I love his mouth on me and it's on the way to mine. When our eyes connect, he murmurs against my lips, "All in good time."

I'm unprepared for the kiss that follows. An urgent possession, he holds me in place by the hand on my chin. I take in his low hungry groan, but have no chance at keeping pace with his tongue. Taking long, deep lashes into my mouth, he pushes until I forget to breathe. Just as quick as the onslaught of his attack, it's over, leaving me sprawled in the chair, gasping for air. *What the hell?*

At the sound of his chuckle I'm drawn back to reality. "One hour, Charlie. Be ready for me."

I'm left, stunned and panting, watching his ass walk out the door instead of in the bedroom. Damn.

After a few minutes recovery time, I grab my phone from my purse to call Mom. She answers after the first ring.

"Hi, Mom."

"You're worried. I can hear it in your voice."

"So you saw the paper?"

"No, the nice reporter outside came by to ask about you," Gram exclaims. Apparently I'm on speaker.

"Already?" I groan. But really, what was I expecting? The media is not going to sit back and wait for information from Colin's team. They're going to hunt it down, find it, and report it to the world. "I'm so sorry. How bad is it?"

"Charlie girl, why are you sorry?" Mom's concern reaches me through the phone.

"I . . . It's hard for me to see my decision affect you. I don't want you to get harassed by the press." I'd vowed after they'd loved and supported me through the hardest time of my life that I'd be the perfect daughter. I want to protect them, as they did me.

"This, sweet girl"—Gram's smiling; I can tell—"is the most fun I've had in years. First, you bring life to my birthday party. No offense, Anna. It would have been wonderful without the eye candy, but it was so much better with it." Gram forges on, talking over my mom's laugh: when Gram's on a roll, there's no stopping her. "And the reporter is the cutest thing to hit my lawn in years. Don't tell your grandfather I said so." And now *I'm* smiling. "I could talk about you all day long and still have more good things to say. And then there's your boyfriend? Good lord, Charlie. That man is so fine, mmhmm . . ."

"Gram, do you have a crush on Colin?" I laugh, and I know she's been trying to make it happen.

"How could I not? His eyes have a way of burrowing into your soul."

"You've been reading too many romance novels again, haven't you?" My grin grows as I follow the rim of my coffee cup with my finger.

"Maybe, but that's beside the point. This Colin fella, you love him?"

"Yes."

"Then there you go. You've lived on a bed of broken glass, easing over it, trying not to get hurt again. Anyone can see that man loves you. In my mind, that's all you need. Stop worrying about the rest of us and love him up good."

When I hesitate, Mom interjects. "We're fine. I'll keep Gram away from the front lawn, so don't worry about her." Gram's huff is loud and clear. "I know something else is upsetting you. Don't let it. Your father took care of it years ago."

I choke on a cry. We *never* talk about this. I can't bear to tell her that Colin's background check found my medical record, and if he can, so can someone else. In fact, someone already knows, judging from the e-mail so many months ago and the red room. There's a good possibility my past is open and waiting for the media to find it.

"Okay. I won't worry," I lie. "Please call me if things get out of hand. I'll ask Colin to do something. I don't know what, but he'll do what he can."

"I love you, Charlie girl. You enjoy that hunka-hunka burnin' love."

I choke again, but this time on a laugh. "I love you both too. So much."

After hanging up, I look around the room, contemplating what must be done before we leave. It won't take long to gather my things; most of them remain packed in my larger suitcase. At some point I'll need to replace the items lost in the red room, including my smaller travel bag. When I stand to head into the bedroom, my knees threaten to give out and the room swirls so I fall back into the chair. I haven't eaten anything in almost twenty-four hours. Combine that with the red room, Colin and the media fiasco, and I'm a mess. Blueberry pancakes are tempting, but just the thought of them has my stomach pitching. Coffee sloshes over the side of the mug as I lift it for a sip.

I need to get it together. This is the first day of the rest of my life with Colin. The media will always be there. For the time he's in the spotlight, I'll be in the spotlight. It's the microscope that terrifies me. Colin's gut may be telling him one thing—mine is speaking a whole other language. My choice, my past is going to come into play. I can feel it.

SIX

ONE HOUR DID NOT lead to sexy times. It brought the airport, a short flight to D.C. and more nerves. We encountered media at every turn. Leaving the hotel was my first rock star experience. Photographers swarmed, questions were hurled, and Colin kept an arm around me as we hurried into the waiting SUV. They followed behind us until airport security refused to let them pass, but other reporters picked us up when we landed. After a short drive, we rolled into Colin's gated community in Georgetown and parted from the paparazzi once again. *This is my new reality.*

For now I'm happily holding Colin's hand as Drake pulls up in front of Colin's early twentieth-century townhouse. A wide three-plank bay window covers most of the first floor, the entrance tucked directly next to it. Two more stories rise above the first, with dormer windows hanging in sentinel watch over the house and street below. Tall trees line the sidewalks, converging together to create a canopy of green.

"Ready?"

Colin slides out first and turns to assist me. His arm wraps around my waist as we make our way up the steps and as he unlocks the door.

I slide away from his grip when we enter the foyer of his home. *Wow.* The ceilings must be twelve feet high. Thick white crown molding pops off the gray walls. Hanging along them are large photographs, blown up and stretched on canvas, capturing nature in its most beautiful and pure state.

I know he's waiting for me to say something, his gaze trained on me as I take it in. I've never seen a home like this before: modern, yet holding onto the beauty of its twentieth-century roots. Suddenly I wonder if Abby lived here, if she designed and decorated this for them. He must see a change in my expression and somehow answers my unasked question.

"I bought this place after Abby died. It needed extensive renovation and took a year to complete. I haven't touched the third floor yet—another project to get to in time." Colin's eyes are hesitant in wait, and I realize he needs my approval.

"It's gorgeous," I say while gazing at the large starburst chandelier hanging from the ceiling. "Did you do it all by yourself?"

His smile is shy, a response I don't see from him often, and it makes me wonder what he's thinking. Dipping his eyes to the floor, he shakes his head. "I had an architect help; I wanted to incorporate the historical character of the house with my style. Come, I'll show you around." Taking my hand, he leads me through the living room and a formal dining room that transitions into a huge modern kitchen.

Wood cabinets topped with white quartz warm the cool monotone gray carried throughout the first floor. Five stools are tucked into a large island, yet there's still room for an eight-person kitchen table. The most stunning feature by far is the floor-to-ceiling wall of windows that bring a shocking patch of green, which is the backyard, right into the kitchen. It's a surprising retreat from the city. A long length of grass expands beyond a granite patio and small trees line a wood fence. One huge oak tree lives in the center of the yard.

My eyes pop. Colin's house is everything I would have done and more if I had my own home—absolutely stunning and perfect for him. "It's breathtaking."

His answering grin is more stunning than the room. "I'm glad you like it," he breathes out, reaching for me. I'm drawn into a warm embrace, tucking my head into my favorite place. I hate that he's leaving again for a last-minute meeting. "I have to change and go. Make yourself at home." He smiles, leaning down to brush his lips against mine.

"You're not going to show me upstairs?"

His chest vibrates with a laugh. "No, I'm not taking you anywhere near my bed. I'll never get out of it once I get you in it."

"Just a quick tour?" I look up and bat my lashes.

Although his hands find my ass and pull me into him, he says, "Not even a minute." I pout, bottom lip pushed out and my chin drops. He laughs again. "I'll be back at seven to pick you up. Look at me." When I do, my pout falls away because you can't be sad when you're looking at gorgeous. "Drake will be here all day. I don't want you to worry about anything."

"I'm not." But I get the distinct impression he is, by the shadows haunting his eyes.

"I want you inside or in the backyard if you need fresh air. That's it, Charlie."

"So I'm on lockdown."

"For a while, yes." My pout is back. Before I can say anything else, he continues, "I'm not taking any chances after Arkansas. We have to believe whoever this is knows we're here. He's known everything else. Promise me you'll stay inside until I get here?"

"Okay." His right eyebrow lifts and he tilts his head. "Oh, for the love of God. Yes, I promise to stay here until you get home. By the way, where are we going?"

"A party at the Montgomerys'. Adam Boeing will be there and we have business to discuss."

I frown at two things. One, the Montgomerys? Now I know he's trying to torture me. And two, I ask out loud, "Who's Adam Boeing?"

"Speaker of the House."

"Oh." I shake my head. Six months ago, I was single and going to parties with college dropouts. Today, my boyfriend is running for president of the United States and my new crowd includes the Speaker of the House. Just whoa. Hold on a second while the enormity overwhelms and buries me in the sand. *Holy shit*.

I lean into my favorite place and take deep calming breaths of Colin. This is all real and really happening. My place will no longer be on the sidelines, but by his side.

"Hey." He tips my chin again and my eyes are forced to his. "It's just a few acquaintances. There's nothing to worry about." When I don't react, he says, "We won't be there long."

"Promise me that."

“How about this,” he says, and repositions us so we're hip to hip. “I promise to repay your servitude.” His voice drops an octave and his eyes go with it, deepening to the color I love. I snuggle closer. Dipping down, his breath warms my lips and then he licks them. I think the moan resonating through the room is mine but I can't be certain, because I've lost all train of thought. My fingers are twisted into his hair with no conscious thought on my part to get there. His breath washes over me—it's like the warmth you feel on the first day of summer when the sun pushes away the clouds and shines just for you. I bask in it and then jump up, wrapping my legs around his waist. We stay still, lips pressed in a light touch, energy humming around us, breathing together and simply being together.

“Take me upstairs,” I mumble.

He laughs. “Later, baby. I have a meeting.” My eyes roll back when his pocket vibrates against my thigh and he reaches down for his cell. He’s reduced me to a pool of hormones.

“Give me five minutes.” His tone has cooled off, as has his look, although he watches me the whole time he’s on the phone. “No, we need to review my speech for Friday night and shore up the weekend schedule . . . I don’t care if Grant is in the same city. I made a commitment. He can rearrange his agenda if it’s a problem. I'm not backing out . . . Yes, I’ll be there shortly.”

I stay where I am, enjoying the last few minutes wrapped around him before he leaves. Now that the call’s over, his attention is averted back to me.

“There’s something waiting for you upstairs.”

"What?"

"You'll see." A quick kiss to my forehead is my cue to drop my legs. "Behave yourself . . ."

I look at him, with a raised brow, my hand on my hip. "When don't I?"

"There's not enough time to list your infractions, Ms. Carter." He spanks my butt and then turns, striding through the living room and disappearing upstairs. I wander around the kitchen, peaking in the fridge, which is surprisingly full, and grab a bottle of water, until he bounds down the stairs about three minutes later. Stopping by the door, fully suited and drop-dead gorgeous, he turns to look at me just as he swings it open. "Charlie?" My eyes drag up from his tight backside to catch his gaze. "I love you, baby."

I'm left reeling from not only his fine ass, but also at the thought of the night ahead. Oh, God. What the hell am I supposed to wear?

First thing's first. I trek up the steps, peeking through the second floor.

Colin's room isn't hard to find because of his suitcase sitting by the door. It's masculine and reminds me of him. Large windows, similar to those in the kitchen, overlook the oak tree. The deep teal gray walls surround a platform bed, framed by a white pin-tucked headboard reaching toward the ceiling. Natural black and white landscape portraits bring the world to D.C. The only other piece of furniture is an oversized 1960s leather butterfly chair tucked into a corner.

He's a minimalist. I laugh and focus on two boxes sitting atop the mattress. A folded piece of paper lies on one of the brown parcel packages.

Dearest Charlie-

You have reached me in a way I never thought possible. My love for you can't simply be expressed in words or touch or a combination of both. It's too profound. It lives within me, reaching even into the darkest shallows of my heart to bring light and a joy I never thought possible. I will savor you and live to bring you the gift you've given to me. You are my life.

-Colin

Closing my eyes, I let the chill sweep through me and clutch his note to my chest. I don't know how he does it, but he always does. He grounds me just when I need it, when I need to realize this is about us, and the extracurricular activities of life are a sideshow.

The boxes are large, one bigger than the other. Starting with the smaller, it reveals a guitar, sleek and brand new. Mine is old and battered from years of use, passed down to me from my dad. Too many nights spent around the fire have left it worn and too special to bring on the road. This is a work of art and must have cost a fortune. A typed note simply says *I want your song to resonate around me wherever we go.*

I shake my head and slip the magenta strap over my shoulder to strum a few cords, humming along to "At Last" before moving onto the bigger package.

It's a huge white box; the centered black satin bow slips easily apart when I tug. Under the heavy layer of tissue lies a mountain of new clothes, everything I lost in the red room replaced and then some. Lingerie, jeans, skirts and shirts and pants—so many I lose count. At the bottom is a new bag, a magenta ribbon tied to it just like there had been on the one that was destroyed.

Sinking onto the bed, I fall back and stare at the ceiling to take it all in. When Colin McKenna asks, people answer. He did all of this in less than twenty-four hours. He's a force to be reckoned with, and I love him for it and because of it.

It's past three in the afternoon, leaving a few hours to get ready for the night ahead. I sit up to decide what to wear and notice a garment bag hanging from the adjoining bath's door. I have a feeling it's mine too and I'm right. Four gowns are inside, one perfect for tonight. Quick to undress, I slip into a pale pink sheath. It hugs my curves to just above the knee, yet there's gentleness in the sheer lace overlay. Obscuring my cleavage and the sweetheart neckline of the tight shift underneath, it graces my collarbone in a boat neck opening and down to quarter-length sleeves. This dress is sophisticated, yet sweet and sexy at the same time.

That's exactly how Colin will find me when he comes home—sweet, with a side of sexy. Bring it, Mr. McKenna. I'll be ready for you.

ooo

"Stop fidgeting. You're stunning."

Pulling my twisting hands from my stomach, Colin drags me behind him to the massive front door. The home is old, maybe built in the early twentieth century, but it's been refurbished to mirror the other multi-million dollar mansions lining the square. It's distinguished and imposing, a lot like the night ahead.

"I'm not worried about how I look, I'm freaking out about the guest list."

He turns and waits for me to step close enough for his hands to rest on the curve of my waist. "And you're worried not because we're walking into a den of vapid women, but because you clearly want to state your opinion on gun control?"

"Yes, that's part of it. A girl doesn't meet the Speaker of the House every day."

"What's the rest of it?"

"I'm also quite intent on proving my ability to nod every eight seconds and pretend to care about the newest pair of Manolo Blahniks lining the great expanse of closets the size of my condo. I've been practicing in the mirror."

He smiles and shakes his head. "That's impossible."

I swat his shoulder. "Now that's no way to build me up. A more supportive response is . . . *you've got this, babe. Your inane, senseless stare is perfection.*"

"You're perfection."

I smooth the collar of his jacket. "Mmm, I'm glad you think so."

"You're my perfection." We meet in the middle, a light touch of our lips. I'm tempted to tempt him with my tongue, but think better of it. The Montgomerys are on the other side of the door and that's enough to deflate any girl's libido.

"Oh, and I can't wait to see Ella. She's at the top of my this-is-better-than-Christmas list."

"Baby," he sighs. "There are many events I have little control over. This is one of them. It's something I have to do. I want you with me every minute, every day. You're my beacon, keeping me sane through all of the daily bullshit. Enjoy this for what it is. We're together—the rest of them be damned."

He's right. This is what I signed up for. Colin McKenna is one big package and I've opened it up: heads of state, fundraisers, ball gowns and people I despise are all part of the gift. He's worth it and giving him a guilt trip isn't winning me a Girlfriend of the Year award.

"You're right." I wrap my arms around his neck and shimmy against him. "Plus you promised to reward my servitude and I plan to hold you to it. Every minute someone drones on about the Affordable Care Act I'll be devising ten ways you can make me scream when we get home." I wink and push around him to ring the doorbell.

When his breath hits my ear I squirm and find his hard length pressing into my behind. "Only ten?" He nips along my jawline. "Why not set the bar higher? Challenge me."

I shiver as if it's winter, but the evening air is hot, his mouth on my neck even hotter.

"Challenge me, baby. I promise to rise and meet your needs." He pulls me even tighter against him. *No doubt about that.* "Give me something to work for."

The shiver remains and sings in sweet harmony with my galloping heart. "Yes . . . please. Sign me up for this whole body challenge. I promise not to follow instructions and be bad, very, very bad."

If his sharp inhale is any indication, I failed to keep my thoughts to myself. "Charlie . . ."

I love when he says my name in that dark, commanding growl and I'm determined to hear it all night long. "Take me home."

He groans and bites my shoulder. "Just a few hours . . ."

"Two hours and I'll let you make me scream in the car."

"Two and a half and you'll scream for me to stop and then I'll do it again."

There's a distinct possibility this game will backfire on me tonight. "Anything after two hours and you'll have to work to get into my panties."

I gasp when he cops a feel, squeezing my breast. Even through the lace of my dress my nipple rises to his touch. Bowing into his hand, my mouth falls open and I stumble for words, but he beats me to them.

"Be careful, or I'll rip them off with my teeth."

I smile and tilt my head to look at him. "That would be hard to do."

"You doubt my ability?"

"No . . ." I kiss his nose at the same time as I ring the doorbell. "Because I'm not wearing any."

The opening door meets his growl and he steps back, just enough to be on the border of appropriate. His left hand on my hip leaves his right free.

A familiar cold blue stare is my greeting, yet the lines around her eyes soften what I've come to know as venom and her smile warms the cool pale of her skin.

"Colin, dear." She breezes past me to encircle him in her arms. "It's been too long." Kissing him on each cheek, she lingers, gripping his shoulders. "Too long, my sweet son-in-law."

He stiffens next to me, his hand falling from my waist. Joan Montgomery is a mirror of her daughter: petite, blond and direct. I brace myself for the wave of hatred sure to follow Colin's kind welcome.

"It has been some time. Always a pleasure to see you, Joan." His eyes find mine, as does his hand, entwining our fingers. "This is my girlfriend, Charlise Carter." His brow falls almost imperceptibly as we wait for her response.

Clasping her hands together, she smiles, a real, genuine smile that has the ice blue of her irises dancing. This catches me more off-guard than an evil stare.

"Charlise." She reaches out and I loosen our hold to take her offering.

"It's nice to meet you, Mrs. Montgomery. You have a beautiful home."

“Joan, please. Come in, both of you.” She waves us over the threshold.

The foyer is immense, but sparse. A lone circular table stands in the curve of a grand staircase with a fresh flower arrangement on top. Differing light to dark shades of tan run through what I can see of the floor plan. A large living room opens to the right, where guests mingle from one group to another. Animated chatter falls quiet and heads swivel to stare in our direction. Mr. McPerfect has arrived. Everyone notices, including the bevy of women I'll soon have to mingle with, although I hope their drool is wiped clean before our introduction.

“Colin, John's been waiting to bend your ear in the library with Adam. Why don't you leave Charlise with me and take care of business?” She huffs when he jerks his gaze toward mine. “Come now. I'm perfectly capable of introducing her to our friends. Off with you.” She shoos him away as only a mother can.

I would laugh at the hint of panic on his face if it weren't mirrored in the rigid square of my shoulders. Suddenly the lump in my throat is the size of a baseball. Alone with Joan Montgomery—*gulp*. Nothing is more terrifying than being left unaided with the matriarch of my nightmares. Speaking of Ella, her nose juts into the air when she spots me from afar, giving Cindy Lou Hoo a run for her money. I can't help but giggle when she stalks away like a child, and it eases some of the tension. *I can do this.*

Relaxing my frame, I refocus on Colin and hope my widened eyes are enough of a hint to bring him back as soon as humanly possible. He nods, as if my hidden message is received. Circling my waist, he leans in and brushes his lips against my cheek. I melt into him when his whispered breath meets my ear. "I'll be with you soon, baby." Standing to his full height, he addresses Joan. "Take good care of my heart while I'm away."

I blush at his sweet words and the fact he said them to his once mother-in-law. With a final squeeze to my hip, he turns and heads through the living room, stopping every few feet to shake a hand in passing. When he's out of sight I look to Joan, whose own gaze has remained trained on Colin as well.

"He's always been such a romantic." She sighs and tilts her head in my direction. "You're a lucky woman, Charlise."

"I prefer Charlie and yes, I am very lucky."

Joan hesitates the shortest moment, but doesn't respond. Tucking my wrist through her extended elbow we follow the path Colin just took.

"Here," she says, handing me a glass of wine from a passing server's tray. "A Sauvignon from California. It's one of my favorites." Taking her own long-stemmed glass, she steers us into the party.

We stroll through a tall vaulted entrance and into a grand, for lack of a better word, ballroom. The space is sectioned off into multiple seating areas; two baroque couches face each other in one, four armchairs in another, and a grand piano situated in a corner next to the biggest fireplace I've ever seen. Famous paintings line the wall; spotlights hang from the ceiling to ensure they're prominently on display. Even with the most expensive furnishings and decorations, the house seems cold. It presents as a museum, not a home. Missing are the personal pictures and knickknacks that would warm it to a family. This is detached and empty, although forty people fill the room.

Most of the guests stand in small parties, discussing one topic or another. We stop at a group made up of all women, who pause their conversation as we approach.

"Ladies, it appears the wine is flowing nicely." Joan's smile is empty, an artificial plastic rise of her lips.

"You always have the best selection, Joany." The rancor in the last word is almost lost in the southern accent coming from a brunette miming Delta Burke.

"I'm sure you would know, missy," Joan mumbles between gritted teeth before dragging me forward. "Won't you all be so kind to welcome Charlise Carter into our little soiree?"

"Charlie . . ." I pipe in, but Joan's already talking over me, introducing each of the six.

As it turns out, Delta is married to Adam and the others are matched up in some way to various politicians or influential families. I don't get the chance to share my views on gun control, but the dull stare and bobbing head come in handy. The latest fashion trends of the First Lady are reviewed and criticized in detail. I mean fine detail. These women make piecemeal out of her choices and throw her to the wolves, enjoying the desecration. Who would've thought an orange blouse was so sensational?

"Excuse us, my dears. It's my duty to show Charlise around." Joan smirks and tilts her chin toward Delta. "Do enjoy another glass, missy. I made sure to increase our stockpile when I learned of your R.S.V.P." On that parting note, Joan takes my arm and leaves huffing whispers behind.

"What was that about?" I can't help my curiosity. Peeking over my shoulder I see the six women in animated conversation, Delta's face so red she's on the verge of a volcanic eruption.

"Nothing but a little tit-for-tat. Missy needs to learn to keep her hands to herself. But enough about that. How are you liking the campaign trail so far?"

"Oh, oh . . ." I look back once more to find Delta stomping out of the room. "It . . . it's a fantastic experience. Each day brings something new." The ease and friendliness with which she addresses me is in direct contrast to whatever just happened and it's disconcerting. Why is she being nice to me? Every other Montgomery wants to bury me in the backyard, yet Joan's sweet as pie.

"I always found campaigning tiresome. The day-in, day-out, city-to-city pace was exhausting."

"You ran for office?"

She laughs. "Not me, John. Several times in fact. All three tries were unsuccessful; that's when he realized he was better suited to behind-the-scenes management of a campaign and advising."

I study her expression. The small smile lifting her mouth belies the disappointment clouding her tone. "Oh, don't look at me like that." She shakes her head and sighs. "I'm only disappointed because

John was. He put his heart and soul into those campaigns. Each defeat broke him just a little more. It's gut-wrenching to watch the man you love suffer through the loss of his dream."

I blanch. Through the fear that my past could harm Colin, I've never stopped to think he would actually lose and what that would do to him.

She pats my hand. "No sad faces here, Charlise. Your Colin is doing superb in the polls. His march to the White House is a clear victory in our minds."

The baseball is back. It's a lump the wine does nothing to erase, but I don't have time to think it through as we stop at a heated discussion.

An aging man, very professor-like in an old-school tweed jacket, huffs when Joan interrupts to introduce me. She's barely finished pronouncing my last name before he nods and jumps back to topic. "There's a gun in eighty-eight percent of American households. It's no wonder they've found a way into the schools."

"Controlling the gun population shouldn't be at the forefront of our minds, controlling the people ought to be," says the man with a eyebrows so thick they've grown into one.

Two other men jump on that statement. I stand back and watch in amusement, not at the topic, but the intensity that emanates from the participants. Hands fly, voices rise and faces get red. It's quite entertaining.

At the tail end of the professor's last statement, I pipe in. "Shouldn't we research—"

"Gentleman, if you would excuse us."

I fumble on my words and with my feet as Joan drags me along to the opposite side of the large living room. *What was that about?* I don't bother to ask because her mouth is twisted as if she just ate an entire box of lemon drops. Instead I focus on the Montgomerys' home. It's majestic, as striking as the highly waxed grand piano to my left. Joan drops my arm and sweeps her fingers over the bared keys, but no one pays any attention to the kaleidoscope of sound. When I look up, my mouth falls open. Raquel Meyers is not ten feet away, clinging to a man who may be twice her age. How did I miss her?

Joan laughs. "You've met Raquel?"

"Ah, briefly. When I first began working with Colin. I didn't realize she would be here."

"I'm sure no one did, dear. Raquel is a surprise addition."

She hasn't changed: tall and statuesque, drowning in caviar and diamonds. Each glamorous curve, from bust to hip, is held captive by ruched cobalt silk. But the blue is overcome with green, namely the nasty green-eyed monster of jealousy. The hair at the nape of my neck stands on end with a chill. She may have had Colin, but he is mine. Mine, as sure as the day follows night. This realization brings with it clarity. It's not just jealousy I feel, but also possession. A sudden need to protect him consumes me. I want to gather him up and steal him away. Hide him from past hurts—hide him from the likes of Raquel who used him for his position and power.

"Why a surprise?" I ask, staring as Raquel tosses her head back in gratuitous laughter.

"It seems she has taken up house with Ramsey Nichols." She points to the tall, handsome man next to her. The patch of gray at his temple is one of the indicators his age overshadows hers by many years.

"And you don't think it's a good match?"

She smiles, a wicked sneer that's all too familiar. This I know. Ella has a good mirrored image of Mommy, dearest. "It's not for me to judge; however, I would believe his wife wouldn't think so."

"He's married?" I'm unable to hide the shock in my high-pitched question.

"Yes, and it would behoove Raquel to remember that. She will not be looked upon with a kind eye when this blows over."

I frown. "Aren't they divorcing? I mean, how could they get back together after he's been with another woman?"

"Don't be so naïve, Charlise." The harsh lilt to my name has goose-bumps spark to life on my arms. "This is not high school. We commit to our men and stick with them through the ugly messes, forgive them for infidelities." Joan laughs at my gasp and pats my hand. "It will happen; it always does. Your job is to forgive and stand by his side during the press conference, send his suit to the dry cleaners so the evidence is washed away, and let him shower you with his sorrow. Every woman in Washington has to decide if they're strong enough for this life."

SEVEN

WHAT? I TURN FROM Raquel and stare wide-eyed at Joan.

"You have a lot to learn and I have little time to school you. Journalism may have been your career at the beginning of this campaign, but it's not any longer. Colin is your job. Everything you do from this moment on is to support his effort to gain the White House. The world revolves around him, and you will do well to remember that. You don't have an opinion—not anymore."

Dragging in a breath, she leans in. "First order of business: learn Colin's. When you speak, it's his voice." She takes my hand in both of hers, squeezing until circulation stops. "Support, comfort, console, and for God's sake stop introducing yourself as Charlie. This is not some backyard barbeque. You're on display, a reflection of him, *an extension of him*. You may think orange blouses are fine, but you won't after the press destroys you the first time. Stop rolling your eyes. If I can see them, so can everyone else. Get smart about this and do it fast. One wrong move on your part could see him slip in the polls, and we work on margins in this business. There's no room for error."

I can only stare, my mouth parted and skin tingling.

"Chin up, head held high. Every day, Charlise. No matter what's said on television or whispered in the gossip columns. When he gets his first girlfriend on the side, brush it off. Deny the allegations and cry in your pillow. If you want to survive you'll become like the rest of them." Her eyes travel the room and she drops my numb hand. "Welcome to the world of make-believe, where appearances are not as they seem and wine is the only cure for it." Just like that, the wicked witch retracts her cape and Joan, the pleasant woman I met at the door, returns. "Will you excuse me, dear? Congressman Williams and his lovely wife just walked in." I continue to stare, dumbfounded, as she leaves, her blond hair tied tight in a bun on top of her head, and her back ramrod straight.

All of this is unwanted food for thought. I chew on it for a moment, focused on the contents of my glass. How naïve am I? Fidelity has never been my concern. Should it be?

Our fight has been to find a way to be together. Now that we are, I've not stopped to consider another woman or how Washington will affect our relationship. The surety of a future with Colin is new and beautiful and exciting. Our love is so fresh, it drips with the dew of early morning. I think of history, a subject close to Colin's heart, as a predictor of what's to come. Just off the top of my head I can think of multiple scandals in the White House, but Colin is different. He's proven that to me time and time again. The nature of his relationship with Abby, or rather the demise of it, is a sure indicator infidelity is the least of my worries.

My gaze is drawn to Raquel, her hand resting on the shoulder of her married partner. What the hell kind of world have I walked in to?

In a very unladylike way, I gulp down my wine and hand the empty glass to a passing waiter. It's time to find Colin. Heading in the direction he took earlier, I steer clear of Raquel, although, I catch her head swivel in my direction as I slip into a long hall. Straight ahead is the exit to a patio, and a set of double doors are pried open just before them, to the left. I slide through the small gap into the library but silence is my only companion. Damn, he's not here.

This part of the house is straight out of a gentlemen's club. It's all dark wood and red velvet drapes. A large, antique desk hovers in the center of the room, and two wingbacks sit in front of it. The faint hint of cigar smoke lies in the air but it's the floor-to-ceiling mahogany bookcases that I'm drawn to. From what I can see they're filled to the brim with just about every genre. I pass world news encyclopedias and political science for an easier one . . . the classics. Running my fingers over the rippled spine of *Moby Dick*, I get lost in thought, Joan's words seeking purchase in my brain.

She wants to change my name. I've always been Charlie. I don't even know who Charlise Carter is. No one calls me that, except Colin. He's done so when trying to make a point and when introducing me. *Wait, what*? I groan. Does he feel the same way? Oh, shit. I am the backyard barbeque to his ten-course meal. A burger compared to filet mignon. Can ground chuck ever become a steak? I laugh at the comparison. At least he appreciates my sense of humor, but will the public?

Taking a deep breath I move on to *Pride and Prejudice*, a fitting novel given the circumstances. It's a mirror of my life—two social classes colliding for love. I've always felt joining Colin's world would be difficult and now I know for sure. His path to the presidency would be so much easier with someone like . . . well, just about anyone he's been with before me.

I jump and whirl around at the sound of the door latching. Ella borrowed her mother's broom and has flown in to meet me. Damn again.

"Make yourself at home," the snide comment slithers from her lips. She circles away from the door, watching me like the Mona Lisa. Her unnerving half-grin remains in place while her eyes stay trained on me from all angles.

The chill along my spine is back in full force and it's not pleasant. But I intend to be. "Thank you. It's a beautiful library; I'm enjoying the selection."

"You'll ruin him," she hisses.

I roll my eyes for lack of a better response. "Ella, seriously. We're both adults, there has to be some common ground . . ."

"You're such an amazing fool, but I didn't think you sunk to stupid. Now I'm not so sure."

"Thanks for your hospitality, but I didn't stop by for a handful of sharp knives." I'm trying hard to be the better person, but after her last stunt I would like nothing better than to scratch her eyes out with my teeth. What would the media say about that? "Have a swell night," I say instead and beeline for the door.

Her hand on my shoulder has me swinging around until we're face to face. I focus on the sight of her fingers burning into my skin through the lace. Revulsion shoots straight to my eyes and they fall to slits. "Don't . . . touch . . . me," I ground out between my teeth, yanking away from her grip.

"You'll listen and listen well. I'm not mincing words any longer. You're going to ruin Colin and his career. He's at a critical point in his campaign. This relationship"—her lip curls and a fang peeks out—"is a farce. The fact you're unwilling to acknowledge how ridiculous it is speaks volumes. I'm astounded by your selfishness. Have you even considered what will happen when he loses because of you? Because you're keeping secrets that when found out will rock his campaign, because . . . look at you." And she does, a long perusal from head to toe that ends with a finger pointed in my face. "You don't belong here."

"That's enough." I shove her hand aside and take a step closer. With my stilettos on I tower over her. An advantage I use to push her backward with each step I take.

I'm done.

"Now it's your turn to listen. We couldn't be more different. I've fought for everything I have and the only remedy for the silver spoon shoved up your ass is a lobotomy." Anger rolls up my spine and out of my mouth. I hate that I'm defending myself to this heartless woman. "You have no idea what I went through. I'm not asking for you to approve of what I did, but it'll be a cold day in hell before I let the likes of you judge me. Until you've been in my shoes keep your mouth shut—"

"Tell that to Amer—"

"You don't get to speak," I scream and lean down until she recoils. One more foot has Ella backed into the wall, eyes widening when she hits it. "Stop interfering," I ground out.

She tries for smug, but the subtle change to her eyes is hinting toward doubt. "Or what? You're not in position to threaten . . ."

"Don't push me. Who do you think Colin would stand behind if it were you or me?"

"He's fought for this his whole life."

"Now you're the fool. You Montgomerys pretend to know him, but that's all it is. A façade. I know what he's fought for and what he needs." Ella's lips part. I snap my fingers in front of her face and she clamps them shut.

"Let me be clear. I'll even put it into simple terms so you can understand. Colin is with me. I warm his bed. He finds release in my body." I laugh at her sharp wheeze. "That's right. Simple, isn't it?" I'm vibrating with fury and from the look on her face she can feel my wrath.

With her nod, I spin and walk away. Stopping by the door I turn to her once more. She has yet to move. "Oh, and one more thing . . . Colin *loves* me. *Loves . . . me*. Sink your fangs into that bone and chew on it, bitch."

I leave as she slumps against the wall. I've had it with this sham of a party. The Montgomerys can take their shit and shove it. I'm consumed with resentment and it's directed at everyone: Joan for her goddamn definition of a Washington wife, Ella for her constant interference and Colin for bringing me here to deal with this asinine family. I stumble to a stop when rounding the corner into the ballroom. Raquel . . . Rage colors my vision red. There, center stage for everyone to see, is Colin surrounded by almost the entire assembly. The broad line of his shoulders stretches wide and narrows to the curve of his fine ass. And just above it, in the indented arc made for my hand, *made for me*, is Raquel. The sight of her manicured claws stroking Colin's back sends me over the edge.

"Cocktail, miss?" A waiter sidetracks me. Grateful for the interruption, I accept his wares and knock back the contents before he can even walk away. Ella's right, I don't belong here. The more I know of Colin's world, the less inclined I am to like it. I can't fathom spending night after night with people like this. Now I know exactly why he needs me. He needs relief from the idiotic droves of people that surround him every day. This experience has driven that point home. He's said all of this before, but now it makes sense.

The second glass of wine eases some of the tension and I drag my gaze back to him and the claw that's still in my place. His deep timbre resonates through the room.

"There's no doubt healthcare reform is needed, but not in the way the current plan is laid out. We're headed down a path to socialized medicine."

Raquel's hand falls when he steps to the side and by the lift and sway of his head, it appears he's looking for someone—*looking for me*. The topic of conversation piques my interest. Not for the same reasons as the other guests, but because he owes me and I intend to collect.

I stay behind; each time he turns I take a step in the opposite direction. I've yet to move past my irritation and right now, I'm feeling reckless because of it. He's kept me at bay for too long. I've needed him, needed the connection, and each time his response was to tease and keep me an arm's length away. Well, it's time he experienced the same distance, the desire to touch intensified by separation. My restraint will surpass his.

Let's see who wins at this game.

Colin continues to volley back and forth about the Affordable Care Act. At the same time he's searching the room, turning to look behind him or peering out into the hall. Time ticks away, minutes, probably thirty, as we play cat and mouse. Eventually he catches my eye. Relief loosens the tight bunch of his brow. He takes a step in my direction until a question from Joan keeps him in place. By the length of this debate I'm going to be screaming all night long. I can't help the slow smirk lifting a corner of my mouth. Make him pay. That's my motto for the night.

A waiter passes by. I help myself to another glass just as Colin's eyes stray from the congregation panting at his feet like puppies, to mine. They narrow, as if in wonder of my insisted distance. My response? Take a sip of the chilled wine and slip my finger in my mouth after I swallow. I've got his undivided attention. Voices become dim noise in the background. There's only Colin, and the mounting hunger between us.

Brazened by the alcohol and banking on the attention Colin commands, I release my finger to caress my body, starting at the hollow of my throat, feathering to my collarbone and over the breast he held not long ago. I can almost hear his growl, my imagination not as good as the real thing, but enough to warm my thighs. His parted lips bring with it a sharp inhale. This I know by the jagged rise of his chest—a subtle hint at his growing need. Now if I could just place my hand over the front of his pants, I'm confident I'd find his body stirring to life, the hard pulse of his erection weighing heavy in my hand.

A shimmer awakens my own arousal, all along my skin and in the violent beat of my heart—everywhere. I imagine his hand taking over for mine in the long sweep against my abdomen and when it falls lower to gather the hem of my skirt.

"Excuse me . . ." His powerful directive cuts into my reverie, and my eyes snap to focus on his. Midnight blue and deadly—a potent combination. The crowd easily parts as the tiger stalks his prey.

I'm not ready to be caught.

Make him pay, the motto sings in my ear. With each step he takes, I move away. A simple game, yet by the storm gathering in his gaze it may become dangerous.

"Payback," I whisper the word, moving my mouth in deliberate slow motion so he can read it.

His nostrils flare and he sets his drink on a nearby table. Loosening his tie, he takes another step forward. Two polished women, one of them a Delta look-a-like, seize hold of his elbows. It takes a moment before his gaze drags from mine to theirs, and even then I sense his distraction. Fawning over him, they paw at his arms, and one is shameless enough to run fingers along his lapel.

It's my turn to growl. Just as it rips from my throat Ramsey Nichols sidesteps into my space and casts a long look up my entire length before landing on my mouth. He licks his lips in clear invitation and my stomach rolls. Raquel, his mistress, is on the other side of the room, God knows where his wife is, and he's staring at me as if I'm next on the food chain. This is not helping my mood.

"Hello darlin'. Having a good time?"

There's no way he could see the disgusted curl of my lip because he's too focused on my cleavage, obscured only by delicate pink lace.

"Not anymore," I snap and hand him my glass. The shocked expression on his face is priceless, but not worth sticking around for more.

Without looking at Colin, or anyone else for that matter, I cut through the living room to the front door. I'm ready to roar when two hands gripping my hips hold me back. That is until I'm pressed against familiar hard planes and the wash of sandalwood fills the air.

"Going somewhere?"

"Take me home. Take me anywhere but here."

"I'll say goodnight . . ."

I whip around, frantic in my pursuit of freedom. I won't go back into the fray. "Now." Even I can hear the demand. It's not a request. Cat and mouse is over. "I'm not playing anymore."

Darkness falls over his features, his jaw clenching as I take his tie in hand. I tug while backing away and let it drop when I hit the steps. Colin doesn't even glance over his shoulder when the hard clasp of the lock shuts us into the deepening night. A slow breeze lifts my hair and cools my anger by a fraction, leaving only longing in its wake.

"Come here." Reaching out, his arm anchors my waist and pulls me close once more. The erection I imagined earlier is brought to life, twitching against my stomach. Dipping down until his mouth hovers over mine, and our breath mingles together, he says, "No more games."

"No . . ." I sigh in agreement when he steers us down the steps. Holding me as I fumble, my hands wrestle into his hair, staking their claim. "I mean yes . . ." I manage, but I don't know what I mean. No more games, but yes I want to play. I want to play with him.

Drake is waiting by the curb, somehow knowing we were on our way out. Colin heaves me into the SUV and I slide over as far away as possible. If I touch him, I will take him. It wouldn't be pretty with an audience. I've never wished for a limo more so than at this moment.

"Home, sir?" I catch Drake's quick glance in the rearview mirror, a stoic expression until the small lift of his lips.

I look out the window when Colin's harsh confirmation barrels through the confined space. A simple "home" has Drake accelerating fast enough to catapult me into the seat. I would laugh, but Colin's face straightens any humor right out of mine.

His gaze is fastened on the road ahead. The rigid set of his shoulders is a catalyst for his arm stretched between us. But it's his fingers that give away the need for separation and keep me in place. They grind together, his thumb rubbing so tight against the others the friction could start a fire. And they do. A simmering glow began days ago within me. Colin's subtle stokes brought it to flame and now, I'm burning up.

It could be minutes, probably twenty, and as soon as we pull into the drive I fly out the door and up to the entrance. He's behind me again, his breath panting in my ear.

"Do you think you can escape, bunny?"

Colin surrounds me, an arm on either side, one reaching to the lock, the other drawing up the hem of my skirt. It's an erotic feather-light touch that stops just shy of where I need him to be.

A groan is my only answer as his deft fingers have us inside in ten seconds. We stumble into the foyer and he slams the door behind us. I turn, watching him watch me.

He stalks forward and instinctively I step back. This is a new look. Dark and stormy I'm familiar with, but now he's downright predatory. As if he could eat me.

EIGHT

I GROAN AGAIN. WITH his jacket thrown on a chair, he's making easy work of his tie, ripping the knot open and now his shirt. Before I can take another step back his chest is bare and rising with the same intensity as my own.

I'm paralyzed by his eyes, by his body, by his mouth, by everything this man does to me. *I give up. The hunter has his prey and I want to be dinner.*

"Dinner?" He laughs at my widened eyes, but his killer look remains.

He's before me now, so close I have to tip my head back to see his face. Dipping to run his nose along my jaw, he breathes deep as he comes by my ear to whisper, "I can hear you."

Oh shit. I clamp my mouth shut, but it's not long before it falls open to gulp in air. "Do tigers bite their bunnies right here?" he asks and licks the pulse pounding in my neck. Then he bites it, hard.

"Ahh . . . yes . . ." I cry.

Backing me into the wall, he puts a hand on either side of my face. Hip to hip, he ensures I can feel every inch of him. Every . . . single . . . inch rubbing up and down at a pace designed to drive me mad. Somehow in my haze I miss the removal of my dress. The brush of his chest against mine pebbles my nipples into tight peaks and I lose a little of myself as desire, swift and shattering, takes over. My knees buckle and my hands tangle in his hair to hold me upright. The sexy-ass smirk is there, lying on his lips, when he lifts his head.

"I could make a quick meal out of you, but this . . ." He rocks into me, ". . . is just the appetizer."

I mewl and lean in to kiss him, but he pulls away, grabbing me so fast a shriek slips from my throat without thought. My tiger becomes a caveman, hiking me over his shoulder and bounding up the stairs and into his room. I barely have time to laugh and whack his ass before he throws me on the bed like a ragdoll. Bouncing and breathless when I land, all of the laughter is driven from my lungs when I look at Colin.

Bare chest heaving, he kneels on the edge of the mattress staring, and drinking me in with those insatiable eyes. He doesn't speak; he doesn't have to. I can see everything written in the tight clench of his jaw, the tension easing as his gaze lingers over my body. He wants me, but it's more than that. More than need, more than lust. The shadow covering his face is not enough to hide his love. I may be dinner, but it's a feast worthy of a king.

An unexpected moan escapes my parted lips, yanking his gaze back to mine. He smiles a feral smirk that grows as he falls to his hands and crawls over me until we're nose to nose.

"I'm hungry, bunny."

I lick my lips and accept his mouth when he crushes mine. The hunger eating away at me for days is released and reciprocated as we paw at each other. I'm desperate to touch, pet and claw my nails down his back. I feel his answering moan in the pulse between my thighs.

It's not enough; it's never enough. Not with Colin. Snaking my hand between us, I unleash his belt. After I fumble at the zipper I settle for palming his erection through his pants. His mouth becomes more urgent, as do his tongue and hands.

But he breaks away, pushing up to his knees and pressing mine apart with the spread of his. The harsh sound of our labored breathing falls around us like the tails of a fireworks display: explosive and ready to start a fire.

"No more games?"

"No." I reach for his fly, with more success this time, moving under his briefs to find his hard length. Taking back a little control, my fingers glide over his penis and squeeze at the base. It's not fair, so not fair, that he's unfazed and hot as hell. A lock of hair has fallen on his forehead, no doubt released from its perfection by my grip. I want him everywhere. I want to become overwhelmed by Colin McKenna, my mouth filled with the taste of him on my tongue, blinded by his beauty and held captive by his touch. I need to break through his implacable self-discipline and I just might know how.

"You've kept me waiting too long. Please . . ."

"Please what?"

"Eat me."

Tipping his head back, he looks at the ceiling while exhaling a deep breath. Sliding his knees further apart he takes mine with them, leaving me open and vulnerable.

Being open with Colin is a freedom. I don't have to think, I just have to feel, and take in each sensation and revel in the pleasure that follows. I'm not embarrassed or self-conscious. I get to want and need and *demand.*

"Now." Gripping him harder grabs his interest and then he's on me, biting and kissing into my neck until I barely remember my name. Any restraint I thought he had is gone and so is my mind when his teeth clamp onto my nipple. I bow from the bed with the unexpected voracity with which he feeds on me. His mouth has a direct line to the apex of my thighs; he sucks until the ache in my clitoris is deep and pulsing and then flicks me with the tip of his tongue.

Oh, dear lord Jesus. I gasp as his teeth sink in. Covering me in his brand, he leaves what I'm sure is a long path of impressions, first on one breast and then the other. But he's not done. Starting again, he sucks and laps at my nipples until they're screaming, or maybe I am, from sensitivity.

More, I need more, and I need him to touch me everywhere, but he follows his design, matching them and deepening the marks that will surely last a lifetime.

It's not just my groin that pulses in a torturous ache, but my skin. My breasts are hot and heavy under his attention, yet the heat has traveled along every nerve and they're begging for the wet glide of his tongue and piercing imprint of his teeth. I've never loved and hated the cool air so much in my life. It's an aching blow. I long for it, want to feel the echoes of the rush and the sting as it skims over my newly formed imprints that drive both pleasure and pain. They bind me, as surely as I'm bound to him.

Whimpers fall from my lips, one after the other, mixing with Colin's hungry groan as he licks his way to my navel. He's greedy and impatient, tugging me down to the end of the bed so he can kneel before me, and spread my thighs open wide. Holding me down with a hand on each one, he stares at me through his lashes.

"Do you like making me hot for you?" The heat of his breath mixes with the damn torturous air wringing out another cry and then a scream when he dips down. That tongue. Oh, how I love his tongue.

"Don't stop," I whine when he does and that damn smirk is back.

"Mmm, I think you do. But what else do you like, baby?" He flicks my clitoris and we both moan. "Do you enjoy this?" Oh God, his teeth and lips, and . . . and . . . holy shit . . . his mouth hollows out when he takes me in without mercy.

Yes, I gasp and then cry out, "Yes, oh, for the love of God, yes." I grip his hair, holding him in place as an orgasm takes over and I lose a little bit of my sanity in the white-hot bliss that surrounds me.

Just when I think he's letting up, when his tongue replaces his teeth and the long slide of it eases against the peak of my high, he starts again. Ravenous and demanding, that beautiful mouth is still hungry against me.

Involuntary jerks take hold of my muscles as I spasm beneath him. His hand snakes out and grabs my breast, pinching it so the ache isn't only centered under his lapping tongue, but all around the depraved branding he gave me moments ago.

"Again," he mumbles into me, his eyes sharp as they pin me down.

"No," I cry and wrench away, but he follows without missing a beat and a pinch of his teeth. "Oh . . . Colin."

"Yes," he growls, forcing his demand into my flesh as he works me over. I'm lost in the graze of his mouth and this time when he takes me in, his fingers, first one and then another, sink inside, finding the spot, the amazing I'm-never-going-to-recover-from-this spot, he rubs in and out, over and over.

"Stop, please," I beg as my knees draw up and lock around his head. But he doesn't let go. He just keeps licking and sucking and . . . *I let go*. I give in to the pleasure at his insistence and welcome the numbing paralysis that seizes and draws me from the bed and into the arch of a ballerina, graceful and poetic. My arms follow the pose, lifting above my head in the rigid form needed to hold the frame as I spiral out of control. My breathing is suspended, as is the scream immortalized with my statuesque position.

Oh, so amazing. As I come down, he pulls me up into the center of the bed and onto his waiting lap. Without thought, I've straddled his knees and just when my fingers find their place in his hair and my arms wrap around his head, he glides inside of me. The stretching fullness, the pulsing depth, the mind-altering moment when we're one stops time and he gives me that minute to just feel him.

"Ah, Charlie. Christ you feel good."

I'm complete and want for nothing. Then it changes. My body takes charge and demands movement.

"Hold on, baby. I'm going to give you everything." He grips my hips, lifting only to buck up as I sink down in a slick, frantic stroke. Again, up and down. I whimper as his mouth finds mine, dipping in long, licking strokes until we're both gulping for breath. "Yes," he whispers into my skin, "tell me what you want."

"I want this forever," I gasp and let my head fall back. Hands resting on his shoulders, I find the arch, the pose that stretches me thin and pulls out every ounce of pleasure my body can reap from his. Colin's growl awakens my wicked imp. I become wild, finding the feral side he brought to the surface not too long ago. Our bodies come together in violent slides of wet and heat and hunger. Leveling my eyes to his, I sink my nails into his back and say, "I want you to come."

"Fuck," he chokes out as I push him down and we roll so he's on top. His teeth find their place on my neck as he sinks in, a long, hard glide.

Oh, shit. What was meant to drive him mad has driven me up the mattress and into a frenzy. I can't get enough. *Please*. This isn't supposed to happen again. It can't be this intense, but it is and oh . . . *Colin, please make it happen . . . one . . . more . . . time.*

"Make me come with you."

He grunts and lifts up on his hands above me, working his hips faster, pushing deeper as my legs round his ass. Sweat beads on his brow and along the strong line of muscles that bunch and pull with exertion throughout his entire body.

I'm coiled like a spring and any minute, with the next thrust, oh . . . *yes*. I jerk beneath him and then around him as pleasure rips through me.

"Christ, oh fuck, baby, I can feel you." He throws his head back and loses himself, taking over my wildness and bucking into me as everything else disappears. I welcome him in my arms when he falls into his own heaven.

"I love you," I whisper and kiss into his shoulder. "I love you so much." Tears cloud my vision, derived from the beauty before me, and the experience we've shared. The pleasure we give and take in moments like this is exquisite and life-altering.

Conscious thought is slow to return and with it, the slick heat of his skin against mine is what I feel first. Then I'm overwhelmed with all things Colin—the weight of him pressing me into the mattress, his head buried against my breasts, the soft feather-light touch of his hair tickling my chin, and our legs tangled together.

His breath levels into a whisper. It speaks to me, offering a lifetime of perfect moments like this one. An invitation to enter a fairytale—dare I dream for my happily-ever-after?

We were different tonight—playful yet possessive, and teasing but desperate to love and express that feeling in touch. I'm not afraid to love him; I'm afraid to hurt him. I fear in some way my insecurities and imperfections will harm his future. Joan's sentiments come back in a rush, taking my breath away. What if he loses and it's because of me?

“I can feel you thinking. Stop.” His gruff voice reaches me just before the pierce of his teeth as he bites my nipple. It hardens and he takes me into his mouth, soothing the sting.

My gasp fills the room and crashes down when he clips me again. I’m quick to pull on his hair, bringing his eyes to mine. His grin is wicked, as are my thoughts. I lean in for a kiss, but he rolls over and takes me with him so our positions are reversed.

“Tell me what you’re afraid of,” he says while pulling me down to face him, my hair spilling around us.

“You read minds now, too?” I ask, sitting up to straddle his waist. “How is it you could pick my brain apart tonight?”

He chuckles. “I’m psychic, bunny.” Laughing louder when my mouth falls open, he sits up and kisses me breathless and then falls back down.

I bat his frisky hands away from my chest and say, “Be serious.”

“You talk out loud, sharing your thoughts.”

Eyeing him with a suspicious glare, I rub his chest. The hair is soft against my fingers. “Not all of the time.”

“No, not everything. But I’m good at reading your body too. You tighten up when you’re worrying. You’re over thinking; I can feel it. Tell me.”

I tilt my head and contemplate what to say. His face falls to serious and I know he’ll never let me go without sharing something. “Tonight was eye opening, that’s all.” I shrug and flip my leg over to lie on my back next to him. Staring at the ceiling, I weave my fingers through his. "It's like another world. One I never knew existed . . . and I'm not sure how I fit into it or if I want to."

I sense his gaze on me, so I turn to find him. Worry draws out the three lines between his eyes. He's on his elbow in a second, pulling me closer as if I've been floating away. "You fit with me."

"Yes, I do, and I'm not questioning us at all. Those people . . ." my voice drops to a whisper, ". . . they're all fucked up."

He laughs. "Is that the clinical term?"

"The closest I can get. I don't even know how to describe them. It's like watching *Dallas* reruns on T.V. All the women are meticulously groomed, with manners to match, but they eat at each other with words and stab daggers with their eyes. And the men . . . it seems they're all sleeping with someone else's wife." Holding his cheek in my hand, I confess, "I lost my mind when I saw Raquel touching you. I didn't like it."

I place my thumb over his mouth when he tries to speak. "It's okay. I know you didn't invite it. I wanted to protect you from her and everyone else. At the same time, I struggled . . . I don't know how to be like that, play the part."

He lets out a breath and squeezes my waist, inadvertently pulling me in even closer, and our legs tangle once more. "You're different than all of them. You're real. It's one of the many things I love about you." Leaning down, he brushes his lips against mine, once and then again. Our eyes lock and he says, "Tonight was a glimpse into what I've lived with for years. I hate the people, but hunger for the challenge and broad scope of Washington's depravity.

I can make a difference, with the people and the politics. I know I can." Passion hums beneath his skin and reaches me. He's meant to do this, meant for the path he has meticulously carved for himself.

"Before I knew you existed, I craved you. Craved the closeness, the contact, and the person who could take me away from the false pretense and feel alive again. You said that I've saved you, but it's simply not true." Scoping me into his arms, he cradles me close. "You saved me from a life of solitude. People surrounded me, yet I'd never been more alone. So, you can ask of me anything and I will give it freely. You have my heart. I'll give you my life, but don't ask me to give you up. I won't survive it, Charlie."

Closing my eyes, I draw him down with my hands on either cheek until his forehead rests against mine.

"I'd let you go if it was for your wellbeing, just don't let my career drive you away." His words are spoken in a desperate whisper against my mouth.

"I'm not going anywhere. Never. I'm only learning how to fit in." For a long moment we just breathe and feel and revel in each other. I'll figure this out.

"What else?" he asks. The warm caress of his breath falls over me, waking me from my reverie. When I find his eyes they're a blurred midnight, his unerring confidence clouded by unease.

I sigh. "Ella."

The ridges lining his muscled arms tense around me. "What did she do?" To say his tone is cutting doesn't quite describe the malice sliced into each word.

“Nothing,” I lie. I'll tell him about it later—no sense inflaming his anger while we talk about hers. “Will you tell me about her and why she’s so crazy?”

Silence stretches on for a minute and I fear his withdrawal, the emotional detachment to anything that happened before Sara. As he lowers me onto the mattress, I clutch his biceps and hold on for dear life. Relief sinks in when he relaxes next to me, propped up on his elbow to keep eye contact. The steady strum of his fingers over the well-played lines of my ribs revolves into reassurance. He’s present and accounted for.

“I don’t know where to start.”

I smile and stroke over the three lines that appear as his brow drops down. “The beginning’s always a good place.”

He nods. “Ella and I met in college, assisting on Bush’s campaign. John was involved, and Ella was a tagalong, but she spent more time volunteering than I did. We became friends,” he says this with a heavy emphasis on the last word. “From the start I suspected she had feelings for me, but I wasn't interested in anything more, and didn't think much about it. She had her life; I had mine. We stayed in touch when I left for Harvard, connected through the various campaigns we both supported.

“When I came back to Indiana, we fell into an old pattern, maybe even seeing each other more than we had before. The college gang had moved on, so Ella was one of a few friends who remained in town.”

"Where was Evan?" I ask, while running my fingers through the hair at the nape of his neck.

"Back home in California. He completed his second degree at Berkeley. A year or so later, he returned to join my team at McKenna Industries. Shortly after that I met Abby." The strum has turned into a clamp, his hand baring the weight of our conversation and holding me in place. I can't tell if it's because of his own animosity toward her or his fear of mine, but either way, I encourage him with touch. My hand is anchored on his hip. "Ella was hurt by my interest in her, but she moved on with someone else—or so I thought."

A haze falls over his features as he tries to hide his disgust, but it's written in every taut line.

"Who?"

"Alex Miller."

I tense beneath him. "What?"

He nods. "They were together off and on throughout the time I dated Abby." The clamp on my hip cinches tighter.

"Okay, so how did being with him translate into Ella terrorizing half of America?"

"Alex left her for another woman." I know my eyes are the size of the moon, big, round and white. "And I believe the other woman was Abby."

"Oh, God." I hold on tight, securing myself even more to his rigid form. "How do you know?"

He bites his lip and thinks. "I don't know for an absolute certainty, but his behavior after her death made me suspect it. At the hospital, after the accident, Sara needed a blood transfusion. I offered to donate because supply was low and I would have done anything to save her." His wavering voice gives away his pain. "As it happened, my blood type was not compatible with hers. It made me believe I wasn't her biological father and after she'd died I had the test run to confirm it."

I close my eyes for the briefest moment. "I'm so sorry."

A terse laugh escapes when he continues. "Alex was at the funeral, too upset for a casual friend. He didn't hide his emotions well, and it made me believe it was him. I asked Ella once and she denied knowing who Abby was with. But my suspicion is that's why she's angry—because in her mind, she lost two men to her sister."

Colin's hair tickles my chin when he covers me with his body, and his head nestles into my breasts. My fingers are there, streaking through the waves, providing any kind of comfort I can.

"I was a mess when Sara died. My marriage had just fallen apart, and as a result of the argument the accident happened. Abby's death, then Sara's—I wasn't in a great place," he mumbles against my skin as he burrows further down. "My control slipped, as did my reason to go on. It was then that I slept with Ella. I'm not proud of it. Abusing our friendship for reckless physical need was appalling."

He looks up when a huff bursts from my chest. "I don't believe for one minute she didn't plan that attack. She wanted you and took advantage of your state of mind. I know enough about Ella to believe it's true."

Shrugging, he lies back down. "Maybe. But it still happened and it fed her desire to change our relationship. Something I could never want."

"So what about Alex?"

"I learned of Abby's infidelity just before she died. My anger over that and the abuse of our wedding vows transitioned into cold detachment. It's hard to explain, but the simplest way is to say I stopped caring. I didn't care about Alex and what he may have done, nor did I have faith in any future relationships. It's why I kept things physical, not emotional. My trust in people was broken, but for a few who I relied on. I left Alex alone to suffer in his own misery; I had my own to deal with."

I squeeze Colin so tight it elicits a breath that wraps around my nipple, as if his mouth were there. His fingers follow to play with the now puckered point. "He's infatuated with you."

"Because I look like her?"

"Yes, that and because you're mine." It's his turn to squeeze until breathing is compromised. Looking up and drawing close, his mouth hovers over mine.

"Colin?" I want everything out in the open. "Is he . . . do you think he's stalking me?"

"I don't know. I had Phil look into him, but nothing tied him to any of the events except his location in some places." He responds to the drop in my brow, "I will never let him hurt you."

"I know," I whisper. "I love you."

"As I love you, baby. More than you will ever know."

The only thing I can do is to kiss him. Kiss away history and the uncertainty surrounding the present. His tongue sweeps into my mouth with the same urgency, until it's not enough and I want more. More Colin.

Breaking away, he rests his forehead against mine to catch his breath. When he does, he says, "I've dreamed about you in my bed." It takes some effort, but I roll him onto his back and straddle his hips once more.

"Yeah? What in particular were you dreaming about?" I kiss and nip along his jaw and neck, taking my time to get to his nipple. His breath catches when I tease it between my teeth.

"This, everything. I wanted you everywhere."

"Here?" I ask licking and kissing a path down his abdomen.

A tremor surges through his body when my hand sinks lower to grab his penis, squeezing the base and pulling up to the broad head.

"Yes," he growls and I smile; my tiger is back and it's good to see him.

"Here?" My breath fans over his hardening erection. I lick around the crown and down and back up to suck on him like a lollipop—my favorite kind.

Groaning, he manages a mumbled, "Yes."

"Then I'm about to make your dreams come true, baby," I say, just before taking him into my mouth.

NINE

THERE ARE MANY BENEFITS to waking up with Colin McKenna. Many, as in multiple. I smile into my coffee and revel in the ache of my muscles and the willowy effect they suffer from, even hours after he left. He certainly made up for the few days of abstinence. I feel him everywhere. When I move, it's as if his fingers follow. Last night his touch was desperate, hinting at a fear I would disappear unless his hold could keep me. The subtle outline of his grip on my hip stains the clear ivory of my skin, as do the ruddy burns on my neck and chest. All are reminders of where he's been. I'll never complain again about attending a party if my service results in that kind of service. I giggle and pull out my cell to text him good morning.

Although I was able to lie around in bed, he's been long gone to work and I miss him.

Dear CM, I love watching the birds nest in your oak tree. It would be a perfect morning if I could sit and watch the show, but I must stand because my vagina is broken from your giving nature. Can't wait to see you this eve. Love you, CC

P.S. Ali and Evan are confirmed for game night at seven.

As I set the phone down on the island counter top, Colin is calling. I barely get out a breathy "Hi" before his words barrel over mine.

"Are you trying to drive me crazy?" I can almost see his jaw clench as he grounds out the words.

"Of course not. It's my life's mission to loosen up your tie and everything else—although now that I'm thinking about it, there are some parts I prefer hard. Very, very hard. How do you feel right this second?"

"Charlie," he sighs, and I imagine him shaking his head. "It's my life's mission to make you happy and give you the world as your playground. That includes any part of my body you wish to play with."

"Mmm, good answer. Did I catch you at a bad time?"

"I always have time for you," he says in a low tone that sets my heart into a pitter-patter. "Dare I ask what you're going to do to keep busy today?"

"I'm making you dinner."

"Don't burn my house down."

"Ha ha, I've heard that one before." I roll my eyes. "Your housekeeper did a good job of stocking the fridge; I only need a few things from the market."

"No, not a chance."

"What do you mean, no? It's a quick run up to the fruit and vegetable market. I saw it a couple of blocks from your house on the way in yesterday."

"I'm not arguing about this. The answer is no. If you need something, I'll pick it up on my way home."

My temper peeks around the corner. "It's not a big deal. I'll have Drake take me."

"I forbid you to go and I'll make sure Drake knows it."

"Wait a minute." I'm pacing now, the sweet ache of last night forgotten in the clench of my knuckles around the phone. "I think I misunderstood, because there's no way you can *forbid* me to go. Let's start again . . ."

"Don't." The growl is back and it's not playful. It rips through me until my anger is front and center. "I'm in the middle of a meeting on the federal deficit, creating a plan to erase it. I'm not in the mood to worry about you outside of the house. There's someone trying to hurt you, or have you forgotten about that?"

"I'm well aware of my circumstances and yours. All I want to do is go to the goddamn store so I can make my boyfriend a nice dinner." I catch the crack in my voice before it completely breaks. "You're making it a big deal and it's not."

He groans. "Your safety is the most important thing to me. I'm sorry, baby. I really am. I can't let you go . . ."

"That doesn't make any sense. I have security. . ."

"They're calling me back in. We'll talk more about this when I get home. I don't care about dinner. Make whatever or order in." He falls silent. Each breath between us sharpens into a challenge. "Charlie?" he asks, when I remain quiet. "Don't be mad."

Who's he kidding? I'm beyond mad. "I'm hanging up now. Goodbye, Colin."

His sigh is loud and clear, "Goodbye, ba—"

I jam my finger as I end the call. *Don't baby me.* Stomping through the house to the front door, I swing it open to find Drake. He's stepping out of the black SUV parked by the lawn, phone pressed to his ear. Another man dressed in a similar black suit follows him up the walkway.

"Yes, sir. I understand . . . uh, yes. Ms. Carter is standing out front as we speak . . . I'll be sure to pass along the message."

A second later, Drake's call ends and we face a standoff. "I'd like to go to the store. I'll be ready in two minutes."

"Ms. Carter, I was given instructions to keep you home until Senator McKenna returns this afternoon." He at least looks remorseful with the sheepish set of his eyes. Mine narrow, and if I had a superpower they would be shooting laser beams.

"Fine." I don't wait for his apology before slamming the door and throwing myself on Colin's living room couch.

I will not cry; I will not cry. That chant works to wrestle away the tears of frustration. I'm not a child and it drives me crazy when Colin treats me like one. He actually thinks he can forbid me to go to the store? Puh-lease. I haven't been forbidden from anything since Ali outlawed *Grease Two* when we were sixteen. My sick obsession with the pink ladies drove her insane, to the point where she tossed the movie into the fire pit and did a dance as it melted in the flames.

Forcing my thoughts away from the lockdown, I plot out an escape route. My cell chirps with notice of a text and it doesn't take a rocket scientist to guess who it's from.

Dear CC, I'm sorry. I'll make it up to you and your vagina when I get home. I love you more than life. CM

His turn at funny and sweet does little to soften my thoughts. First thing's first: I need a plan. It's just the market, for the love of God. Two blocks down and to the left. If Colin and Drake won't help me get there, I'll go myself. A quick examination of the backyard reveals a padlocked gate opening to a neighboring sidewalk. Scavenging through the kitchen drawers uncovers a key.

It doesn't take long to learn the security pattern. Drake and his sidekick stay out front and at the top of the hour they walk the perimeter of the house. I wave when they peek in the windows, which has them scurrying for the cover of the trees because the laser beams are still quite piercing. I'm good at being mad. When it settles in, I can take it with me for days and sometimes longer. Mom says it's a skill I should refine, but I learned it in foster-care and it served me well.

After they declare the yard safe and return to the front, I slip out the door and then the gate. The walkway is clear, and in less than a minute I'm on the street behind Colin's house. So much for Phil's top-of-the-line security—it's certainly not Charlie Carter-proof. I giggle and it lightens my mood, taking me through the easy walk to the market. The day is full of bright sun, heating the air into the upper eighties. It feels good on my skin. Dressed in a white tank and jean skirt, I soak up the rays and enjoy the warmth.

The store is small, but clean and quaint. It's midday in Georgetown and still it's filled with patrons—mostly women, and it seems they cater to that crowd. Along the front wall is a rack of handmade aprons. One catches my eye and sparks an idea that grows into another plan, one that *will* drive Colin crazy.

As the concept takes shape and kills the last remnants of irritation, the weight of a stare prickles along my neck. The awareness stiffens my shoulders and I turn, slow and with a caution that screams *you should have brought Drake*. My breath rushes forward in relief when there's only chef Rocco DiSpirito's picture in a mass display of his latest cookbook. I'm alone and fidgeting with the ruffles of the fabric in my hand. Unease expands in my stomach and I hurry, spending the next five minutes in the vegetable aisle.

Checking out should be simple—it should be, but it's not. My smile falters when the cashier and woman behind me won't make eye contact, but I catch their stare on more than one occasion. Two others waiting in a nearby lane have their cell phones pointed in curious angles, the perfect angle for a picture. Well, shit. What I thought would be a speedy visit to the market has turned into a hair-raising, look-at-Charlie-Carter festival of fun. After paying and a hurried 'thanks,' I rush from the store and then down the street into Colin's neighborhood. He was right. I should've stayed home, yet my need to remain true to myself overcame my desire to fit into his life. It's a balance I need to find. I'm back at the house twenty minutes before anyone could become aware of my jailbreak, ingredients and utensils ready for battle in the kitchen.

I relax into the day and forget the unfortunate morning. When Drake walks by this time, the wave is friendlier, as are my eyes. And the next time I even offer lemonade.

ooo

Wine poured. Candles lit. Steak grilled. Salad made with ingredients fresh from the market. Charlie Carter? Sizzling in stilettos, black panties, and some kinda teeny 1950s replicated ruffled apron. Colin McKenna? Due home any minute.

We haven't spoken since our disastrous phone call, so I'm unsure what mood he'll be in, but if my vamped-out version of June Cleaver doesn't bring him to his knees, I don't know what will. I've long since drawn all the shades, pitching the house into muted sunlight. The candles flick and lash out with fevered flames on the dining room table, practically begging for romance. Evan and Ali aren't coming over for another three hours and I know exactly how to spend our free time.

The slamming car door is just enough warning for me to get in place, or at least try to look sexy. I fumble for the right pose, choosing the stool at the island, legs crossed, one hand lying on my knee and the other lazing around the rim of a wine glass. The most nonchalant look I can conjure masks my face, giving Colin's expressionless expression a run for his money.

"Char . . . lie?" he stutters, and I hold my grin. If someone can stumble to a stop, he does, right at the entrance to the kitchen as his gaze finds mine and travels the length of me, slow and hitching on my chest and then along the line of my legs and back up again. My pulse quickens at the sight of him.

"Welcome home, dear," I say, with not so contrived breathlessness. Even after a rather sleepless night and a long day at work, he's stunning, with his tie loosened and his hair masterfully disheveled, as if his hands raked through it a hundred times today. *Well hello Mr. McPerfect, my dinner is served.*

Holding back a giggle, I hand over his Zinfandel as he takes a measured step toward me. "I hope you worked up an appetite."

His lids lower and he looks skeptically at the wine, as if maybe I've slipped something inside the glass. Eyeing me over the rim, he drinks down a good amount and watches as I slip from the stool with as much grace as Charlie Carter can muster. Squeezing between Colin and the island, I make sure to rub the pretty frills of my apron over his chest and arm without looking purposeful. As I make my way to the fridge, I can feel the weight of his stare on my barely-there, just-as-frilly-on-the-ass briefs.

"I thought we'd start with an appetizer," I say, while bending from the waist at the opened door. Most definitely I planned out the vegetable tray on the bottom shelf, and for sure I take my time and wiggle my ass in the air. Absolutely I expected the sharp inhale that follows this show.

His tie is completely gone when I stand and turn, shirt loosened by three buttons. *Oh my, did it get hot in here?* My heart rate spikes, as does the pulse in a certain body part that needed repairing earlier in the day. I force my eyes to his, but his gaze isn't diverted from my frills as I place the tray on the island.

"Carrot?" I ask, handing one over. When he shakes his head, I tip it into my mouth and practice my oral skills—tongue, lips and teeth engage in a delicate yet thorough nibbling. Who knew fellating a vegetable would cause such a stir? It's not just the spiked breathing, or the parted lips, or even the flared nostrils that give him away. The not so subtle hand stroking the growing bulge just below his belt might be my biggest clue. And I mean big.

It's not time to giggle, so I refocus on the carrot and his hand and my body's already in the game. The heat just got turned up one more notch. I squirm under his scrutiny and rub my thighs together, wishing his hand were a little closer to home.

"If vegetables aren't your thing, can I offer you something more appetizing?" I mean for the words to come out in sexy confidence, but they're more liked a panted whisper.

His chest rises on a deep breath and his exhale rushes against my cheek when he steps before me. "What the hell are you wearing?" he asks while running a finger down the side of my breast, left exposed by the narrow cover.

"Cooking's a messy affair. I had to protect myself."

He grunts. His free hand is quick to wrap into my loose bun, tugging so my head falls back and our eyes meet. "Why do you challenge me?"

"I'm a big girl, Colin. You don't get to make decisions for me."

His fist clenches in my hair and my hands rise to do the same to his. Talk about a standoff: guns are about to blaze. "I'm going to draw conclusions for three hundred million people who will trust me to do so. But not my girlfriend?"

I was expecting anger and frustration, but not the wound bleeding out in his eyes. Because of that, I soften my retort. "That's just it. We're a part of a democracy, one where I get a voice. And let's be clear—I'm not a constituent and you're not my president. I *am* your girlfriend and I love you with all my heart. But I'm not a woman who'll just do as you say without question or some kind of negotiation. If that's what you need—"

I'm cut off by his growl and crestfallen face. Our eyes collide, his blues peak and level into an intensity that calls to me. I've seen this from him before, the need, the passion and the panic that our relationship could slip out from under him in a heartbeat. I want to reassure him, to exude a level of confidence that sends my own message, but his thoughts mimic my own. We're on shaky ground, committed to a future that blurs each time we try to find our way. I won't let him or his position overpower my will. I've fought too hard to salvage a piece of my self-respect and carry on with what little dignity remained before. What I will do is compromise. Bending is my concession, but I won't lose myself in the new world he's introduced me to or to Colin himself.

Moving my hands to cradle his cheeks, I press my thumbs over his lips. "Shh, if that's what you need then we'll discuss other security arrangements. I need some freedom, Colin. I'm not the kind of woman to stay home and knit while you're saving humanity."

"I need you," he whispers, his hands moving to cradle me as well. "I need to know you're safe. The thought of you out there, alone, without me, is driving me insane. I've never had to rely on others to do my job. I'm supposed to protect, slay the dragons breathing fire at your door, but my hands are tied." He squeezes his own and then drops them to my waist and pulls until I'm nestled against his hips. "I don't know how to navigate through this in the back seat, with Phil and his men leading the team to manage your safety. I'm drowning in fear, but at the same time I don't want to suffocate you."

He looks miserable and maybe a little nauseous. "Listen, we've always found our way and we'll get through this too. Here's my compromise." I drape my arms around his neck and tip my head back. "I'll have four guards go with me, five if that's what makes you feel comfortable when I'm out."

"Ten," he says, eyes easing for the first time since he walked in.

"Four and I'll call wherever I go. How do you feel about that?" I ask, tipping my pelvis into his, because really I'm hoping to feel something else.

His mouth lifts in a sexy smirk. “I like your negotiating tactics,” he says while playing with my ass.

“I thought you might.”

He laughs when I flutter my lashes, but the light in his eyes is quick to dim. “I don’t know what I’d do without you, Charlie,” he whispers, just before his lips clamp down on mine. There’s a moment when we just breathe together and another when he’s slow to lick into my mouth, taking his time to savor and repeat in action what he just whispered in words. His tongue speaks for him, a soft lance piercing my heart. I know he loves me, and fears for my safety. It’s real, and I need to remember that at times like this afternoon, when I was angry with him for dictating my actions.

What started slow turns into a quick defiling, with him first biting into my mouth and then on my neck, followed by a desperate drag of his teeth to my chest, where he strips me of my pretty ruffles. His shirt follows and soon we're left skin against skin.

My nipples peak to the point of pain when he squeezes my breasts together and laves first one and then the other with his tongue. It feels as if all of the blood in my body rushes to those two points, poking each nerve into responsiveness and sizzling under the attention of his mouth. I let him take me, claim me as his, because he needs this. And I do too.

His mouth parts from my breast, but his hands continue to knead and pull the tips. Watching me through the dark shade of his lashes, he says, “You . . .” He bites down, and I cry out. “Are . . .” He does it again to the other. “Mine.”

I yank hard on his hair, pulling him up to meet me, and our ragged breath crashes between us. "Say it," he growls, snaking one of his hands down the length of my torso and around to skim over the remaining ruffles. The pulse between my thighs has taken on its own rhythm and I'm obsessed with it.

"I'm waiting," he breathes into my mouth, twisting the delicate lace into his fist.

"Colin . . ." It comes out more like a whimper than an actual word.

"Say it, Charlie."

Oh, God. The pressure of the lace is digging into my hipbone as he wrenches it from behind. It gives way to the force of his will and takes a little of me with it. I will do anything for this man, *even if it means bending a little too far*.

Just as I move to respond, he grabs my shoulder and has me turned and bent over the counter. My hands are splayed out on either side of my chest, my cheek pressed to the cool stone, nipples pulsing from the absence of his mouth and hands.

I'm positioned for his every whim and ready for his command. It comes in the simplest breath fanning over my skin, a silent directive to fall under his spell, to grant him access, not just to my body, but also to the farthest reaches of who I am. The path of wet kisses from my waist to ear is an order to let him in—don't look back, not now or maybe never. Our future is ahead of us—give it to Colin, give in to him and he'll see us through. Bend Charlie, bend a little farther . . .

"When I left this morning it was clear you were mine. I liked it." My gasp turns into a moan when he dips to suck my shoulder, a long, hard drag sure to leave a mark. "I want you to know with the shadows on your neck and chest that you belong to me."

The light touch of his fingers skirts along each side of my spine and down to my ass. A shiver follows, chasing the desire he ignited. It explodes at the sound of his belt snaking through the loops and silences all further thought. All I can do is whimper *please* and *hurry* because I'm so empty without him kissing me, touching me, pressed over me and thrusting into me. *Please, please* . . . A flush spreads over my skin, which is only overcome by the throbbing ache between my thighs.

Touch me, touch me please, I chant in my head and roll my hips in search of his, in search of any contact.

"Ah, Christ Charlie." He's almost reverential in his exclamation when he finds me wet and ready.

He bends to suck a new sting into my shoulder as he spreads me open and his fingers, three of them, roll over my clitoris in a circular motion clearly meant to drive me insane. I groan and move with him. But I want him, all of him, desperately. I want to feel the thick slide of his erection fill me—a fullness which when left to the imagination is inconceivable. I need to feel the rush of his breath heating my skin and the piercing of his teeth on my most sensitive flesh. The harsh but encouraging words he spits out as he rockets into me aren't nice, but necessary.

"I can feel how much you want me." His voice reaches me in my haze of carnal appreciation. Scooting my stilettos further apart with the spread of his legs, the breath I've longed for is warming a path along my neck and to my ear. "But do you want my fingers or this?"

"Colin . . ." I gasp as his erection presses just inside, spreading me open in the most delicious way, and then he's gone.

"Tell me."

I'm lost to the pleasure of his fingers.

"What do you want . . .?" he grounds out.

"Both. I want it all."

I feel his smile against my shoulder and then his teeth as he bears down. "Let's do it together," he says, reaching for my hand and bringing it down to my clitoris. My pulse stumbles and then sprints as he guides my fingers to replace his own.

Suddenly he's there, inside of me, pressing deep as he glides in before stilling to allow me time to catch my stunted breath.

"Colin," I moan and twist my hips, loving the depth of his reach.

"Together, baby," he murmurs, and his fingers find mine. In one second he rocks his hips and in another, we're rolling, both of us, over my clitoris with a speed purely meant to get me off.

"Oh, God." It all feels so good and so fast. "Colin," I whimper and search for something to hold onto, but there's nothing to do but press back into each thrust and let it happen.

"Let me hear you. Tell me what you feel . . ."

"I . . . so good."

"Say it so I can hear it and feel it." He's breathless, as am I.

"Oh . . . oh, I'm . . . coming . . ." And it's sharp and fast, uncoiling like a loaded spring down my spine and all around him. I jerk and rear up off the counter, riding the wave that was swift to sweep me away.

Colin holds on. He groans but never lets up, pushing onward in short, stabbing thrusts meant to see me through my orgasm and to chase another. His arm is wrapped around my ribcage and between my breasts so he can hold my neck in a tender yet strong embrace as he punches me forward with each stroke.

"Charlie . . . baby," he breathes into my hair before his head falls onto my shoulder. We work together. With each drive forward, I push back into a deepened intensity. It's not just our bodies that heat with the connection, craving more. A silent understanding passes between us as we try to devour each other. *Mine, mine, mine*. I'll never let him go. My heart is on the verge of bursting. His whispered words reverberate inside of me, filling me up just as his body does: *so sweet, need to feel you again.*

He pushes me down until my forehead finds its place on the cool quartz. One hand fists in my hair, the other digs into my waist, and his hips piston and pull. Fast, faster, and I can't help but follow his command.

"Come for me, my sweet girl." *Yes,* I will and I do. Every muscle in my body draws into a stretched rubber band, humming in an explosive vibration, and with one last thrust I snap, my silent scream expressed to the rock beneath me because I haven't the ability to speak or breathe or think. I lose all sense of self, and Colin's roar is the only thing left between us before we melt together into a boneless pool on the cool tile floor.

Our breath is splintered, my heart mimicking the pattern. "Mine," he whispers into my ear, as he wipes sweat-drenched curls from my brow. "Say it."

"Mine." I reach behind me to latch my fingers into his hair, pulling him forward as I tilt back. "You belong to me," I say and then kiss him senseless.

TEN

ALI'S BRILLIANT MIND IS wrapped around an anniversary bottle of Johnnie Walker Black and the plethora of decanters Colin has housed in his lower level bar.

"They really drink this stuff?" she asks, sniffing the opening before gagging and looking for something more palatable.

With her attention occupied elsewhere, I swivel my stool around to watch Colin bend over the pool table, sinking first one then another solid over Evan's stripes. His easy laugh warms my insides like the whiskey in Ali's hand and leaves me a bit unsteady, and a little drunk on love and all things Colin McKenna.

He changed into a T-shirt and jeans. One is stretched tight across his chest, leaving little to the imagination. The other is fitted to his ass and my imagination is working just fine. I'm studying him like a science project, the most important one of the year. It's as if I didn't just spend three hours glued to him, running my tongue and lips along his shadowed jaw. Or that this same stubble didn't cause the abrasions between my thighs I can still feel burned on my skin.

"Why do you look like you're about to devour him?" I catch Ali's lip lifting in a smirk when I swing around.

"Do I?" Her giggle is greeted by my scowl.

"Uh, yeah. As in swallow him whole."

I sigh. "It's not funny."

"No, it really is. This coming from the girl who shied away from all things male for years is now an animal." She pops an olive in her mouth. "I love it."

My bottom lip pouts out. "I think I'm addicted."

Ali throws her head back and she laughs, her hand propped up to hold back the olive juice threatening to coat the granite bar-top.

"I'm serious. Swear me in, give me the oath. The first step is to admit the problem, which I'll do. It was confirmed when I prayed my favorite sister would cancel on the one night out of a hundred I'll be in the same city as her. It's just not normal."

She takes my hand and squeezes. "It is, Charlie girl. It's called love and you're in deep." She tilts her head, hazel eyes shining. "It's a good thing . . ."

"Are you crying?" I ask, with a pitch that could break glass. "Al, don't, please."

"Shut it. I'm only tearing up from your funny face," she says one thing, but has to turn and wipe away a well of water.

I'm distracted by Evan's yelp. Glancing behind me confirms what his shout implies. "I kicked your boyfriend's ass, Charlie. He might need grief counseling after losing to me for the last year." Evan's eyes light with amusement and seek me out. "I'm passing along the warning so you can hold his hand through the trauma."

Ali giggles and his gaze is drawn to her, along with a grand smile. *Hmm, very interesting.* The tilt of his head and his lowering lids are screaming lascivious thoughts. My guess is he's devising a plan to get her into bed tonight. When he runs his hand through his hair, ruffling what was already a sexy disaster, I know I'm right. Evan has set his sights on my sister.

Colin's laugh cuts through my laser beams currently directed at his best friend. I'm drawn to him and his own sexy-ass smirk. "Every game I give you is a gift. Your loss equates to incessant whining that would institutionalize the sanest man, and I don't have time for a break in a padded cell. Let's do it one more time so I can give the girls an example."

"Whatever you say, chief, but I don't want any tears when I kill it again."

It's easy to forget about Evan's plans for Ali with Colin relaxed and leaning on a pool stick. Holy mackerel, his muscles flexed into hard lines and rigid perfection cause a warm noodle feeling, as if I'm Jell-O, left out for hours in the sun. Add his perfect smile to the picture and I want to drag that mouth back to my abraded thighs and sink into a pool of whipped cream.

Ali's laugh cuts into my drool-fest. "I take it things are good?"

With Colin and Evan's banter behind me, I turn to contemplate her question. Nodding, I say, "We are. It's all the other stuff I'm trying to work through."

She huffs and sniffs another bottle, this one more appealing based on the shot she pours for herself. "Please, your little finger has more class than Ella Montgomery. She's obnoxious, as displayed by her behavior at the party." She nods, as if thinking about the information I shared with her earlier. "Don't let her make you second guess your relationship with Colin. Cheers." Lifting the glass, she doesn't wait to clink my bottle, but shoots back the content and hisses, "God, that's awful."

"It's not that. I'm solid with Colin."

"What then?"

"You saw the paper?" When she nods, I keep going. "I can't hide anymore. Where he goes, I go. Everyone will expect me by his side and if I'm not, reporters all over the country will speculate why. The party was just the first of many encounters I'll have with Ella. If it's not her, it'll be Raquel, or someone exactly like her. But I'm not worried about women necessarily. I mean, the real question is how do I go from standing in line at Starbucks to standing next to the leader of the free world?"

"You're thinking way too much about this. What does Colin want you to do?"

I shrug. "Be myself."

"Well then? That's logical. He fell in love with Charlie Carter, not some powder-puff, fruit loop like Ella."

"Yes, but I don't know how to do any of this."

"Any of what? Be a girlfriend?"

"Well, that too, but it seems to be coming along naturally," I say, and she laughs at my blush. "Would you quit enjoying my sex life so much and focus up, Sister?" Her back straightens, and she tries to do the same with her face but fails to hide her smirk. "I'm more worried about how to act on the campaign now that I'm front and center."

"Sounds like you don't trust Colin."

I gasp. "Why would you say that?"

"*Be yourself*?" Leaning across the bar top, she grabs my shoulders in a playful yet frustrated shake. "It can be that easy. Think of it this way. Compromise when you have to, ask questions when you need direction, wave if you're told to and have some fun with it. My only advice? Don't let them put you in pearls."

I laugh. "Pearls?"

"You hate pearls, so don't get badgered into wearing them. Be Charlie, remember? Do all of the things expected of you, but do it your way. Colin's advisors will want you scripted and coiffed." Ali's narrowed eyes speak a million silent messages. "Do it all by being the same Charlie he can't stop staring at."

"Okay," I say, but even to my own ears I don't believe it.

"You know what? I think what you're really afraid of is turning into a powder-puff fruit loop."

She hit the nail on the head, and I bob mine up and down in agreement. "I don't want to lose myself, like I did when we first came to Mom and Dad. I feel like Colin has opened me up and given me the confidence needed to really be myself. I've only ever felt that way with you. Now, with his support, it's so easy to be exactly who I want to be. I laugh and cry and get mad and . . . I don't know, I just get to be me and I love it so much. I'm figuring out who I really am without worrying if Colin will accept me, because I know he does. Oh, Ali." I grab her hand and I think the shine is back in her eyes, but I keep going. "I'm not afraid he'll give me back."

Her lips part on an unintelligible gasp. I struggled for years, and to an extent I still do, with security. Driven by years of disassociation, given up from one foster home to another, I never felt worthy of a family. A shiver rolls up my spine, remembering Mr. Jennings's finger wagging in my face. I still can't eat peas. When I was nine, and with my first foster family, I refused them. He left me at the table all night, a battle of wills he expected to win. It was a small defiance on my part that meant much more. I wanted my mom. I needed her reassurance they weren't that bad and when I was done, dessert would be so much better. But what I got was Mr. Jennings's hand on my cheek and the kitchen chair for a bed. They served peas for a week and when he couldn't break me, he sent me back. Non-compatible. The first time the Carters' served peas I verged on a panic attack, until Ali taught me how to swallow them whole.

Perfection was my goal. To find the freedom to live and truly be myself without fear of abandonment is liberating and terrifying at the same time. Terrifying because the candidacy demands a different Charlie Carter, someone different than the woman I'm just discovering and loving. That is the crux of my problem.

"I do trust Colin. I believe he wants me to be myself, but his life, his career aren't as simple as that. If he were selling cars I wouldn't feel this way; I know how to fit in with that crowd. But he's negotiating contracts with Middle-Eastern leaders. There's a bit more pressure when Sunday dinners are with the Sultan of Sudan. It's kind of hard for me to picture myself in that kind of situation."

"Charlie girl, I get it. I really do. I love that man almost as much as you do because he's given you this gift. Don't let his job muddy your water. I'm sure there's stuff you'll have to do that won't come naturally, but you can figure it out as it comes." She glances behind me, before catching my eyes. "Stop worrying and enjoy your super-hot, not a car salesman."

I close my eyes and automatically lean back when strong arms snake around my midsection. The heat of his lips on my neck has my eyes rolling so high they'll meet God in two seconds. Lord, this man can send me from zero to sixty on the needy meter with a simple touch.

"What are you girls whispering about?" His breath fans against my ear and I hear God talking. Heaven is a lot closer than I ever thought possible.

"Nothing much." I'm distracted by his mouth again, this time nibbling its way down my jaw. I've officially lost my train of thought when my hands find their way into his hair.

"Wouldn't be the latest edition of *Cosmopolitan*, would it?"

"Mmm, you wish. Now that you mention it, I can think of some interesting articles." His growl reaches me in familiar places and I like it.

Turning into him, I find his eyes and smile, our lips an inch apart. With his eyebrow hitting new heights, he says, "Care to share?"

"Maybe I'll show you later," I breathe out, before falling into him for a kiss. Colin's not shy, his mouth hungry against mine, and I feed off of his appetite. After a minute, Ali and Evan's voices pull me from the angels singing.

"I'm betting on January," she says.

"I don't think so. That's going to be a busy time of year for Colin. My bet's on December."

"We'll see. I do have some influence you know, being the maid-of-honor and favorite sister. Keep in mind, I look good in navy."

"That's total girl department. I'm comfortable in my tux, so no problem there. I'll let you and Charlie worry about the dresses."

When thought actually returns and their conversation is processed through my now functioning cerebral cortex, I shove against Colin's chest, mouth agape.

"Wh . . . what are you two talking about?" Colin's deep rumble vibrates into a full on chuckle against my back as Evan starts humming the wedding march. I yank my head in Colin's direction, not at all enjoying his laugh or the Bobbsey Twins plot, currently titled *The Adventures of Charlie Carter*. I can't decide whom to glare at, so I start with Colin because he's encouraging them and end with the two blond beauties. Why can't anyone see how wrong this is? We literally just started dating and they're picking out colors for a wedding that will never happen? Has everyone forgotten that Colin's not interested in getting married again? Of that he's been very clear. Ali and Evan's joke is hurtful on many levels because . . . because why?

Because I want to marry him and love him for the rest of my life, that's why. Crap. I do want him forever, but marriage? I can't even think about that right now with all of the other stuff going on.

"Come on. Let's play Pictionary." Twisting out of my seat, I grab Colin's hand so he has no choice but to follow.

Ali came prepared for game night. A Carter family favorite is already set up in front of the sectional in the corner. Just as I sink down into the cushion, she begins the instructions.

"Okay boys. Let's have some fun." She rubs her hands together while taking her place by the makeshift easel. Ali's devious, and it comes out in her twisted competitiveness. Freshman year she played a full-tackle football game with the high school varsity squad just to prove she could do it. The next day she could barely walk and she had to seek treatment from a chiropractor. Pictionary is no exception. A product of her own warped upbringing prior to becoming a Carter, she strives to be the best. That's why she's a great doctor. Determination is set in her eyes as she takes stock of her competition. Oh, boy.

"Evan, it's you and me against these two losers."

"What? You know I kick ass at this game, Carter," I tease.

"Not tonight, Charlie girl. I've got the updated version. You are so going down."

"I like the sound of that." Evan sidles up to her and coaxes a high five from my beautiful sister. I hope she knows what she's doing. A wink from her is my answer, and it reminds me a lot of something Evan would do. Maybe the two of them will be good together. Or, they just may suffocate each other with their arrogance.

Shaking my head, I fall into Colin's side when the cushion dips from his weight. The length of my body tingles from his touch. Rolling my eyes to the heavens, I keep them there until he tips my chin up. His blues are dark and hint at mischief. "Ready to play?"

The deep timbre of his voice does things to me. Needy things. I groan and if the trembling line of his mouth is any indication, he thinks it's funny.

The swift crack of my hand against his thigh straightens it out. "Why are you doing this to me?" I whisper.

"I love working you up—that's why." His breath on my ear sends a shiver down my spine. "It makes my nights so entertaining."

"Grrrr," I growl, and he kisses my nose.

"Charlie, you're up." I drag my eyes from Colin's and pop off the couch, thankful for the distance. But it doesn't do much good. His gaze is hot, his smile hotter, as he stares first at my chest and then down the length of my legs. To get him back, I turn and bend over to grab the markers from the floor, shaking my ass as I did earlier to drive him crazy.

"The Carters play with three rules. Gentleman!" Ali claps. Colin jerks his attention her way and I'm happy to see his dazed expression.

My phone, which I left on the bar, interrupts Ali's instructions. I leap for it with what I hope is gazelle-like grace, but in reality, it's probably more like a galloping donkey. Without checking the number, I run my finger along the screen.

"Hello."

"Charlie?" The voice is rough and somehow familiar.

“Yes? May I ask whose calling?” I ask, stepping toward Colin as I do.

“I’m coming for you.”

I stop in my tracks. “What did you say?”

“An eye for an eye. Get ready, sweet-face,” he says, and then starts to laugh.

My gasp is loud in my ears, filling the space between both of them with nothing but the audible symptom of my fear. The hair at the nape of my neck is on end and it’s followed by a long, jarring shudder.

“Sweet-face.” I choke on the whispered word. His laugh is soon replaced by a baby’s wail, loud and shrill.

The phone falls from my fingers, yet my hand remains in place. Cries fill the room. Haunting echoes bounce off the walls when the phone’s speaker is activated upon landing. All heads snap in my direction and Colin launches from the couch. He’s by my side in a heartbeat, Evan not far behind to pick up the dropped call. The familiar warmth of Colin’s arm surrounds me, yet I remain rigid, paralyzed by the past.

“Who is this?” Evan demands, but the bawling continues.

Colin’s quick to dial a call. “Phil, he’s got her cell number,” he barks. “He’s still on the line, can you trace it? . . . Do it. Do whatever you have to do.” Both arms are around me now.

Drake, who’s been planted outside of Colin’s house, barrels down the stairs.

"Give it to me." He doesn't wait for Evan's response. Snatching it out of his hand, he bolts back up and out the door. We're left with only our panted breath filling the deepening silence. Minutes tick by and no one moves.

"What just happened? Who was that?" Ali's incredulous questions finally break the creeping tension. Colin tightens his arms for a second and then he pushes against my shoulders to look at me.

I stare, unable to move. He's worried. I know this, the fingers digging into my arms is one clue, the other his eyes. The beautiful blues I love stretch on with endless anxiety. My mouth falls open, but no sound escapes. I squeeze my lids shut and drop my head. The draw to fall into the faraway place is great. *I need it.*

"Charlie?" My sister's voice. Ali.

"Baby?" Colin's whisper. *My heart.*

For both of them, I stay in the present instead of slipping away to a place that can ease the horror one phone-call brought back in an instant. I can do this. Straightening my shoulders and spine, I level my sight with Colin's.

"It was Shane Roberts."

ELEVEN

IF THE CLOCK IS correct—and there's no reason to believe it isn't—I've only slept for an hour. Colin's breath is steady beside me. Rolling onto my stomach, I wrap my arms around my pillow, and stare at his prone figure. He's sprawled out, legs fanned across the bed. His muscles are defined, but relaxed in sleep, carrying the definition as if they were tense. I take him in, loving the drape of the sheet that barely covers his ass. If one must have insomnia, it should always be with Colin McKenna, but I'm grateful this is a one-woman show.

Sleep came slow tonight, and it's no wonder it didn't stay long. There are too many thoughts, too many subjects pining for airtime in my brain. The thought of Shane Roberts is the most disturbing of them all. He found me. I spent fifteen years trying to forget and one phone call brought my fourteenth year back in Technicolor.

Colin had lost a little bit of his mind after I told them who was on the line. The war had played out on his face and in his actions. Stay with me or go with Drake to slay my dragons. He had taken a step in the direction of the stairs and then came right back to my side. His eyes had betrayed a calm demeanor, a wild, but aching blue blurred into his enlarged pupils. He'd tried to console me, but the rigid set of his shoulders against the same sharp lines of my body hadn't left much relief for either of us. In the end, he'd left me with

Ali. It was Evan who'd filled her in on most of the details because my voice had been adrift in a sea encompassing the last fifteen years.

I hadn't been able to talk. At first anxiety had caught my tongue. Although Shane had sounded different, the rough whispered word he would grunt in my ear back then, that he had repeated tonight echoed without stop: *sweet-face*. One word convinced me of his identity. My stomach heaved, remembering how he would say it then and with the knowledge he'd found me to say it now. It was foolish to believe I'd be through with him. If I were honest with myself, I knew he'd come back to torture me, but now I feel doubly bad because it's affecting Colin.

Pity had given way to anger. Ripping my hand from Ali's, I'd jumped from the couch and immediately doubled over as an outraged scream barreled up my spine. Two sets of wide eyes had followed me with barely contained anxiety as I paced and slung insults at the bastard who ruined me. I'm quite certain I even rocked my fist at the ceiling in silent condemnation. For all that's holy, what in the hell do I have to do to escape this pervert's invisible arms that hold me down?

I'd railed at fate and at the walls and anything that would listen. Poor Evan and Ali took the brunt of it, until Evan excused himself and left my stunned sister to deal with the crazy in the corner. Hours had passed; Colin had worked with Phil's team and Ali had stayed with me. Evan had eventually returned to sit in silent wait with us in the game room, Pictionary abandoned for another time.

Nothing had been solved tonight, other than the identity of my assailant. We don't know where Shane is, and we suspect his timing is based on my visibility from the campaign. Colin believes he's kept tabs on me my whole life. When I was thrust into the spotlight, he used it to his advantage and began following us as we traveled from city to city. It's all speculation, but it makes sense. Using Colin's past as part of the persecution would be easy to do. Sara's death was front-page news at the time, as was Colin's devastation. But what's Shane's end game? Has his obsession carried over from childhood to present day with an intensity that could lead to more violence?

The only conclusion the night had brought with it was to drop every available resource into finding Shane Roberts, the boy-turned-man who won't let me go.

When I push past the newest blast of Shane Roberts images, the red room is there, Joan and Ella not far behind. Raquel and the media follow suit. There's just too much, and even the God lying next to me can't chase them all away. *"Sweet-face." Babies and red rooms. Washington wives. Ella's glare. Raquel's hands.* Oh, God.

I contemplate waking Colin. One thing for sure will take my mind off of everything, but he needs his sleep and I don't want him to worry about my worrying. Lord knows it took him ages to find the peaceful state he's in now, and he needs it. Tomorrow morning we're back on the campaign trail.

After another hour, I slip out of bed. It only takes a second to find one of Colin's T-shirts, which is enough for the unseasonably hot weather in D.C. I pad down the stairs and to the backyard patio where

I lay on his lounger. Security is tight. Two men remain out front, others circling the street constantly. There will be no more escape routes through the locked gate. I'm resolved to my fate and happy to remain prisoner in Colin's jail.

I get lost in the layered midnight sky. Purple and navy wrap around the smallest hint of a star. I pass time searching for constellations and remembering the magical stories they were named after. Sleep may have claimed me, but if it did, it was fleeting and too light to remember. All too soon the layers change from purple to the barest tinge of pink and then orange as the sun begins to rise.

"Hey." Colin's whisper is in my ear, as he lifts me from the chair. "What are you doing out here?"

"Star gazing." I tuck my head into my favorite place without complaint when he settles back down on the lounger.

"You should have woken me if you couldn't sleep," he says, while tangling his limbs with mine.

"Mmm, trust me, I thought about it." I kiss a path up his neck and jaw before whispering, "But you need your rest."

He pauses a beat, dipping his nose into my hair. "You okay?"

I sense the hesitancy in the question. We both know I'm not. Peace, the kind I find with him will be fleeting, with my nightmare stalking my every move.

My safety, and his limited involvement in it, is hard enough for Colin to deal with. I won't remind him of my angst. "I am. I know you'll never let him hurt me." This is true. I feel it with every breath I breathe.

His growl is confirmation. "I will protect you, Charlie. That bastard will never get his hands on you. Believe in me." The tightening of his arms is the exclamation to his point. Tipping my head back allows me a clear view of his jaw clenching to go along with his impassioned statement.

Running my fingers down the side of his face only brings a certain amount of relief to the strained muscles. "I do. Now, stop worrying about me and focus on the day ahead. You've got a busy schedule." I can see the battle rage behind his eyes. I'm pretty sure he's weighing his options—steal me away to Timbuktu or continue on with the campaign. "We've got this covered. Drake and half of Phil's security team will be with us. There's no reason to believe everything won't go on as scheduled from here on out. Let's just try to forget about Shane Roberts and concentrate on work. I don't want to think about him. He's taken up too much of my life already; I won't give him anymore of it. Please?"

He nods. "Will you promise to listen to me when I ask you to stay locked away somewhere or do something, even if you don't understand? I've only got your best interest in mind, baby. I couldn't live with myself if something happened to you." Sitting up straighter he pulls back to study my face. "There are times I won't go into details and I'll need you to follow direction. Can you do that for me?"

I know he's referring to my flat-out refusal to stay home yesterday. My natural instinct had been to derail any train that forbade action on my part, even if the steamy locomotion was Colin McKenna. The flight-or-fight instinct was cemented in my psyche in foster care. But I don't need to fight for my safety alone any longer. I know he'll never let anyone hurt me.

"I promise."

Burrowing against his side, we sit in peace as the dawn becomes day. When the sun is past the horizon, Colin rises with me in his arms and heads to his room. He sets me down when we reach the bath, and only steps away to start the shower. Slipping from his T-shirt, I yelp when the cold water stings my skin and then eases into relaxing warmth. Pulling my back against his chest, he holds me close and massages my abdomen and then my breasts. I sigh and tilt my head to allow more room for his lips roaming my neck. It's not long before my troubles are blotted out by a pleasure so intense it blurs the lines of reason and responsibility.

ooo

My mouth falls open when we pull up to the plane. It seems in the last forty-eight hours it's doubled in size. *McKenna, for the People* remains on display on the side in red, white and blue, yet it's also grown.

Colin chuckles beside me and I swing around to find his eyes. "You've been holding out on me. What's this?" I ask, as he helps me from the SUV. Dread unfurls in my stomach. Surrounded by security, we climb the steps to the open door.

"If I didn't mention the new plane, it was only a forgetful omission. There'll be more people traveling with us from here on out. Not just Phil's men, but more campaign staff." His hand rests soundly on my lower back. The media set off to the side of the stairs happily capture every minute of our relaxed joining. The shutters of their cameras mimic a swarm of insects and suddenly I feel the need to swat them away. The press is very beneficial to Colin, but it can also be the opposite. They have the power to sway the voters with lies or hyperbole.

Turning on the top stair, my hair catches in the wind and whips off to the side. My gaze lands first on the swell of reporters below us and then on Colin, who's stopped on the step under mine. I'm not sure why, but my trepidation has grown with each minute we've drawn closer to the plane.

Before we enter, before I succumb to the inflexibility of the campaign trail, I take one last minute to reassure Colin, or maybe myself.

Straightening his tie, and running my fingers down the length of it and then his lapel, I find his eyes. There are few things I'm certain of. One, Colin's a force of nature. His power will lead him to the Whitehouse. The path is laid before him, he's made it, and with or without me he'll rule this nation. Two, my future is unknown. Shane Roberts has returned and with it, my sanity lies in the balance. He nearly broke me when I was fourteen. I'm stronger now, stronger with Colin by my side, but I'm not sure how to move forward with Shane in my way. Three, and most importantly, I'm for all of time lost in love with Colin McKenna. He is my knight in shining armor. Whether he knows it or not he's already slain my biggest dragon. I've slowly found myself. Each day with him has allowed my voice to grow without fear of retribution. My body, at one time a wilted flower, has budded with the exuberance of spring. It's fully open now to the fruits of his ministration, and greedy for the rain, the fluidity of his hands and each caress.

For some reason, the need to let him know his importance consumes me. I grab his lapels and force his eyes to stay with mine. "From this moment forward, you will never be alone. My heart will protect you, my body will cherish you and I will forever love you. Take this with you each day and during the minutes when we're apart."

His mouth parts on a sharp inhale. Without thought to our audience, the droves of security and reporters, I wrap my arms around his neck and pull him into me. Our lips taste, never hesitant, but familiar and hungry. When his tongue reaches out to mine, I sigh and welcome him into my warm embrace. With Colin, passion reigns. It's easy to forget time and space and the demands placed upon us, but as usual he regains control and presses our foreheads together.

Our breath meets in a soft pant. "I lo . . ."

I push my fingers over his mouth. "Promise me you'll remember that even through the darkest of times." The words tumble out. I'm not sure where they came from, I only know they need to be said. When his head tilts in question, I move to kiss him quickly and then turn to walk through the door.

This plane is similar in some ways to the last one and I'm grateful to see Mrs. Brenner and Captain Greene are there to greet us. The kitchen set-up, although larger, remains behind the cockpit and beyond that are eight rows of first-class leather seats, three on each side. Behind them is a sitting area composed of a sectional and recliners. Tables and chairs are just beyond that, with a door leading to what I assume is a conference room. It's all very familiar, just bigger and filled already with passengers, many of whom I don't recognize.

Colin stops to shake hands, introducing me to some people. A wave catches my eye. It's Evan, stepping out from the conference room door to garner my attention. Excusing myself, I eagerly head to the back, hoping to learn of his evening with Ali. She had started her shift at the hospital this morning when I called, so I couldn't drag a lot of information from her. She was more insistent on knowing if I was okay and wouldn't give anything up. I'll need to focus on Evan for the goods.

"Hi. How was your ni . . ." Before I can finish the question, he's grabbed my hand and hauled me into the conference room. It's bigger, but relatively the same. Unfortunately, the similarities don't end there. John Montgomery's irate scowl waits for me at the head of the sleek wood. Staggering to a stop behind Evan, he releases my hand. "I'll get Colin. Wait for him." He glares at John, but his eyes don't lose the edginess when they find mine. Oh, shit. What happened now?

As soon as the door closes, John's on his feet and in my face so fast I don't have time to step back. His breath punches into me with each word. "This isn't some campfire where we're all singing fucking 'Kumbaya'. It's his life. Everything we've worked for. This is his chance to lead the goddamn free world and you're going to fuck it up for groceries? Get your head out of your ass." His anger is palpable, and I feel it in every muscle I've tensed in protection. He takes a step back and slaps a newspaper on the table. The room spins as I look down.

My groan dulls the sharpened silence. A picture of me at the market is below the headline, but the words don't register—my appearance does. I've worn that skirt a hundred times and never thought twice about it. When in print it appears to barely cover my ass. It's short, as in Daisy Duke, and the white tank leaves little to the imagination.

"Stupid girl." He elongates the vowels so they hit home. "Do you get it now? Every move you make is witnessed by millions. When you step out of the house you're judged, and the jury will convict you with the slightest wrong move. What in the fucking world possessed you to leave the house in that?" Spittle has formed at the edges of his mouth and he doesn't move to wipe it away. Each word is a slap, my head jerking with every blow. Instinctively I back into the wall, but he rounds on me. Not done. "And who in the hell were you with? Care to explain that?"

Colin walks in. His eyes find mine and then he frowns at John who's holding up at least five more papers, tossing them down as he names them off. "*The Post*, the *Times*, the *Tribune*—the list is fucking endless. McKenna's floozy out on the town with someone else."

"No, I was al . . ."

"Shut up!" The spittle is back and he's turned into Cugo. My hand covers my neck to protect it from a sudden attack.

Colin stares at the table where the many papers have landed. His eyes fall to slits of steel, his jaw more tense than I've ever seen before. I'm afraid the vein on the side of his neck will explode as it pumps up and down with the grinding of his teeth.

More disturbing than any of that is his silence. I stare at his hands, clenching and re-clenching into fists by his side.

Still holding my neck, I whisper his name but he flinches at the sound of my voice. Evan glares at the table and then at me. Although I can see compassion his brand of anger overrides it. God, I'm really in trouble this time.

"If Colin is insistent on keeping you around, then from this moment on you'll follow my ground rules or I'll see to it you're left on the street where you belong. There'll be no more traipsing around in barely-there clothes with some man. Who is it anyway? Alex? Is that Alex Miller?" John holds up another paper and this time my widened eyes glass over the outline of a man. He's standing next to Chef Rocco's display. I remember the inexplicable dread that came over me at that moment, while looking at the aprons on the wall. I'd thought someone had approached, and apparently someone had. Alex Miller. The way his hand is reaching toward me, it appears from the angle of the image that he's touching me. It looks as though the sassy smirk on my face is meant for him, and not in anticipation of the night I had planned for Colin. My stomach heaves and my hand leaves my neck to hold the bile in. Pressing against my mouth, I retch again and again until I stumble toward a chair and sit.

Colin just stares. His eyes are light and empty when he finds me. Nothing, no emotion. Not the expressionless expression that usually is given away by the intensity in his gaze. There's nothing there when he looks at me.

"Colin." It comes out like a whimper. I'm afraid. Afraid I've done something not only detrimental to his campaign, but to us. I would never step out with another man, let alone Alex Miller. Not when I know what Abby did, and whom she did it with.

The rigid set of his shoulders straightens even further and his lip curls up. "Take a seat outside of this room, Charlise."

Oh, no. No, no, no. "Please, Colin. Let me explain . . ."

"Take a seat." He backs up to the door, opening it with a jerk. "I can't look at you right now."

I close my eyes in defeat, wishing I could melt into the fine leather and into non-existence. Evan's next to me then, the hint of his cologne filling the small space between us. When I look up, his compassion has expanded, but the frustration hasn't totally dissipated either. Taking my arm, he helps me up and carries most of my weight when leading me to the door.

Breaking free, I throw myself at Colin. He dips his head away, closing his eyes as he does. With his hands fisted, he remains stiff underneath my seeking grip. "Look at me," I whisper, wincing at the desperation that clouds my tone. "Please."

A single tear falls over my lid, cool against my heated cheek as it drops in slow motion and with the movement of his head. The man I love beyond reason blurs like a hologram before me, as if he could disappear in an instant if I make a wrong move. Fighting against the tears, my fingers clench into his biceps. When our eyes meet, I choke on a cry. He's buried under too many emotions to understand them all, but one is very clear. Revulsion. His mouth trembles with it.

"I can't be near you right now," he says. The words are a train, barreling at full speed and slamming into my chest.

TWELVE

"COME ON, CHARLIE." EVAN pulls me from my paralysis by tugging on my arm.

I crumble, emotionally and literally. My knees go first, my fingers failing in their grip on his arms. What have I done?

If not for Evan I'd pool to the floor. As it is, I allow him to move me into the belly of the plane where I'm met by a wealth of strangers. There are no sympathetic eyes to ease my anxiety or a friendly shoulder to lay my head on. Drake is in the front, but he's probably furious with me too. I can't imagine the trouble I've brought to his door. I hang my head. My company is my own and I tunnel into myself as I slip into a seat, far away from any other passenger in the back row of the eight.

I recoil, as does everyone within eyesight, at Colin's ferocious roar behind the now closed door and the following diatribe that's lost in the thunder of the engines. Time is nowhere to be found, the entire length of the flight is spent replaying my jailbreak and hoping Colin gives me a chance to explain. I never meant to hurt him. The whole outing signified my freedom, and I hadn't stopped to contemplate what I was wearing or who I could run into.

I'm jerked from my trance as the wheels find purchase on the earth, the brakes wrenching the plane to a slow pace. My stomach, which has been on shaky ground since I boarded, rolls again. It's a good thing I haven't eaten since lunch yesterday. I close my eyes as they well with tears. *I will not cry, I will not cry*. This seems to be turning into my new mantra. Sitting taller, I will the waterworks away and look out the window. My lips tremble when I think of the stupid trip to the market. We didn't even eat dinner. After Colin came home we found nourishment in each other and dinner went to waste. Then fucking Shane Roberts called and the night went to shit. Now my day has followed suit and I wonder what my next hand will be.

The men and women in the rows before me are piling out as John stomps his way down to the exit, a gruff nod given to the captain in farewell. Evan's next. He glances my way in passing and eases into a sad half-smile, but I'm drawn to the door of the conference room. My heart stops as Colin fills the frame. His nostrils flare as he stares, pausing to take me in. The heat flashing in his eyes is better than the blank existence that filled them when we last saw each other, yet his silence slices into my chest. Finally, he steps to the end of my row and waits without a word. The vein is popping again, along with the clenching jaw, but at least he hasn't left me.

My eyes fill again as I slide out and take my place before him. He doesn't touch me and my lower back aches for the hand that normally rests there, steadying me as we make our way down the stairs. I'm on my own.

I hide my head, tilting it down and to the side when more cameras flash. All of the others board a bus, but Colin and I are ushered into a waiting car with Drake at the helm. I find myself pressing against the far door, leaving an expanse the size of Mount

Olympus between us. When I chance a glance at Colin, he's pulling on his lower lip and I know he's contemplating a decision. I can feel it in the shaking of my shoulders and in the odd energy that exists between us. Clamping a hand to my mouth, I hold in my cry and stare, dazed, out the window. It's only when we stop I realize I'm rocking myself back and forth in short, simple movements.

Colin's out and at my door before Drake can open his. Afraid of what I'll see if I look at him, I keep my head down as he ushers me into the hotel. Every minute spent checking in and the ten stories in the elevator to our floor becomes an eternity stretching before us.

Flashes of the red room assault me when we walk in, but the paint is blood and the babies are real. It's the same every time, in every city. I expel all of my breath in a rush like a punch to the stomach when I look into the bedroom. *Oh, God. What's wrong with me?*

Holding in a cry, the silence of the suite becomes bitter, as is the taste in my mouth. I'm being punished by my mind and Colin's reaction. Each moment of hushed reticence is a strike against my flesh. It hurts as certainly as if a whip were lashing the ivory skin of my back, leaving it open to bleed.

While I stay paralyzed by the door, he's at the bar, pouring a thick glass of whiskey. It's gone in one gulp and he's doling-out another before he looks at me. This time when he brings the glass to him lips, he's trembling.

Covering my eyes with my hands, I force my tears into tremors. I will not cry. I let myself do it too often with Colin, but I know better. Crying will not change what happened and it will not ease my pain now, so I let the physical ache take over. One day at a time and I will not cry—a new mantra to sit side-by-side with the old one, murmured from my lips.

"Baby," the whispered word hits me, a physical blow to go along with the lashes to my back. When Colin's arms find me his fingers sink into the flesh that was a moment ago bleeding and a violent shiver races down my spine. My knees give out and he holds on. I claw into his hair, pulling until I'm buried in his neck, gulping in his scent. I'm desperate, as is he. His grip is just as deep, bruising into my back and butt in a fevered race to stake his claim.

"I'm so sorry," the mumbled words are lost against him. I feel him swallow a lump. "Please don't be mad at me."

He sighs. "Charlie." When he tries to pry me away, I fist his hair. You want to see defiance? I'll give you defiance. I'm not going anywhere. "Baby."

As gingerly as he can, he works at my arms and hands to garner enough distance between us to make eye contact. My chin quivers when he does. "Don't hate me." It's out before I can stop it.

Tilting his head back, his brow burrows down and he takes a few deep breaths before looking at me again.

"I didn't go with him. You have to believe me. I would never, never go anywhere with that man. Please . . ."

"Charlie." He pushes my frazzled curls from my eyes and I find his. Holding me tenderly, he says, "I never thought you went with Alex."

“Then why . . . why are you so mad at me?” My voice cracks, even though I’ve promised not to cry.

His lids fall closed and he leans his forehead on mine. “How will I ever explain this so you understand? I’m never mad at you and it’s impossible to hate you. Don’t ever think that.” He’s back to staring, boring into me really, as his fingers nest in my hair, holding me still. “You’re my life. When you put it in danger voluntarily I lose my mind.”

I think my heart stops when his mouth finds mine. If a kiss is worth a thousand words, then this one is valued at a million. A million broken pieces come together with the touch of his lips and then in the seal of his tongue. I can’t get enough of him, and before I know what’s happened my groans are met by his, and I’m ripping at his shirt to find his skin. I need to know we’re okay and feeling him inside me is one way I’ll know for sure.

“Charlie, stop. We have to talk about this.”

“I don’t want to talk. Please. I don’t want to feel anything but you.”

“No.” He grabs my wrists and wrestles me to the couch. Lying on top of me, he says, “Not like this.”

I fear the tears will come now in a waterfall. “I just want you to know how much I love you.”

He shakes his head. “I do. You don’t have to do this for me to know that.” When my chin quakes, he says, “Charlie, this is so hard. Harder than you could ever imagine.”

I can’t speak, so I let him continue.

"I've never been in a position where I've had to work so hard to keep someone safe, and I can't do it with my own hands. I have to rely on others because mine are tied. I struggle everyday not to rage against those that hurt you. I want to find Shane Roberts and work him into the ground." The tightening of his fist punctuates the truth to his sentiment. "But I'm bound by my dedication to this country, and the campaign to get me into a position to make it a better place. I couldn't survive it if you were injured because of me. To think of you broken, to never hear your voice or your laugh or to see the flush spread over your skin when you're under me . . ." He shudders, ". . . it's inconceivable."

Taking a deep breath, he licks his lips and says, "I was so angry at the situation and at myself. I forced you into going out alone with my inflexibility. When I saw Alex was there . . ." A low growl rumbles in his chest, and I swear if he wasn't lying on top of me he'd be ripping a hole in the wall with his bare hands. The energy coursing through him is staggering. "God, Charlie. I want to kill him. The thought of him touching you . . ."

"Nothing's going to happen."

A pain deeper than the lashes to my back sinks into his features. "How can you be so sure?"

"Because you always save me," I whisper.

He shakes his head and buries his nose against my neck. "You have too much faith in me."

"No, I don't." I pull on his waves to bring him back up, nose to nose. "A very smart man once told me that history predicts the future.

Sound familiar?" I try for a smile but it's more like a wobbly preschooler learning to ride a bike. "You're one of few people who've always been there for me. Always Colin. When I stumble, you catch me. When I'm lost, you find me. I know you'll be there every time I fall."

"What about when you sneak out of the house without protection? I'm not there to save you, nor is the security I have set in place to do it for me." His eyebrow is sky high, and I have to give him credit for keeping the resentment out of his voice.

My bottom lip pops out. "I had no idea a jailbreak would result in all of this. I'm so, so sorry. I promise not to do something so stupid again, and I'll do better. I will Colin. Please don't lose faith in me. I can do this."

His mouth finds mine again, but it's more of a presence than a kiss. We remain fastened together for a long moment.

"I can't live without you, Charlie," he murmurs into me. "Please keep that in mind when you make decisions to go off on your own."

Nodding, I say, "I'll do whatever John wants me to. He just has to tell me—"

Colin cuts me off. "I don't want you to change. I only want you to think differently about your security and how you present yourself in public. Shane Roberts is stalking you, and the press, to a certain extent, is doing the same. Smart decisions and following the advice of the experts will suffice. I'm sorry about John and I'm even sorrier I didn't stop him. You have no idea how terribly I regret my reaction. I . . ." The cringe slicing his beautiful face is deep and mournful.

"There's no excuse. I was wrapped up in what I saw and the reality of what happened. What could have happened . . ." A long shudder travels up his spine and into the width of his shoulders. Sitting up, he takes me with him and tucks me into his side. The warm abrasion of newly-grown stubble scratches against my forehead and I almost miss the slightest whisper of sound as he says, "I feel so much, too much with you."

When I look up, he's quick to glance away and then back again. Running a hand over his face, in apparent exasperation he says, "Tell me what in the hell Alex Miller was doing with you." Colin's entire body has tensed. The arm circling me is now digging into my side.

I shake my head. "I don't know. I never saw him. There was a moment when I thought someone was behind me and from the pictures in the paper, it was him, but he didn't approach me. I promise." Scrambling onto my knees next to him, I grab his cheeks and then, because I don't want any distance between us, I straddle him. Shifting my skirt up to my hips, I sink closer until he's lodged between my thighs.

"It just seems like Alex is everywhere I go."

He tilts his head and stares through me. When his blues refocus he grabs my butt and wrenches me closer. "Are you absolutely sure it was Shane Roberts who called you?"

"Yes, why?"

"There are two men, besides myself, that I will trust with your life. Evan and Drake. Do you understand?" Wrapping my arms around his neck, I nod so he'll keep going. "I don't want you anywhere without one of the three of us present. Even if it's another one of Phil's men."

Frustration wells in my stomach because of his diversion, so I tug on his hair. "Tell me. Are you thinking Alex has something to do with this?"

He nods. "I don't believe in coincidence. Alex has been around too often since Blake's, and I don't trust it. I don't trust him. There's something, but I can't put my finger on it. I'd believe he was behind all of this if I didn't have someone tailing him."

"What?" The one-word question comes out in a punctuated puff of air. "Why am I always the last to know everything?"

He grunts and a reluctant smirk lifts his lips. "He's attracted to you. I get that, because who in their right mind wouldn't be? But when he showed up at each event in Florida I became suspicious it was more than that. I asked Phil to tag him. He was nowhere near Arkansas, and even though I knew he was in D.C. there was no reason to suspect he would see you."

"He wouldn't have if I didn't leave." Tucking my head into the crook of Colin's neck, I kiss the sensitive skin under his jaw as another apology. "If Alex is such a pig, why do you put up with him? Blake and his family remain friendly with him."

"Hmm." Colin rubs his chin into my hair and I hold on tighter. "The Kellys don't know everything. I left it alone, not because of Aiden's long-standing friendship, but for something along the lines of, keep your friends close and your enemies closer. Over the last few years I've wanted to keep tabs on him—that is, up until now. Phil will monitor his whereabouts, but he'll no longer be welcome at any event I have control over."

"I don't get it. Why does he hate you?"

His calm tone belies the fury simmering just under his skin. He's shaking with it. "I've long suspected his affair with Abby was more about me than her." When I sit up with what must be an incredulous look, he throws out a ruthful smile and sighs. "Alex has always despised me, whether it was my popularity or his sense that I had more than he did in college that began the envy. It's hard to understand the enormity of his animosity. His resentment is beyond anything I've ever experienced before, and I'm not sure what caused it. Alex became my fiercest competitor through college and beyond. Constant failure on his part to best me drives his hatred. I think he sought out Abby, at least in the beginning, to take what was mine."

Colin's fingers clench into me now and his eyes fall into lethal slits. "If history does repeat itself, then he's around you for the same reason, and this time"—His hand reaches into my hair, drawing me an inch from his mouth—"I will kill him before he takes what belongs to me."

THIRTEEN

"STOP PAWING MY ASSETS." My response to his hands on my ass and the teeth nipping the rounded swell of my breast is more breathless than I'd anticipated. This man knows how to get me worked up, but now is not the time.

He chuckles. "Stop showcasing them in black silk and I may be able to keep my hands off. Until then . . ."

I moan, and tug on his hair to loosen his grip on both parts. "I'm about to stand by your side while you speak to four hundred of your closest friends. Who, by the way, paid thousands of dollars to hear what slides off your wicked tongue. Let's make sure they can't tell where it was five minutes before we walk on stage." I yank harder and finally find his eyes. *Wicked is right.* "Come here."

We melt together. This kiss is simple and yet it speaks volumes. Colin and I could not be closer. We came out of the jailbreak incident stronger than ever. Enormously stupid escape plans lead to killer make-up sex. That should be a national headline.

I giggle and Colin pulls back, a brow raised in question.

"I love you," I say, and straighten his bow tie.

His brow reaches new heights. "You find that funny?"

"No. I find that extremely gratifying. Your obsession with my breasts is hysterical."

"Hmm." He smiles and it's more than wicked, more like the devil himself come to take me away. "You won't be laughing tonight when I have them in my hands. Held tight while I kneel over you . . ." The rest of his words are lost as he dips to take a bite of said flesh, murmuring his decadence into the now flushed skin.

He looks up through his lashes. "Tell me, would you like to feel my cock slide along your skin?" Tickling a line along my cleavage with his tongue, he then says, "Right here?"

Just as my breath rushes forward and I feel a new beat pulsing in my groin, a knock resounds through the small anteroom and the door bursts open.

"Senator? We're ready for you." His campaign aide glances at me and then to the floor. I try to hold back the blush ready to rise on my cheeks. Honestly, I don't know why I have a reaction anymore. I'm used to Colin's hands and his mouth and his imagination on every part of me. It can't be much of a surprise to his staff either.

"Hold that thought." Colin winks, and then his face falls to serious. "Are you ready for this?"

I nod, because what else can I do? My place is by his side. "There's nowhere I'd rather be."

He smiles and brushes his lips against my forehead before turning and pulling me behind him as he navigates the hallway. It's not a bad place to be. His broad shoulders and tight ass look fantastic in a tuxedo. I'm caught in that thought when bright lights force me back to reality. For a moment I'm blinded. And when I'm not, I wish I were.

The crowd is immense, no doubt seemingly larger when you're the focus of its attention. Men and women, tall and short, all of them elegant in formalwear, huddle in small groups in front of the podium, although the room is grand. It's two stories high with windows lining the walls and crystal chandeliers lighting the space as the sky sinks into dusk. My answer to the nerves creeping up my spine is to hide behind Colin's shoulder. He's all ease and friendliness, a smile and a wave for the masses as he's done hundreds of times before. I have not. This is my first. The first time I've stood by his side while on a platform—and I'm not just talking about a raised stage—but in support of his opinion and the fundamental values he campaigns for the people to believe in.

His smile reaches me as he drags me forward, squeezing my hand. I'm not alone. When our eyes meet, it all melts away: the crowd, the anxiety and the embarrassment over his rousing introduction of the woman, Charlie Carter, he's proud to call his own. *Charlie*. Now I blush. Tilting my head down, I accept his praise and only relax when it's over.

I've adjusted to the spotlight enough to scan the faces staring in rapt attention. As his speech begins, I search and recognize many from television, some politicians, most notably the Governor of Indiana. Others are activists and some celebrities. My gaze sticks on the Montgomerys, all of them—John, Ella and Joan. Of course they'd come, Ella, because it's hard for her to stay away from Colin and the spotlight surrounding him. Joan, because today's event is a highly sought-out ticket. The most influential residents would be in attendance and she wouldn't miss it. Not the Hamilton County Republican Committee Memorial Day Dinner, where everyone who is anyone comes out to play.

She catches my eye and smiles. It's warm enough, as is mine in return, yet it slips when her lips purse. One look at the low-lying dip in the bodice of my gown and she resembles a sourpuss. When her gaze hits the high line breaking the fabric mid-thigh I can almost hear the click of her tongue in admonishment. Talk about holding back a blush.

My shoulders stiffen, as does my back. I may have missed the mark on my dress, but Joan's posture on all things is hard to forget. *Listen, obey, forgive*. The strings on the marionette pull taut as I turn to Colin.

The passion is there, as it always is when he speaks. Connected to his beliefs, he shares them without doubt. It's easy to fall into the sway of his voice, and support his values. Yet my heart stumbles when he says, "And together we'll fight for the right to life." The new topic pulls the strings tighter.

I feel the weight of a stare, or maybe many, prickle along the goose-bumps on my arms. A quick glance confirms it's Ella, with Joan's head tilted to inspect the dark paint of her fingernails.

If I could hide from the topic I would, and I try to, by sliding just to the left, farther behind Colin. The air chills and I know it's not from the temperature, but the flashback to that day—going to the clinic, trembling and alone, although my new mother clenched my hand. Lying on the table, numb to what they were doing between my thighs, the need to scream overwhelming but gulping it down because I didn't deserve the release. And then the emptiness that filled me when it was over. I couldn't cry; there was just nothing left, except I was alive.

Am I a hypocrite? Can everyone see the twitch flexing my right eye? Is my secret evident to those surrounding us with their pledges to bring him into the White House?

Obey. His beliefs are mine.

I let the strings take me. That's my job.

When it's over, my applause beats out anyone in attendance, my smile a beam of light to drive away the darkest fears. When Colin's eyes find mine, I step forward and take his hand. Dipping down to my ear, he whispers, "Thank you for being with me." My breathing accelerates when his lips brush my cheek. He's more than a job. Colin's my life.

After another moment, we step down and walk into the crowd. I welcome a glass of champagne from a passing waitress. Taking a long sip, I swallow down the emotion threatening to creep up and as I do, a long-ago-seen smile warms my heart. Molly.

An easy feeling takes over and I tug on Colin's jacket. She's waving now, and the giddy feeling of being near an old friend pulls out my own grin. "Looks who's here." I point and his gaze follows my finger.

He looks from her to me and he eases into a chuckle. "Say hello for me too." My breath stumbles when his mouth finds mine. I close my eyes and lean into him for just a second. *Mine*. It might as well be tattooed on my forehead.

"Go," he whispers. "I'll come for you soon."

I'm giggling and wrapped in a hug three steps later. "What are you doing here?" I ask, squeezing her just a tad harder before our release.

She looks over her shoulder at a man straining the seams of his tux. "Brendan Carlyle. He couldn't leave home without me."

I mimic Colin's raised brow. "Brendan Carlyle? *Hollywood* Brendan Carlyle? Star of every romantic comedy this side of 2010?"

She laughs. "That's the one."

"Husband material?" I ask, never expecting the flush rising on her cheeks.

Shaking her head, she says, "I don't know about husband, but boyfriend yes. Speaking of which . . ." Her mouth gapes open and we both look at Colin, catching him checking out my assets. His answering grin is breathtaking, and I falter as we raise our glasses to mirror his salute.

"Ah, about that. There's something going on between us."

"Yah think, Sherlock? It didn't take a super sleuth to figure that one out. I told you from the very beginning he was into you. Why do you ever doubt me?"

We collapse into a giggle and it feels so good. "Lesson learned. Now tell me about Hollywood."

Just as I say it, Brendan turns from his conversation and his eyes assault me, dark brown and intense. Smoldering has taken on a new meaning. I glance at Molly and she just shakes her head and says, "I never had a chance."

"Now you know how I feel." We laugh again and spend the next twenty minutes playing catch-up, Brendan joining in our fun. It's only when her shoulders stiffen, that mine do the same.

"Ella," Molly says in a tight greeting to the woman sliding into the spot next to me. "It's been a while."

"That's what happens when you're traveling the country in support of our candidate. I'm sure you understand." Her voice grates against the nerves I'd been holding at bay. I seethe at the hand she holds out for Hollywood. "I don't think we've met. Ella Montgomery."

Brendan's smile transitions from natural to big screen in a second, Acting 101 apparent in his practiced demeanor. "Molly O'Donnell's boy-toy at your service."

Champagne sticks in my throat and I hold onto Molly's arm as I force it back down on a laugh. She leans over and whispers, "I warned him about Ms. Bitchy."

The lift to Ella's lips doesn't do much to soften her features or show that she shares in the joke. "How fortunate for all of us you could come tonight, Mr. Carlyle. Your support bridges a path for the McKenna campaign into California."

Ah, I didn't even think of that. "Charlie was just telling us about the upcoming trip to the west-side states," he says, covering for me. The campaign was not a topic we'd discussed.

Ella's eyes fall to slits and her smile is more sneer than compliment. "Charlie?" She glances my way and the taunt grows. "I'm sure she's filled you in on all of the important details, like where she got her dress? Do tell, *Charlie*, I'd love to know where to find such a steal."

I'm ready for the jab. Ella's false pretense is not lost on me. I knew she couldn't hold back her feelings for long. We'll never be friends. "It was a recommendation from your stylist."

There's little time to appreciate her narrowed eyes and prepare for her comeback. All of our attention is drawn to the entry of the ballroom and a hush falls over the crowd. Everything is suspended as a middle-aged man saunters in, un-lit cigar in one hand, a twenty-something's fingers held in the other. Her flaming red, spring-loaded curls fly haphazard down and around slim shoulders that barely hold up a sequined gown. They walk on a sway, her high-pitched narrative louder than the hushed murmur now sparking to life.

She stops her story long enough to ask, "Howard, won't you be a dear and find me a drink?" Two of Colin's aides intercept the couple and guide them to the far side of the room. I'm stuck staring, following the train wreck that is now huddled in a corner with plenty of attention drawn their way.

Molly's explanation is in my ear. "Howard Mane and his intern-turned-mistress. He lost his Congressional seat last year when they got caught red-handed in his car."

"Red-handed?"

"Use your imagination. The police were not thrilled by the antics going on in the front seat. She tried to escape and save him the embarrassment, but rolled down the hill into a ditch instead. The press had a field day."

"Oh."

Ella turns from the wreckage in the corner. "Oh, is right. Don't you find it interesting how a woman can change the course of one's career?"

A growl burns in my throat, but Joan waylays it. She stops just shy of Hollywood's elbow to accept a glass of champagne from a waiter. He also hands over a card and points in my direction. Using it to fan herself, she steps into our circle, leaning in to brush a kiss on first one of my cheeks and then the other.

"Charlise, dear. It's so good to see you again. Don't let Howard Mane interrupt your mingling. I'm not sure how he would have come across an invitation to tonight's gala. I'm sure heads will roll over whoever let it happen." She smiles as if she wants to watch the spectacle. "Oh, I almost forgot." Tipping the card my way, I barely have time to grab it before she's latched onto Hollywood.

Molly waves before getting swallowed up in a discussion and the addition of more guests, leaving me alone with an envelope addressed to Charlie Carter in calligraphy. It's the size and weight of a formal wedding invitation.

When I pull out the card, blood leaves my face like a weight sinking into my stomach. Not because Shane found me here—somehow he always knows where we are—but because of the contents. My fingers tremble as they feather over a picture. It's me. Last year I went out with Ali when she was in Michigan on break. I'm obviously drunk, too many margaritas and if I recall, a shot of tequila to go along with them. It's her friend that's the problem. His arm is draped over my shoulders as he leans in, mouth open. A dare I accepted from Ali to allow him to lick salt from my neck for a silly body-shot. She's always devising something to drive me out of my comfort zone. That night, it was mission accomplished.

I flip the cardstock over and my breath hitches at the written words.

It won't take much to ruin him. End it or you will.

In one minute my world turns into crisp clarity. Will I let Charlie Carter ruin Colin McKenna's chance at the presidency? I feel his eyes on me. Colin. Tucking the photo back in the envelope, I shove it into my clutch and glance up in time to see him striding toward me. The Governor and his wife are in tow. I close my eyes for the briefest moment. To anyone watching it's a second, but to me it's the dawn of a new age. *Bend, Charlie, bend a little further. Now is the time. There is no other way.* Fear of discovery is replaced by determination and a serene smile. I won't hide in fear of the past. *I will not be his downfall.*

"Baby," he whispers, tucking me into his side and my hand falls into its place on his lower back, digging in. "I'd like to introduce—"

Straightening my spine and pulling back my shoulders, I speak before he can. "A pleasure to meet you, Governor Bernard." Holding out my hand, I clasp his in a tight grip. "I'm Charlise Carter."

FOURTEEN

JULY

PEOPLE SAY EVERYTHING IS bigger in Texas, and I think they're right. Colin's broad shoulders definitely stretch across a time zone today and his ass? Damn, his ass looks fine in dark jeans. A weathered navy T-shirt with the American flag expands across his chest. I snap a picture as he walks the line, shaking hands next to the mayor of one of the oldest cities in the state. Turning away, I allow the setting sun to hide the blush that desperately wants to warm my cheeks. Colin McKenna sure knows how to heat up my engine and rev me up like a car in the fast lane. I roll my eyes and laugh out loud.

I spent way too much time with Ted Langston, NASCAR driver extraordinaire, in Louisville yesterday. So much time, I learned all about his cars and got an invitation to ride not only on the track, but in his back seat. I think Colin had a mini stroke, confirmed by his ever-twitching eye that lasted until we were in the air heading to the Lone Star State. Oh boy, did he ever teach me a lesson, one which left my legs weak and my groin aching for more.

I have to stop thinking about him or every person at this event will know what he did to me all night long—delicious-I-must-go-find-someone-to-flirt-with-so-he'll-do-it-again-tonight kind of love.

I smile and pack up my camera. Over the last month, the press has vacillated between sensationalism and painting Charlise Carter as the picture of understated elegance. I won't lie. I prefer the elegant pieces more centered on the truth, even if they do lend an air of dignified polish I don't really possess.

I'm sure those articles have everything to do with how John has chosen to 'spin' me toward an audience. After Memorial Day, I asked Colin to hire a coach to transform me into the ideal girlfriend. John handed me over to Joan, who was more than willing to take on a pet project. I went from Charlie to Charlise overnight, with her leading the way, along with a hands-on trainer. Therese please-don't-call-me-Tessa-or-Terri Wainwright is a bulldog I'd never think of crossing. I've already hidden a few bite marks from Colin. She's not shy when letting me know I've displeased her, or more so, that I've done a disservice to Colin and his campaign. The thought of injuring his dream has me crossing my T's and dotting my I's, using the correct fork at all dinner parties, and standing ramrod straight through every event. Straight enough Joan should throw a ball in my honor.

I haven't come close to leopard print in weeks. Nothing belongs to me anymore, not my hairstyle or the clothes I wear. It's robotic perfection. Still, pretending to be someone I'm not is harder than I expected. I long to be myself, to find Charlie again, and leave the prim, tight-lipped Charlise behind, even if it's just for one day.

My past remains hidden, as does Shane Roberts. It's too hard to have his name run through my head every day, so I started referring to him as Freddie. Like Freddie Krueger. Other than a couple of intercepted messages at various events, he's been absent. I fear the inactivity, because it feels like the calm before the storm. He's out there waiting, waiting for the perfect moment to strike. Thinking about his next attack is terrifying. I'd never tell Colin the depth of my fear or how it's affecting me, but it's taking a toll. Sleep is evasive and eating is secondary due to the nerves constantly rumbling in my stomach.

We're days away from the Republican convention, where Colin will officially accept the nomination of his party. It was concluded he would run for president after he secured enough delegates last month. Going into the convention strong is our focus, so the momentum is carried over into the campaign for the presidency. Because of it, our schedule is even more hectic than it was when I began working for him. We're typically at three events per day, sometimes more, working from the break of dawn to twilight and beyond. Once the nomination is official, he'll keep moving at breakneck speed through to the general election in November, taking only three days off in late July for his sister's wedding in Ireland.

Speaking of taking days off, Evan is in D.C. Two days ago he asked Colin about a quick trip over the holiday weekend, claiming he had personal business to attend to. Hmm, work on Ali is what I suspect, but neither will give up any specifics. Something is going on with those two, and I aim to find out what it is when he returns tomorrow.

The Fourth of July in Texas is hot, really hot, ninety-five degrees to be exact. Our tour brought us here to enjoy a Texas-size party to celebrate the nation's independence. Tonight's agenda is relaxed. In an hour we'll enjoy the much-heralded fireworks. The quaint, picture-perfect American town is painted in red, white and blue and everyone is wearing it too.

This morning I pulled my hair into a high ponytail, that along with a white cap-sleeve T-shirt and ankle-length jeans, and I feel close to Charlie. Today's the day to be myself. I brought my guitar and throughout our visit I sat with different groups of children to sing songs, even "Kumbaya". It has a new place in my heart after John Montgomery's tongue-lashing.

A well-known country band is playing on a makeshift stage in the courtyard, and a loud but not unpleasant twang fills the cooling night air. Another area is sectioned off for our small party and a crowd has gathered to meet Colin. He and the mayor are moving along the barricade, shaking hands and talking it up with residents eager for an up-close glimpse of the presidential hopeful. Always gracious, he's taking his time with each one. I move behind him, because they want to meet me, too. Colin McKenna's girlfriend is apparently newsworthy and fascinating.

Colin grabs my attention, as he does so often. The crowd has grown even larger for the impending fireworks, bringing with it many female admirers. Their unabashed flirting always makes me laugh because he clearly doesn't know what to do with it. In most cases he'll flash a friendly, jaw-dropping smile, murmur a polite hello and move on. Today a bold buxom blonde has gripped his hand and hasn't let go, talking a mile a minute about God knows what. Turning his head to find me, our eyes connect, and I laugh out loud at his staggered expression, silently pleading for help. I take a few steps toward him for the rescue and recovery effort to begin.

"Hi," I whisper, saddling up next to him, my arm snaking around his waist. He's sinfully handsome and hard muscle wrapped up in all-American goodness. For a second I melt into him and squeeze, filling my lungs with his musk and glorying in the fact that he's mine. Blondie can't hide her irritation at my interruption and my smile grows larger, as bold as her grip on his hand.

Pressing his mouth to my ear, his close proximity and whisper cause a shiver to spread down my spine. "Some help here, please?"

"What's in it for me?" I tease, just as Blondie tugs on his hand. Her latest move has security stepping closer and I laugh again.

A low growl only I can hear vibrates through his chest and the shiver spreads lower, creating a slow fluttering in my groin. Oh, he's going to be bad, really bad, and I like it.

"I'm going to ride you like the bucking bronco at the rodeo, all night long. I promise you." A wicked smile brightens his chiseled jaw as he straightens.

"Uh . . . yup, o . . . okay," I stutter, and my grin slips from distraction. A bucking bronco, huh? He sure knows how to give a girl motivation. When our eyes meet, his dark with longing and a hint of sass, I say, "I love your promises and I love you. Just for that I will save you, Mr. McKenna."

"Please do," he grounds out while Blondie moves in for the kill, pulling him closer.

"I just love your hair," I gush with overt excitement, drawing her attention away from Colin. "I wish mine had as much volume."

Blondie releases his hand with obvious enthusiasm at the compliment, using it to plump up the already mountainous curls. Nodding, Colin manages a quick escape and moves on to greet others waiting to meet him. Catching my eye as he slips away, he mouths silently with a devilish grin—hinting at a promise he will definitely keep—*I love you.*

His smile is contagious and I stick around long enough to learn how Blondie volumizes each morning. Who knew there's still a market for Aqua Net and hair picks? After a few minutes, I excuse myself and catch up to Colin, moving beside him and chatting casually as we work the line. As always, I get distracted, this time by a group of young girls off to the side of the large gathering playing hopscotch, a game I vaguely remember playing with my best friend prior to the death of my biological parents. Intrigued, I step to the other side of the divider and ask if they have room for a fourth. When they agree, I don't hesitate to jump in and surprise myself at how much fun it is.

The girls are blissfully unaware of what's going on around them, unconcerned Colin is making his rounds and that I'm his girlfriend. They laugh when I teeter on my foot, almost losing balance. The squares are much smaller than I remember, or maybe it's because my feet are so much bigger. As I'm heading back to pick up my rock, I barely hop into a square, landing just shy of the edge.

Balance isn't my strong suit, so I topple, landing on my hip and giggling with the girls at my misfortune.

When I glance up, Colin's watching me from afar. The once wicked smile has transitioned to one of tender appreciation. His eyes are alight with happiness and suddenly I wish we were alone, not to ride the bronco, although that thought makes me giggle anew. I wish we were alone so I could enjoy the fireworks with my boyfriend, kiss him under the bright lights and snuggle into his arms. Not this year at least, so I wave and return his smile. Before making my way back to his side I stand to dust my pants off and shake each of my new friend's hands in farewell.

Stopping for a minute, I admire the sky. It's on the verge of nightfall, and dark orange and deep red layer in the horizon. One on top of the other, the colors melt into dusk, a shadowed crimson. The color has taken on new meaning and seems to claw its way down my spine in a shudder. Shaking off the trepidation, I glance at the growing crowd. I'd bet every resident is here for the firework display and probably out of town visitors too. Our once segregated space is filling with onlookers. Security is pushing back those curious to meet Colin, trying to keep them behind the barricade, but many are edging in. Drake, who has kept his distance for most of the evening, hedges closer to me. Removing his ever-present sunglasses, he roves the crowd. I follow his gaze, yet I can only see a mass of people.

On my way back to Colin, firecrackers startle me. The loud, incessant pop bites into the air over and over again. Someone began the celebration early and is setting them off close by. Bodies crowd around me, twisting and turning to get a closer look at the personal show. They're louder now—*bang, bang, BOOM.*

My whole body jerks from the enormous explosion. *What the hell was that?* Swarms of people scream and push, seeking an exit in an unobstructed configuration so they're moving in every direction. More firecrackers—*bang, bang, bang*—ending with another explosion.

"Charlie!"

It's Colin calling for me. Twirling, I look for him everywhere, but his voice vanishes amongst the chaos. Screams echo in my ears as the crowd parts. A blur flashes out of the corner of my eye and then Drake is diving toward one man who slices through the tangled masses.

Time slows. I'm living in an alternate reality watching, paralyzed, when Freddie raises his arm and fires two bullets in quick succession into the man sworn to keep me safe. I suck in a breath as Drake falls to the ground in an unmoving heap. But I have little time to process events. Freddie's sure steps are leading directly toward me. Stopped dead in my tracks, a deer in headlights, I'm mesmerized by him. His low baseball cap is pulled around his eyes, but I can see them. They've taken on the red hue of the sky. Intent on his target, he plows through the confusion. People rush in every direction, and I'm pushed toward him in their haste to escape.

Stopping not ten feet away, a corner of his mouth lifts in a snarl. "It's time to pay up, sweet-face," he says, but I don't hear it. I read the words as his lips move in slow motion.

I'm transported back fifteen years, when his voice was not leveled at me from a distance, but ground into my ear when he made me scream. I remain silent and staring when he lifts his gun. Holding up my hands in weak defense I turn to run and just as I do, two things happen. *BOOM!* A crack so loud my ears ring and then the force of it hits me. Hard and pummeling I fall to the earth, dead weight pressing me down.

FIFTEEN

WARM BREATH PUSHES INTO my neck and one whispered word has fear gripping my heart. "Charlie."

The darkness of night descends around us, constricting the flow of oxygen along with Colin's full weight. Sinking into me, my body welcomes him, drawing him down in comfort as his breath becomes labored. I'm struck by the sheer terror glazing over his eyes. Dropping his head into the crook of my neck a small wheeze sharpens the air and heat passes between us. Soft and flowing, a stream runs through, coating my T-shirt and his, gluing us together. My hands find his back and hair, frantic in their search, touching him everywhere.

"Colin?" I cry, panic raising my voice to manic heights.

It's only then I recognize the chaos surrounding us. What felt like minutes is a second, and in the span of another, Colin is ripped from me. Two of our security men grab him under the arms and heave him up and into a waiting car that then speeds off. Gone. Just like that he's gone and I'm left to lie in the ruin of the red evening sky. Hidden by commotion, I become lost to everyone, enveloped completely by red. I'm drowning in it. The sickening metallic bite of it reaches my nose and my stomach heaves as the red sinks in deeper, covering me. It covers everything around me.

Shocked, I stare, fixed on the billowing gray clouds mingling with the fire of night, extinguishing the flames into a smoldering burn.

The flames have moved to my chest, burning with each breath. Pain flares deep, not because I'm injured, but because I know Colin is. Lifting my hands in front of my face, they're coated in his blood. It rolls down my fingers and drips thick and heavy back to the earth. A long whimpering cry transitions into a piercing scream and I hold my hands against my ears to make it stop but it goes on and on.

Tucking myself into a fetal position, I tunnel away to a place where there's no sound. The outer rim of my sight is fuzzy and I realize how quickly I've come to the faraway place. A sweet numbing takes over in a blur. Opening my eyes, I'm transfixed by the ambulance racing Drake away and then the pile-up to my left. Freddie. Ten men have him pinned to the ground, with his face facing me. Our eyes connect—the evil pitch of red has left his, but they remain sharp and angry.

He is my living nightmare. He has been since I was fourteen years old. A low mewling cry bubbles in my chest as memories flood and threaten to break me. The rough force of his thrusts echo in my mind as my body remembers the pain. Shane Roberts. He's come again to hurt me, but he's hurt Colin instead. This bastard has stolen so many things from me: my innocence, my virtue and my sanity. At least for a period of time, I lost myself. With his return, have I lost love, too? Staring into his eyes, it hits me square in the chest. A villain from my past bears me so much hatred he would kill over it.

Why? I mouth, waiting for an answer. When it comes, it's jumbled because of the pressure placed on his jaw from the multiple sets of hands and knees holding him down.

"You took my life."

Of course. It's been about me all along, and the child he fathered out of anger and aggression. The life I ended to save my own. He stares, darts of hatred spewing from his eyes, until he's hauled to his feet with his arms cuffed behind him. Others begin sectioning off the scene, pushing bystanders away and off the property.

BOOM! A loud crack explodes and I jump, screaming again while a multitude of starbursts light up the night sky in pink, purple and green.

The show must go on.

BOOM! Surreal events play as a rerun in my mind; it's a constant loop circling over and over. *BOOM!* Freddie and a gun. *BOOM!* Colin pushing me out of the way. *BOOM!* Breathless, glassy eyes falling away into darkness.

"Ms. Carter?" A young Barnie Fife stands above me, with a cautious expression. The overly large police uniform declares him safe, and I nod.

"We need to ask you a few questions."

"What?" I choke out.

"Uh, I need to ask you about what just happened. You know, about what you saw. It should only take a few minutes," he explains.

"Oh, I . . ." I don't know what I thought would happen. Standing slowly, my own questions run through my mind, yet they go unanswered. Is Drake alive? Why has no one come to take me to

Colin? Where did they take them? Are they okay? "I need to get to the hospital."

"Are you injured?" he asks, fumbling to click his ballpoint pen open.

"No, I . . . I don't think so," I say, and for the first time I glance down at my shirt. It's no longer white, but covered in a pink and red tie-dye. Blood. Colin's blood. *Oh, God. Not Colin.* I groan and close my eyes. All I see is red. Grabbing my head, I bow under the pressure.

A chill settles deep into the night and into my bones. Wrapping my arms around myself to stave off the cold, I'm reminded of Colin and his generous nature, always offering his coat or his body for warmth. I begin to see him everywhere, in the face of everyone, and I think, for just a second, sanity has left the building. *One minute at a time.* I start my mantra and concentrate on it for focus.

"You don't look so good. Let me call my lieutenant for some help. Just stay here and I'll be right back." Walking away, Barney finds a large man who bears an air of authority and the two begin a heated conversation, looking at me periodically while the big guy's brow furrows.

"Miss?" Barnie's back.

"I need to get to the hospital," I say louder this time, hysteria bubbling to the surface. "I don't have a phone or my purse; they're in Drake's car. How is he? I need to get to Colin. Do you know where he is? Where did they take him? He has to be okay. Do you know if he's okay? Have you heard anything? Do you know how they are? Please. Help. Me."

By now Barnie's hands are out in front of his chest pushing away the barrage of questions. "I just have to ask you a few things and we'll get you over to Baylor."

Leading me to the side of a police car and near the big guy, he hands me a bag of wet wipes and a non-descript navy windbreaker. I pull it on as he begins the interrogation. While I clean my hands and face, Barnie surprises me with the details he's able to draw out. A few questions turns into many, and the minutes tick by. Each second away from Colin and not knowing what's going on has my anxiety level reaching new limits. When Barnie takes a breath, I take control.

"Listen to me," I start off calm, but my voice rises with each word. "A nut job just shot my boyfriend right in front of my face and I need to get to him. Are you going to help me, or do I need to find someone else who will take me to the goddamn hospital?" I scream and it gets their attention. With it, things begin to move quickly. Herded into the back of a police cruiser, lights on, we tunnel through the night. Both men are quiet; the static of the radio is the only noise to breach the silence. I can't make out what's passing through the airways so I stare out the window, drawing further into myself. The night replays in my mind: Blondie, bronco, hopscotch, Freddie, *BOOM*, Colin, Barnie—repeat and again. It gnaws until my psyche is raw and bleeding.

By the time I'm ushered into the hospital, it's crawling with police and people. Barnie and the big guy send me into a waiting room, promising I'll find my answers there.

When I approach the counter, the triage nurse demands, "I.D. and insurance card."

"I . . . I don't have any I.D. I just need to check on Colin McKenna and Drake Eaton." I grip the chest high desk to support my weakened knees.

Barely looking at me, she replies, "Yeah right, you and a hundred other people."

"No, I'm sorry. I should have explained. I'm Charlie Carter, his girlfriend."

She purses her lips and stays focused on her computer monitor. "Listen, lady, I'd think if you were his girlfriend you'd have come in with him, *if* he's even here. So save the drama for someone who cares. Hospital policy dictates we can only give information about patients to immediate family members, anyway. Are you family?"

"No . . . I . . . I'm Charlie. Please . . ."

"Are you injured?" Her tone hardens as she glances at paperwork on the desk and begins typing on her keyboard without looking at me again.

"No, I'm fine. I just . . ."

"If you're not injured you need to leave this area. It's for patients and family only. Step aside." Her face darkens in frustration and she levels her eyes at me. "Did you hear me? We have enough going on without McKenna's crazies trying to pimp for information.

You're the worst kind. The fifth one pretending to be his girlfriend. You should be ashamed. Go, get on with yourself and find the rest of your media lackeys. You'll receive status updates if and when they're given to the rest of your sorry lot."

Turning, she greets a young patient struggling to the desk, gripping his stomach, but I won't give up.

"Please, just tell me where his security team is, I'll—"

"Do you have any identification?"

"No, it's—"

"Mmhmm, thought so. This is the last time I'm going to say it. If you don't get out of this area I will call hospital security and have you escorted off the property."

Fear grips me again; I need to be here. I need to be here for him; I can't get kicked out. Stumbling out of the room, I find a smaller waiting area on the other side of triage and tuck myself into a hard chair in the corner. There are only a handful of seats in this room, probably for an overflow of patients. A soda and snack machine line one wall, a pay phone on another. Siding up to the phone, I dial my parents collect to let them know I'm okay and ask them to reach out to the McKenna's for me. After the operator connects the number it rings and rings until the old-school answering machine picks up.

"There's no one to accept the collect call. Miss, would you like to try another number?"

"Um, yes. Ali Carter at this number . . ."

"I'm sorry, I can't send a collect call to a cell number. Is there someone else you would like to reach?"

"Uh, no," I say, deflated.

A quick glance confirms Nurse Rached remains at the desk. Squeezing back into the corner chair, I wrap myself into a tight ball, head falling against my drawn-up knees. What was once faint is now overpowering, and I drown in the smell of Colin's blood. My stomach heaves and to stave off the nausea I find myself, once again, seeking out the place where troubles are left behind, where events don't happen to me, but around me.

The local station has a running commentary as breaking news playing on a television in the large lobby. *Colin McKenna shot—critical condition* rolls along the bottom of the screen. Critical condition. I groan and try to listen to the story but it's too far away. The commotion of the emergency room drowns out all other sound, but I can watch it and I do. I'm riveted by what cameras caught in still pictures and video. There's a picture of Blondie holding his hand. I choke on the sudden lump in my throat; minutes later he would once again save me and pay the ultimate price for his instinctive protectiveness. Bile rises from my stomach at a picture of the hopscotch game. If I hadn't been sidetracked, maybe this would never have happened. I begin running through the *what-if*s, second-guessing my actions—if I hadn't of, if I would have, I should have and maybe, just maybe Freddie wouldn't have gotten to us. Rocking back and forth, I know I look crazy, and it's a possibility that's where I'm headed.

People coming and going draw my attention away from the television. Some are sick, others are family seeking information, and many ask for Colin McKenna updates. *Colin.* I groan and tip my head in my knees again. Thoughts of him and what he's going through are agonizing. I just found him—have I lost him so soon? His eyes, clear and glassy, haunt my memories. My chest constricts, but I push that possibility to the furthest reaches of my mind. I will not even contemplate it. No, absolutely no.

Happier times prevail and I run through our brief history. Has it only been six months since we met in January? It has, but it seems like a lifetime. He introduced me to love, a concept so deep and expansive I couldn't image it. The pure, unadulterated emotion is an experience, a journey that comes along with loving Colin McKenna. Joy, awe, desire and passion, so much intense passion, is all part of the adventure. I realize my life before him was obscure. Maybe it's because I never really started living until we met, or maybe it's because life is more vibrant with him in it. Either way, I want the chance to have my happily-ever-after with him.

"*I have no heart to give*," he'd said to me once. Clearly, it wasn't true. He didn't know it at the time, but his heart was full of love and he gave it to me. Maybe unwillingly at first, a protection against past hurts, but with time and patience his heart was given as a gift. The truth of our uninhibited connection is woven indelibly between his heart and mine. We belong to each other, mind, body and soul. There is no other man who understands me and knows without a doubt exactly what I need to be whole. Colin offers me the perfect balance of self-discovery and forgiveness. Without his instant acceptance of my sullied past I couldn't have found the freedom to live my life with the enthusiasm I do today. I *need* him.

And with that, I couldn't have found a better man to love. I've always feared my past would prevent the future he's dreamed of. Colin's never held my choices against me, even though he's very opposed to one of them. He's only wanted to give me the world, new experiences, and protection. All of which he has done in spades. I've only ever wanted him; he's the only man to elicit a physical reaction from me, my body bending to his every desire. I *want* him. *Please, God* . . . I pray as I haven't done in ages. Focused and intent, I plead for his health and safety, losing myself in the constant mantra of prayer.

Two employees in scrubs interrupt my reverie. A coin dropping into the slot of the vending machine draws me into the low hum of their conversation.

"Yeah, I heard he was rushed into surgery after Dr. Silva saw him. Like, they didn't even stop in the ER, just took him right into surgery because he lost so much blood during the drive here."

I freeze. They're talking about Colin. My heart punches a thousand beats in a second and I stop breathing.

"Betty from surgery told me they called a code while he was on the table."

"It's sad, you know. He was so young. I feel real bad for his girlfriend. How do you live the rest of your life knowing your guy died trying to save you? Sucks bad."

"For sure. I wonder what happened . . ."

A long, cold cry escapes my lips, and the room chills noticeably as the sound reverberates against the walls. The two employees jump and whip their heads to my hiding spot in the corner, taking in my appearance.

"Uh, come on, Tara, we gotta go. Our break's over."

As they hurry out, comprehension is swift and earth shattering. I've experienced plenty of loss in my life, but nothing, nothing could prepare me for the excruciating agony slicing through not just my heart, but also every fiber of my being. I'm breathless, unable to draw in oxygen to sustain life and I don't care. Death would bring with it a welcomed peace.

Colin, NO! God damn it, not him. Of everything taken from me—my birth parents, my virtue and with it the possibility of children—this loss is too much to bear. The instant reaction is to funnel the pain physically and I begin to shake. Large, rolling waves of grief rock my huddled frame while I find a numb space in my mind. Drawing so far away from reality, I block out everything, staring sightless into a world that continues to revolve around me. But I don't. My life ended the moment Colin's did. Not in the physical sense, as my lungs continue to draw in air, but emotionally I'm gone.

Time continues and people move, like a silent movie passing before me, while I stare. I stare with unseeing eyes as staff and patients remain unaware of the crazy in the corner. No one comes for me. No one cares that Charlie Carter is suffering in silence, alone. So unbearably alone, without the one person I need more than anything in the universe. The grip on my sanity loosens. I'm sitting in his dried blood that crackles on my skin when I move, and unwilling to wipe it off because it's all I have left of him. I'm never to feel his heat, his body, his kiss, his strength, his *love* ever again.

I fall slowly over the cliff of reason. Hours fly by, and it's not until I hear a familiar voice that I struggle above oblivion.

"Where is she?" Colleen McKenna's shrill pitch pierces my subconscious, her petite frame rising over the triage desk in anger.

"I . . . I'm not sure who you're referring to, ma'am," Nurse Rached replies, trying for her haughty tone, but she trips on the words because Colleen's eyes must be on fire.

"Listen to me and listen well. I want Charlise Carter brought to me this instant. I know she's here; the police dropped her off eight hours ago and they saw her talking to you. Now, either you tell me where she is or get a hospital administrator to find her. Which option do you prefer?"

"There's no one . . ." She clears her throat. "I don't have any record of Charlise Carter being admitted as a patient."

"I didn't say she was a patient; she came in looking for my son, Colin McKenna, and I would like to know why she wasn't taken to him immediately?" Again, Colleen levels a blazing stare at Nurse Rached. For a second, my heart actually beats with Colleen's animosity. Go get her, Colleen. If I could smile I would at least attempt it, but I can't. If I move I'll fall apart, so I stay still, watching through my movie lens.

"Oh, well . . . ohm," she stumbles to answer. "I'm just following hospital policy. We aren't able to give updates to anyone but family. I can't give private information to a girlfriend."

Colleen leans in, capturing the nurse's gaze and says something so low I can't hear it, but based on the widening of Rached's eyes, it hits home. The conversation ends with Colleen saying through her teeth, "Find her *now.*"

Pointing in my direction with a shaking finger, Nurse Rached says, "Is that her over there?"

Colleen's head swings in my direction, anger immediately dissipating to compassion when we connect, her eyes widening as she takes me in. Before moving toward me she tilts over, pulling her frame up and into the desk. Whatever she says to Rached is unintelligible, but it has the crotchety nurse paling and shrinking away. Silently I cheer for Colleen tackling something I wish I had the courage to do hours ago.

Turning, she walks quickly to me. Empathy radiates from her every pore, her hazel eyes glazed from crying. I envy her in this moment. I envy the ability to cry and release emotion, emotions that are suffocating and strangling the very life from me.

"Charlie. I'm so sorry." Bending to her knees, she grips both of my hands in hers. How she is able to provide comfort when she just lost her son is beyond me. I should be comforting her, but I can't. I have no words. "Come with me. I'm sure you want to see Colin before they move him."

See him? Oh, God. I groan and slip deeper, barely holding on at the thought of it. He will be cold, not hot—still, not strong—frozen in time—*not living*. I don't have the strength for that. Seeing him will bring with it a final goodbye and I'm not ready to say it. Small whimpering cries begin to beat out of my throat and I push them into tremors. If I lose it now, I will *lose* it, and I don't want to do that to Colleen. She has so much to consider as it is—she doesn't need Colin's girlfriend adding to her list of woes.

Standing, she pulls me into a hard hug and I sink into the soft comfort, needing to feel life in some way. "It'll be okay," she whispers.

How? I finally open my mouth to speak, but realize the word came out in silence and I mouthed it into her hair. My voice is lost within myself, just as Colin is lost to me.

Taking my hand, she tugs me into the first shaky steps down a hallway, and after a short elevator ride the doors open to a nursing station. Employees come and go, walking with purpose down one of two hallways, where doors open every twenty feet on either side. Colleen guides me to a smaller, quiet area. There's only one door here and there aren't any employees. I suck in my breath at the knowledge that it's because there aren't any patients to care for. Pulling on Colleen's hand, I silently beg her to stop. I can't do this.

"What is it, Charlie?"

Staring down at my shirt, I touch his blood, running my hand over my stomach until I clutch it, as I would normally do his hair. *Colin.* I mewl until tears coat my eyes, pooling heavy at the rim.

"Oh dear, you probably want to change before you see him? I didn't even think of it, but of course you want to get out of those clothes." Sympathy weighs heavy in her eyes, but she doesn't move. "Why don't you go in and I'll ask someone for a gown you can wear. I'm afraid it's the best I can do until I get my bags from the car. Go on, Evan's inside too."

"I can't."

"Why ever not, Charlie?" she asks, clearly dumbfounded by my hesitancy.

"I . . . I can't." And then I lose it. Mumbling more to myself than to her, I let it all go. Colin and Shane, the gunshot, blood, and the last thing I saw of Colin alive: his glassy eyes. A horrified expression dawns across her face, a shade falling and settling still.

"Come with me." Taking my hand, she tugs me along, talking in a soothing monologue, but I'm not listening, absorbed in my own memories and trying to prevent new ones from forming.

Pushing through the heavy wooden door together, the first thing I see is Evan, pale and anxious, hovering over the body on the bed. Michael is seated next to him with his own haunted grief. Blue eyes, so much like Colin's, glance at me. Sympathy, dawning like a new day, shrouds their clarity.

I'm not prepared for this. I can't—I just can't do this.

Gripping my head between my hands, I escape into myself. I feel nothing when my legs weaken and crumble beneath me, taking me to the floor. My heart rolls in my chest, galloping ahead of me into a future I don't want to have. Alone. A page turned to close out one chapter and open another. It's never been more final than in this moment.

SIXTEEN

THE SLAP OF MY hands on the cold tile barely registers. I recognize my breath is punching forward too fast and may verge on hyperventilation, but I can't stop it.

"Hey, hey, hey." Evan's quick steps turn into a slide on his knees until we're face to face. He tips my chin and our gazes lock. I've never studied his eyes before now. They're a true gray, no hint of any color. Black shards spike from the pupil as if to prove there's an inherent sorrow he constantly battles. I've always thought of him as the amusing and fun-loving friend that balances out Colin's natural philosophic tendencies. I'm wrong. He fights his own demons. In that briefest moment, I vow to know him better and understand the connection the two of them shared. A friendship so deep it would drag him hundreds of miles away from Ali in D.C. in the middle of the night to stand vigil alongside Colin's parents. He's more than a friend, adopted into the McKenna family as sure as Ali and I are Carters.

"Everything's okay, Charlie," he says, but his voice is hoarse and comes out in a rough whisper.

"How can it be?"

"Take my hand." When I hesitate, he grabs both of mine and helps me to my feet. Keeping my head down, I allow him to maneuver me to the bedside and to the body that is not so still after all. Sheets rustle and a low hum vibrates through the air. I still can't feel anything—relief would be too simple, joy not enough. Fear transitions into doubt and the smallest inclining of hope. That's too much to wish for, so I construct a wall of numb disinterest around me. The well of emotions that could swing either way is too deep to deal with. I'm afraid of them, afraid to feel anything, so I stare without acknowledgement at the bright blue eyes I love so much.

Colin McKenna is alive.

"Charlie?" He reaches for me, yet my only movement is to tilt my head as if in contemplation. I'm not thinking, I'm stuck, paralyzed by the raw sting of a new reality that's hard to believe.

"I thought you were dead." The air stills around us and no one moves. I allow my eyes to rake up and down his body, taking in details of his prone figure. He's bare, except for a bandage wrapped around his shoulder and a blue brace to keep it in place. His chest moves with each breath. *Thank God*. The sheet is pulled up to his waist, hiding the rest of his body from my feasting eyes, but if I can believe the outline, he looks whole and untouched. Other than the obvious injury, my concern becomes the multiple tubes snaking down from an I.V. pole into his arm. That and his pale complexion—he's white, close to the shade of the sheet.

When our eyes connect, his are strangely cold. Anger heats his cheeks and brings in some of the color I just worried over. "What's wrong? Are you in pain?" I ask, fumbling my hands in front of my stomach, unsure if I should touch him.

"What happened to you? Are you hurt?" he grounds out.

My brow falls and I step back, more than a little confused. "Nothing, I'm fine." Running a hand over my face, down to my chest, I feel the starched stiffness of my shirt. "I just got lost." More figuratively than literally, but I don't know what else to say. It's the closest statement to the truth and I won't admit to how far I drifted . . .

"I won't lose you again, Charlie." He reaches for me, and this time I take his hand. Warmth radiates into me and it's only then I recognize how cold I am. A shiver snakes down my spine and I can't be certain if it's from the chill or his simple touch. Colin. Now I'm found. I see him and feel him, yet an air of disbelief still hovers close by.

"I'm so sorry, baby," he whispers and I whimper, the closest I can get to a wail. I want to cry, the emotion so close to exploding from me. I can feel the shiver turn into a shake, but I push that down too.

"Easy, baby. We're okay."

The soft thud of the door closes and a quick look around confirms we're alone. When I find him again, I see my heart lying on the bed. All I want to do is curl up next to him, hold him and never let go, but I'm afraid to hurt him more.

"Come here." He tugs, still strong enough to pull me easily to his side, and I scramble onto the bed next to him, taking caution to keep my distance from his injury. My lids flutter closed when his heat envelopes me and I sink into the hard lines of his body. Home.

I breathe him in—deep, healing breaths. Exhaustion takes over then. I feel the slide into sleep with each long inhale and the soothing monologue he's whispering in my ear. Surrounded by him, I welcome the surrender into oblivion where Shane Roberts doesn't exist and Colin McKenna is whole.

ooo

This dream is heaven. Colin's deep timbre rumbles underneath me, whispering comforting words and bringing with it a serenity I never hoped to feel again. I revel in the cadence of his words, letting them soak into every crevice and wash away some of the pain.

Wait . . . his hands . . . feel him? Heat expands not just at the site of his touch, but around and through me. Where I was cold, I am now warm and comforted. The electricity ever present between us travels down my spine and into each extremity. In the soft exploration of touch I feel the hard length of his body next to me, my arm draped over his mid-section. Solid, defined muscles of his abdomen rise and fall beneath me and I can't help but burrow into the crook of his shoulder. I clutch him tight. A small gasp, and warmth presses into my hair.

"Stop hovering, Mom, I'm fine. She's waking up; at least I can attest her strength is returning." A tired chuckle resonates and I sink in deeper, trying desperately to feel him along the path of every nerve. A sudden rustling around us moves the air.

"Leave Charlie where she is. I won't have her taken from me."

"Let me know if she's too heavy and we can move her to the sofa. Do you think she's all right? She's been out a long time; should we call a nurse?"

"She's fine, on both accounts." He follows this with a weak squeeze, drawing me in closer, and I breathe in his scent, yet it's almost overpowered by the antiseptic smells of the hospital. I don't like it. "Why was she left in the emergency room? They should have brought her to surgery so she could wait with you and dad."

There's a long pause, then Colleen's soft words break the silence. "Promise me you'll listen without getting upset?"

"Just tell me."

"Fine, but so help me if your blood pressure rises I will call the nurse in to sedate you."

"Okay, I get it. I'm listening."

"As far as I can piece together, the hospital has a very strict confidentiality policy and will only release information to family. Charlie couldn't produce identification and if she did, it wouldn't have done any good because she's not your wife . . ."A growl rips through her statement. "We're done here. I warned you."

"I'm fine. Keep going."

"Colin, listen to me. You're not doing anyone, including Charlie, any good if you're laid up longer than need be because you won't follow doctor's orders. And his orders are to rest, keep your fluids up and your blood pressure down. What happened last night is . . ." Her breath hitches, "incomprehensible. Both you and Drake are lucky to be alive, and he's barely hanging on. So please, for both Charlie and me, follow the damn doctor's orders," she finishes in a rush of breath.

"I'm sorry. You're right. I just slept for an hour and I'll calm down, but it's hard for me to relax when she's exhausted and covered in blood."

"The police kept Charlie for questioning and when she got here, you had already been moved to surgery. I looked for her as soon as we arrived at the hospital, but she'd been alone with no information for over eight hours." Colleen exhales. "Everything's fine now. We've found her and you're healing, or you better be." The sharp, admonishing tone is back. "If I find it's too much to have her here, for you or Charlie, I'll take her back to the hotel. You both need rest."

"I'm healing, almost as good as new. Stop worrying."

She mumbles something under her breath and a shadow falls over my eyes, the subtle hint of her perfume clouding Colin's scent.

"Send Evan in on your way out." Colin says. "I need to confirm the time of the press conference."

"Don't you think that can wait until tomorrow?"

"No, it can't. I have to reassure everyone I'm not dead."

She huffs. "Fine, but remember your blood—"

"Mom." Colin is clearly exasperated and I smile into his chest. The first hint of happiness cracking through an otherwise downright shitty day lightens my thoughts. "You think that's funny?" he whispers into my hair, brushing his lips along my forehead.

Relief is liberating. An almost physical weight lifts from my heart. Colin is really here, really with me, his chest rising and falling in time with my own. I believe it now. I feel him next to me. I hear his voice inside of me, yet relief can't erase the sheer terror that held me hostage throughout the night. It's hard to escape from it, but I have to let it go for his sake and mine. He's already moving on with the campaign and I need to drive forward at the same speed he does. *Put the past where it should be, Charlie—don't think about it. Shelve it for another time.*

With that thought, I open my eyes. Harsh white light assails my vision and I blink it back to focus on what I know with certainty is Colin's hand. I've studied him, every part of him, to know it's his immediately. His arm is held tight to his body in a sling, leaving only his wrist and hand exposed from the blue nylon reaching up along his shoulder. There, just below his collarbone, is a large white bandage, stained pink in places. Tubes snake out from underneath it with a pinkish fluid drawn into bulbs at the end. His chest is partially shaved, from surgery I presume, and the sight of it rising and falling brings new life to my heart.

Lying half on him, the other half on the bed, I move subtly so as not to hurt him. Lifting my head, I search and find the most beautiful blue eyes, clear except for a sliver of brandy floating in the left one. My hand travels unbidden to his pale, yet handsome face. Fingers lighting over the soft thickness of his lips, top and bottom, remembering the hard lines of his jaw and the brush of his now thickened beard. I only tremble a little while I re-explore and memorize every feature, brow, nose, and eyes, as my mouth moves but words fall silently from my lips.

Are you in pain? What do you need? I should move; do you want me to? I was so afraid. I thought I'd lost you, I . . . I . . . so many questions, so many things to say and none of them are verbalized. The only thing that stumbles out is, "I love you."

A tired but bright smile meets my statement and he replies, "As I love you."

Conscious of his injured shoulder I scramble up until I'm tucked into the crook of his neck, my nose under his ear. I breathe deeply and intensely, taking him in at the same time as I push away tears.

"Everything's okay," he soothes with words and the hand at my back.

"Your shoulder?"

"One clean shot through. It clipped my lung on the way in; otherwise I'm fine."

"I'm so sorry," I say, squeezing my eyes shut against him.

"You have nothing to be sorry for."

"Drake . . ."

"Shot twice in the midsection. He's holding his own."

Ice forms in my blood, and a chill comes along with it. It's all my fault. Running my hand through Colin's hair, I pull back until our eyes reconnect. "Shane . . ."

I'm met with a stiff nod. "I'm sorry he got so close to you." Colin stops and tucks me back into his neck. "It's over now. You won't have to worry about him again. I'll make sure he rots in prison for the rest of his life."

I don't doubt it, based on the sheer hatred wrapped around every word. "Thank you for saving me. It's not enough, it'll never be . . ."

"No. I won't let guilt eat at you about this. I made a choice to keep you by my side and protect you—that's what I did, and I'd do it again a thousand times, Charlie." It's my turn to nod and cling tighter to his neck. "I'll live the rest of my life to see you happy and complete. If that includes taking a bullet, so be it. This is the depth of my love for you."

Just as I look up to see the stirring of emotion in his gaze, the door swings open and Evan slides in. "Is now a good time?"

Colin's arm holds tight for the shortest second and then he releases me. "Come in." He waves him to the chair by the bed.

"Hey, Charlie." Evan's smile is warm. "I called your parents and Ali with an update. They're fine for now, but hearing your voice will go a long way to reassure them."

My head spins. "Thanks. With everything going on I forgot to . . ."

"No problem. I thought you could use some time." As Evan sits, I slip from the bed, conscious of the state the night left me in, and the stench now rolling off my clothes. If Colin's face is any indicator, he's not pleased with the separation, but I point to my shirt and he nods. Without any conversation passing between them, Evan pops up and peeks out the door.

Colleen is not far behind, a stack of clothes and a makeup bag piled in her arms. "I think you'll find everything you need here." She beckons me over to a door tucked next to the entrance. I'm loathe to leave Colin for even a minute, but we both know I have to shower. Bending down to his hair, I press my nose there and rub my mouth over his forehead. Too many feelings are battling for victory inside of me and with each attack I slip into tired confusion. I'm so happy Colin's okay, yet I'm devastated my past brought this on him and Drake. I'm still afraid of Shane, even though he's in jail. His hate-filled stare a constant companion. It all seems so impossible. All of this and more roars behind my eyes in silent combat.

I stand abruptly and stumble into the bathroom where Colleen has already run the water to hot, steam clouding the small, white tiled room. Her smile wobbles and fingers tremble with the slightest touch to my hand. "He's going to be okay, Charlie. We all are." Slipping out the door, she leaves me to the heat.

Shedding my nauseating clothes in record time, I step into the stream. The water is a welcome distraction and I let it beat into my aching muscles. What I'd hoped would soothe my raw emotions only ripens them into open wounds. I almost lost Colin. It's the only thing I can think of and the mantra is suffocating. Falling against the tile, I bang my head against it, as if the battering will loosen the tentacles of fear. When it doesn't work, I slide to the floor, knees up, locking my arms around them to rock under the water that mimics the tears I cannot cry.

Life is fleeting or maybe it's happiness that can come and go in an instant. For so long I sought it out and at the same time, never believed I would find it. When I did, it came in a demanding whirlwind called Colin McKenna. There are many defining moments in life; I've had my fair share. When his eyes met mine for the first time was one of them, another when I knew I loved him, and the last when I thought I'd lost him. The truth is, love is a puzzle piece. It either fits or it doesn't, and we do. He became my life so easily, and with a resounding pop every other possibility vanished from existence. All of my tomorrows lie in his hands. The thought of losing him is . . . unthinkable.

So why am I thinking about it? If I've learned anything throughout my life, it's that I can't change the past. It is what it is. I'll move forward from it or let it stifle me. I've always found my way forward and I'll do it again, with Colin by my side. For now.

Gloom folds over me like a thick blanket, and I have to poke my head free to breathe. Pushing myself to stand, I focus on washing it away, along with every other remnant of the night. I clean my hair twice, scrubbing it until my scalp tingles as does the skin on my arms when I have a go at them with the washcloth. When I'm pink and waterlogged and stripped clean not only from grime, but sorrow, I step from the shower to towel off. Taking my time, I blow-dry my hair with the small hospital device attached to the wall. I let the loose curls hang free around my shoulders and revel for a minute at the vision in the mirror.

I'm not the same girl who attended the press conference in January. The woman before me is well loved, used daily in a rabid hunt for pleasure. I'm toned because of that and the pace of the campaign. My cheekbones appear higher, given that my face has thinned out. The paunchy baby-weight is gone to the sleek lines of a lioness. When I'm left unsmiling, as I am now, secrets haunt my eyes and add a layer of mystery. A photographer captured this look once and the picture ran on every magazine in the States with captions asking *what is she hiding?* Afterwards, Therese Wainwright's verbal flogging had a smile plastered on my face at every event, whether I felt it or not.

Loosening my own hold on my eyes, I look from the mirror to the clothes Colleen gathered for me. After slipping on the bra and panties, I stop to stare at the single strand of pearls lying on a plain navy shirt-dress. The press conference will be soon, and these items indicate I'll stand next to Colin. I push them aside and focus on brushing my teeth and covering the circles under my eyes with much-needed makeup. After the last touches with liner and mascara, I dress and wrap the pearls around my throat. In an instant I'm transformed into Charlise, the enigmatic girlfriend. Ignoring the restriction of the tight strand, I head back to Colin, only to find a female nurse placing a bowl of water next to the bed.

"Ready for your sponge bath, Senator?"

SEVENTEEN

"THAT WON'T BE NECESSARY." Three sets of eyes—Colin's, Evan's, and a quick glance to the badge on her left breast confirms the third set belongs to Nurse Stewart, spring to mine.

Evan has the audacity to laugh, but covers his mouth when my laser beams rake over his gaze. *I'm not playing.* Colin was ripped from my arms last night, shot and bleeding, and I've been scared shitless for the last twelve hours, fearing he was dead. Now some black-haired, doe-eyed, ruby red-lipped nurse wants to bathe him?

"You've got to be kidding me?" I can't keep it to myself, or maybe I don't want to. With a touch more control, I lower my tone, and peer once again at the badge perched on her double-Ds, and then to the barely contained displeasure in Ms. Stewart's eyes. Oh, I know what she wants and it's not happening.

"Thank you, Ms. Stewart." I step forward and remove the towels from her hands. "I can take it from here."

She smiles and it doesn't reach her darkened specks. "I'm afraid that's not possible. It's my job to ensure Senator McKenna's wound is washed and re-bandaged, along with his full body bath. So, if you'll both excuse us, I'll get down to it."

I hum out a growl and Evan whispers next to me, "Jealous much?" Waving him away, I focus on the task at hand and the bright white gauze on Colin's shoulder. "Well, it's lucky for us that you've already taken care of his shoulder and I'm highly skilled at taking care of all things McKenna." My own grin levels hers and I take the last step to Colin's side. His shit-eating smirk is not lost on me. If my rapacity is what it takes to lighten his mood, I'll give it to him in spades.

"Shall we get started, Senator?" If I could purr, that's how it would sound. Evan barks out a laugh again and Ms. Stewart's mouth falls to the floor.

"I . . . you don't have the authority . . ."

"Hmm, yes I'm quite certain I do, and you've seen about all you're going to. Thank you for the warmed water. I'll call if I need anything more." Turning my back on both of them, I shout over my shoulder, "Pull the curtain closed on your way out and make note, we need privacy for the next twenty minutes." The door closes on Evan's now rolling hilarity, but my focus is on the sexy but tired man before me.

"It's just a bath by a highly-skilled, professional nurse. I'm quite certain she had no intention of abusing her authority," he chides with his own subdued humor.

"Just call me Nurse Carter." I fluff his pillows behind him and then lower the bed. "You're about to see just how skilled I am."

His smile lightens my heart and my chin trembles until I have to close my eyes. "Charlie, baby. Come here." He tries to pull me down, but I shake my head and push the emotion away.

"I'm fine . . ." I bat at his hand. "Relax and let me take care of you." My voice cracks on the last word and I crumble onto the side of the bed, clutching his thigh.

"It's over. We're fine," he whispers, but it feels as if I'm stuck in the beginning of something new and beyond frightening. After several deep breaths and just as many soothing words from him, I straighten. "Don't do this to me again. Promise me." I grapple for his fingers and press them to my cheek. "Please."

Our eyes lock. His are unreadable, yet he's studying mine, and his face falls into serious contemplation. "I promise to always do what I need to for your health and safety."

"Stubborn man," I say, and grab for the washcloth.

"I'll do anything for you." He jerks back when the water makes contact, or maybe it's my hand on his lower abdomen.

"I know. Just don't let it take you away from me, okay?" He grunts when my finger skims over his nipple. "Don't get any ideas. We're cleaning you up, not getting you dirty. How long before the press conference?"

"An hour."

"Then I better be thorough and quick." I wink as I wash his uninjured arm and along his side.

He's an ideal patient until I lower the sheet. I'm a good nurse, a halfway chaste one at least, when I spend only a minute longer than necessary below the belt.

"You'll be the death of me yet," he grounds out between his teeth. "I'm going to be harder than a rock in front of America if you don't watch it, or at least do something about it."

I laugh and shake my head, "You were shot not twenty-four hours ago and you want a blow job?"

"If I was in a coma I would want your mouth on me."

"You're a sick man, Senator."

With more speed than a man in his condition should have, he grabs my hand and pulls me close. My nose brushes against his and my heart-rate spikes, as does the monitor throbbing out his pulse. "No, I'm a man with a hard dick and the sexiest mouth in the world is inches from it."

I lick my lips because injury or no injury, I like the taste of him, but I know this is not the time to play. Maybe tease, but not play. "It's written somewhere I can't raise your blood pressure."

"And you think having your hands all over me hasn't raised it through the roof of this God forsaken hospital?" He groans and relaxes back in bed. "It's your responsibility now to bring it down to an appropriate level."

Feeling an ounce of pity, I bend to kiss the tip of his growing erection and a knock resounds through the room as I do. "Colin, dear?"

"Fuck," he whispers and throws his head back against the pillow. "Yes, Mom?"

I giggle because we're caught in the act like high schoolers, and I race to finish his bath. "Agent Fitzgerald is here for you. He'd like to meet you before you go downstairs."

"Give me five minutes to get dressed."

I laugh again at his thwarted expression as I raise him up and he leans forward so I can get his back. Kissing his shoulder, I whisper, "If you're a good patient I'll make a house call."

"Tonight?"

"I'll have to check your vitals and if relief is medically necessary then by all means, you'll receive every attention needed to alleviate your condition."

"I'll hold you to it, Nurse Carter."

All kidding aside, he's weaker than both of us expect. Getting dressed leaves him winded, with a sheen of sweat covering his brow. Worry lines dig into mine as I assist him with his suit coat, draping it over the arm that remains tethered in the sling. He's downright exhausted after rising from the bed and into the wheelchair left by Red Lips a moment before.

Colin insisted on sitting to meet the secret service agents that will take over his security. Apparently the government doesn't take kindly to a bullet slicing through their leading presidential candidate. Hours after he arrived at the hospital, agents were deployed for his protection and they're here now for formal introductions. According to Colin, they'll be closer than members of his family for the remainder of the campaign and even closer if he's elected.

"Ready?" I ask, wiping his forehead one last time.

"As I'll ever be." He sighs and straightens his shoulders.

"You've got this, baby," I whisper, and press my lips to his. He holds me there with his free hand for a minute. It doesn't deepen to the passion we're used to, but in a sense, it's more intimate. Love, devotion and the deepest commitment passes from him to me in this simplest of moments. When we break away, I stay close, hoping he'll take strength from me, and the breath I breathe into him. "I love you." One last brush of my mouth to his and I stand to open the door.

"Gentleman." I wave six dark-suited men into the room.

"Ma'am," the first five of them say as they pass, tipping their heads in my direction. The last one lingers by the door. His wayward honey-colored hair sets him apart from the short, perfectly-placed cuts that the others have. The black sheep, I'd say, although his eyes are far from a dark shade. The piercing swing of his gaze catches mine and I'm startled by their sheer transparency. They're not blue, but not gray either—a transparent waterfall where my face is reflected in the falling cascade.

"Kyle Sommerton, ma'am." His hand shoots out to mine, a sassy smirk lifting one side of his mouth.

"Charlise Carter, and don't ever call me ma'am or I'll use your gun on you."

His laugh slices through the other stiff introductions to Colin, and the tall man in front cuts him a snarl. Kyle leans into my side and says, "Don't worry about Fitz. He'll stick close to the big guy so you won't have to deal with his downright surly disposition. No fun at all, if you ask me."

The unexpected rough gravel of his voice makes the whole sentiment funnier than it should be, and my giggle reaches Colin, who is not only staring at the two of us, but growing redder and redder by the minute.

"Damn," Kyle says. "Lost that bet already."

"What bet?"

"The guys bet it would take me less than a minute to piss the big guy off. I thought it'd be at least five."

I wave my hand as if to brush the thought away. "Oh, he's not pissed. He's infuriated." I laugh again when he pales. This agent is easy to like, and I hope Colin moves past his pique and doesn't send him packing before he gets to know him. "Just go introduce yourself and he'll get over it. That and keep your distance from me."

Not moving to take my suggested path to Colin's good side, he looks at his feet and shuffles them back and forth. "That'll be kind of hard to do."

"Why's that?"

"Because I'm your secret service agent, ma'a . . . Charlise," he corrects after my laser beams find their way into his clear water.

"What do you mean *my agent*?"

He raises his right hand. "I do solemnly swear to defend Charlise Carter against all enemies and that I take on this obligation without any mental health issues—well, maybe just a couple. I will faithfully execute the duties of my profession with professionalism most of the time. So help me God."

"You're kidding me, right?" I look from him to Colin, whose brow is furrowed in a scowl.

"I never kid, ma'a . . . Charlise. Right. I'll get that right by the end of the day, I promise."

"But I thought only family members are assigned an agent?"

"Wives, yes. However, I understand the big guy can be pretty persuasive when it comes to you."

Laughter bubbles up my spine and rolls out of my mouth with the irony of this situation. Colin has inadvertently placed the one man by my side that will drive him crazy and make my nights oh so fun. I bend over and hug my stomach, trying to suppress the giggles. The campaign trail just got a little more interesting.

ooo

Colin's health consumed my time for a week, but the first day was a blur. After the press conference, Colleen and I rushed him back to bed. The thirty-minute ordeal reassured America he was alive and capable of leading the country, but it had taken its toll on him, and he slept for the next fourteen hours. I caught naps in the chair or on the couch or sometimes, at his insistence, next to him.

Those days were grueling for both of us. Given his status and his displeasure with my treatment in the emergency room, extra care was taken to ensure not only his wellbeing, but that his overall stay met the highest of expectations. This meant a move to a VIP suite and a constant revolving door to his room. Hospital administrators, physicians, service excellence consultants—you name it and they visited. Well-wishes poured in from all over the States. There were cards, and so many flowers we donated them to other patients.

Campaign headquarters seemed to move in as well. From his hospital bed, Colin made his rounds via Skype and conference calls. He didn't miss a beat. The shooting and his injury didn't set him back in the polls—it propelled him forward. Colin's heroics resonated with voters and instilled an even greater confidence that with his mental and physical strength he could work through even the greatest obstacle.

Shane Roberts was officially charged in federal court with stalking and attempted murder, amongst other things. I overheard Fitz, Colin's new agent, relaying details of what they found at Shane's home in rural Michigan. Fourteen years ago, the Carters reported my abuse to Social Services, and Shane was arrested for rape. A plea deal was negotiated so I never had to testify and he was sent to juvenile detention until he turned twenty-one.

He was convicted, not only for the abuse leveled at me, but for others. I was not the only one. This news broke my heart. Knowing there were others that suffered the same fate was difficult to accept, and that I was the last victim hurt even more so. Could the cycle have been broken if someone had come forward before he was placed with the Kerrs? It's a *what-if* question I can't contemplate. It's occurred to me if I find the courage to open up about my past, I may be able to help others find their voice as well. I've tucked the thought away for another day. My priority right now is Colin; when the time comes, I'll revisit the idea.

From what authorities can piece together, Shane's been obsessed with me throughout his incarceration and beyond. The night he shot Drake and Colin, he said I'd taken his life. I'd thought he was speaking of my pregnancy, but he wasn't. He used the knowledge of my abortion against me, a way to berate my psyche. Over the years his hatred toward me had grown, blaming me for his arrest and the ruination of his future. Apparently his home was filled with all things Charlie Carter. He'd been stalking me from afar, just as Colin deduced, for years, and his house was filled with evidence to confirm it.

Drake's condition improves daily, yet his road to a full recovery will take much longer than Colin's. His wounds are not so clean. A second and third surgery took place over a forty-eight-hour period and he remains in critical but stable condition. I was only able to see him for five minutes, and even then, I'm not sure he was awake enough to hear my plea of thanks. I'll forever be in his debt.

Our first flight post-discharge from the hospital was to Cleveland and the Republican National Convention, where Colin graciously accepted the nomination. He's officially running for president. His goal now is to keep the momentum up. Mine is to slow him down. Although he likes to downplay his injuries, they are severe and will take almost two months to fully heal. It's only been seven days. He needs to rest and I have an idea to keep him in bed all night long.

The doctor's orders had called for a week with limited physical activity and I'd held Colin to it, much to his dismay. He'd tried just about everything to break my resolve, but I'd remained steady because having him for a lifetime is more important than one night.

The McKennas stayed with us through our time in Ohio, leaving on a commercial flight to Boston at the same time as we headed out to Virginia and the beginning of our tour of the east coast. We'll hit fifteen states in fifteen days, and countless cities before leaving for Ireland. After Ryanne's wedding, we're scheduled for a Middle Eastern and European tour taking us to Great Britain, France, Germany, Kuwait and five other countries. Talk about a whirlwind.

I've not only cared for Colin over the last week, but stepped up his online campaign as well. Besides my normal forums to keep America abreast of all things Colin McKenna, I added a texting and e-mail component to keep voters directly connected to him. Sometimes, because we're moving at high-speed, I feel as if we're on a runaway train that won't slow down, even at the dangerous curves. Texas still haunts me—my dreams are full of the replay. I can't get past it, so my answer is to lie awake next to the man I almost lost and pray that it never happens again. Tonight is the exception.

Preoccupied, I stumble to a stop in front of a door I wasn't expecting to be closed. Colin's midday speech ended an hour ago, and I only left the anteroom to confirm my plans with Kyle. Apparently five minutes is sufficient time for voices to rise loud enough that I can hear Colin bark out "get me answers".

The door handle is ripped from my fingers. I stare wide-eyed at a flushed federal agent, his parting "yes, sir" muffled as he storms by.

My gaze swings to Colin and his heaving chest. "What was that about?" I ask, stepping to the table in the corner, only to be grabbed and tucked into his side. His chin nuzzles into my hair.

"Nothing. It's nothing."

Tilting my head back, I stare into his troubled blues. "It didn't sound like nothing. No secrets, remember?"

He sighs. "I've asked for answers. I need the specifics on Shane. His court-ordered psych evaluation was yesterday and I want the report."

I tighten my arms around him and squeeze in. "Will that tell us why and how he knew so much about you and the campaign?"

"Maybe. But more likely it'll come through interrogations. All of those questions were put on hold when he flipped out at his arraignment. A psychiatrist will have to clear him for trial and further questioning."

I snuggle into his embrace as the shiver takes hold. "They won't let him out, will they?"

"No. He's not going anywhere. Baby, don't worry about this."

"But you are. You're worried because you don't think he did this alone." I peek up when he doesn't answer, but his heart rate accelerates.

His thumb brushes against my lip. "I don't know. Anything's possible."

ooo

I left Colin with Evan. Suspicion filled his eyes so I had to take him in a private office to assure him I'd meet him at the hotel in two hours.

Kyle had to promise to return me in perfect condition. I can't be sure if he's petrified of Colin or if he finds his over-protective nature amusing. Cajoling him to keep our original plan and take me to the mall was hard to do because of Colin's reaction. I won him over with promises of Gram's chocolate cake and other sugary treats. Kyle has a sweet tooth, something you'd never know by looking at his lean physique. Learning of his obsession with sugar days ago has come in handy and allowed me much more freedom because I've found his weakness.

"This is an abuse of government resources," he says, but the smile lighting his face gives away his apathy toward my idea and the directions I'm relaying as we go.

"Aren't you bound to do everything I want to?" I ask, and point for him to take the next left.

"Eh, you've got this whole bodyguard thing wrong. Safe yes, servant no," he says, taking a drink from his Coke bottle.

"Isn't the definition of servant an employee of the government? If I have it correct, you, my friend, are employed by the government, and therefore you're my servant for the duration of time they've saddled me to your side. That makes me the boss and I need to visit . . ." I check my phone, "Lover's Lane at Tyson's Corner Mall."

He spews soda all over the steering wheel. "What? Jesus, Charlie." I laugh and hand him a tissue. "No. This is not funny. I can't take you into a store like that. You'll be on the Five O'clock News at four. It'll be a fucking special report."

"Who said I was going in?" I look at him with doe eyes and bat my lashes as his face pales.

"No, no way. You're taking this servant shit too far, boss lady. No way in hell am I buying you a sex toy."

Laughing with Kyle is easy. He's been my comic relief amongst all the stress. Colin's learned to appreciate his lighter side too, which makes it easier for me to enjoy our banter. It didn't take him long to figure out I hated the name Charlise, and he was quick to transition to Charlie without a special request from me. He's like the big brother I never had and didn't know I wanted.

"I never said anything about a sex toy. Anyway, I've already called ahead. Everything I need is pre-purchased and awaiting your pick up at the counter. Pleeaase."

Shaking his head, he mumbles something unintelligible under his breath, but it sounds like *you owe me one* and *I don't know how I get myself in these situations*.

"Thank you." I clap my hands under my chin. "I thank you, and Colin does too. Trust me. He'll submit accommodation paperwork to your boss for a raise."

"You're full of it, you know? He's going to kill me before he's even close to knowing what's in the freaking bag."

"Trust me on this one. It's going to end well, really well."

"Oh, enough already. No more. Can we talk about baseball or something?"

“Okay.” I think for a second. “How about them Ravens? Good season so far?”

“Seriously?”

“You’re from Baltimore; don’t you know anything about your team?”

“Yeah, I know the Ravens score touchdowns and the Orioles hit home runs.”

“Smart-ass,” I say with a smile as we pull into the parking lot.

EIGHTEEN

I BEAT COLIN BACK to the suite with just enough time to get everything in place, including the five-inch platform heels that may cause my early death. These things are lethal but coordinate well with the open-up-and-say-ah nurse's costume that provides very little coverage across the chest and below my ass. I giggle at my reflection in the living room mirror. If the media caught sight of this concoction John Montgomery would have a heart attack.

Speaking of that, my heart skips a beat and starts again with a big wallop when the door to the suite swings open and Colin walks in. "Stephens will sleep with the entire female population to garner vot . . ." He stops mid-sentence when he spots me by the couch, tapping a pen on a make-shift medical record that is really my notebook. "Damn," he says, trying to slam the door behind him and whacking Evan in the chest as he does.

"What the hell?" Evan pushes forward, but Colin's quick to turn and place a hand on his chest.

Backing him into the hallway, Colin's says, "This conversation will have to wait for another time. Tomorrow at the earliest."

It's hard to keep a straight face when Evan calls out, "Oh, geez, Charlie. This is an important . . ." The rest of his rant is muffled as he's locked in the hall.

Colin doesn't turn around. Resting his head on the door, he takes two deep breaths and then lifts and drops it once before rounding on me. His eyes blur into a midnight storm, dark and rolling with emotion. The light bounces off them, stirring visions of lightning and hinting at danger. My heart races as they devour me from head to toe, taking in the heels and white stockings that stop three inches shy of the skin-tight, zip-up short-sleeve dress that leaves little to the imagination.

As he stalks forward, I rub my thighs together in anticipation and then remember I have to take control here. Glancing at the clock on the wall behind him, I say, "You're ten minutes late for your appointment, Mr. McKenna."

Nostrils flaring as he runs a hand through his hair, he's quick to respond. "Had I known the importance of this engagement, I wouldn't have kept you waiting."

I tap my pen in time with my foot and purse my ruby-red lips. "Well, now that you're here I suppose we should carry on. Wouldn't you agree?" I peer at him over my fake reading glasses and his mouth falls open. My stomach curls into a flutter as the prospect of touching him becomes greater by the second. He's all mine. "Hmm, we'll have to check your throat for laryngitis as well as a head-to-toe inspection for injuries."

He coughs and sways a little when he stops before me. Raising my hand to his forehead I lay it there and then move to his cheek. "No sign of fever, although you're looking a tad flushed. Are you feeling all right, or should we remove your clothes?"

"Clothes?" he asks, dumbfounded, and then his head jerks when it hits him. "Yes, clothes. Take them off."

I help him with his tie and jacket. The whole time his good hand fumbles against his belt, and then he gives up and gets hands on with me. When his fingers brush over the swell of my breasts, I push them away. "Behave, Mr. McKenna. If you need something you have to ask and ask nicely."

The storm clouds roll in and never leave my chest when he asks, "Nurse Carter?"

I flush at the heavy rasp in his voice. "Yes?"

"I hurt."

"Oh? Do tell me where." This game, this new position, has allowed me a certain amount of authority over him—a slight domination. His obedience is arousing, and my skin tingles with the heady knowledge that for once I'm in control. "I may be able to alleviate any discomfort you're feeling."

Removing my hand from his shirt, he places it below the belt. His jaw flexes when I make contact with his pulsing erection, the taut seem of his trousers restricting it. "Here," he says, and licks his lips while staring at mine.

I love this about him. I love how easily we can play and his willingness to concede authority. His comfort allows me to explore my sexuality safely and build the confidence that has lacked with my inexperience.

"I'll take this into consideration. Tell me though, what is your biggest ailment? Is it this?" I ask, unzipping his pants to free his penis. Pushing his underwear aside, I take him in hand and squeeze. "Or has something else been bothering you?"

The rush of his breath fans my cheek as he dips down to my ear. "Does bossing me around make you wet?" He nips my lobe until my pulse is pounding in my throat. "I've wanted you on the tip of my tongue for the last week and it's time I get my fill. Take what you want, Carter, but know I'm going to have you in my mouth before the night's over." I whimper and the façade falls for just a second as I sink into his chest.

"Let me taste you," he whispers. Moving my hand off of him, he guides my fingers behind my G-string. "Are you wet?"

I groan as I feel my way along the silk glide of my skin. Warm and lush, I slide further down and coat my fingers in the evidence of my arousal. "Yes." Without thought I bring the proof to his mouth and he sucks my fingers with a deep moan. Teasing with his tongue, he flicks the tips as he would my clitoris and my legs grow weak at the thought of him taking and tasting me.

Closing my eyes, I count to three and steal my hand away from him. "In bed, Mr. McKenna, now." I want to keep control, yet I want to give in to him at the same time. Maybe I'm happy to submit to his will or is it possible to have a little of my own? Before he can comply, I strip him of his clothes, easing around his shoulder, and then guide him to the four-poster king spread out before us. With the slightest touch, I push him to the mattress and he free falls, knees over the edge.

Breaking from character for just a minute, I unleash my mother hen. "If you are in pain or re-injure yourself for even one second, so help me God I'll abstain for two months, not a week. Got it, McKenna?"

His sexy-ass smirk settles nicely on his lips. "You done with my tongue-lashing?"

"Yes," I say, kicking off the disastrous heels.

"Good, because I'm about to give you yours."

"What . . .? Oh . . ." I sway, even though I'm on solid ground.

"Take off your dress."

"But I'm not done." I pout, bottom lip popping out because I'm already lost to his commands and I like it. *I really, really do.*

He growls and sits, hauling me into his chest and ripping the teeny dress from my body. "Neither am I."

He falls back to bed with me in his arms, and I squeal and slide to the left to avoid his injury. "Stop treating me like an invalid, baby, and get up here. I've enough strength left to reward you for your house call."

I pop up on my elbow and remove my glasses. "I didn't even get to my full treatment plan." Throwing them to the floor, I kiss him until we're both panting and my hand is wrapped around his pulsing erection.

"Ugh," he grunts when I pull up and then run my palm over the tip, smoothing a drop of pre-cum around his bulbous crown. "That's funny, I thought you were about to give me my medicine—every last drop. Up." He tugs on my hip and I kneel next to him. "Swing your leg over my shoulder."

"No." My brow falls and I shake my head. "Absolutely no way."

He growls and drags me up and over with such force I fall forward, my hair splayed around my hands as they grip the sheets. "Colin," I whisper, breathless from the fall and his nose that brushes along my dampened panties and against my clitoris.

Biting the meat of my inner thigh, he sinks his teeth into my flesh and marks me as his. My brand is back. I hiss when his tongue makes its first drag. He's wrenched away the silk and is taking his time to lick the length of me. Once, twice and he groans, pulling me down onto his face. Gripping the tiny lace thong, he rips it off and owns my hips, wrapping his arm around one to manage my movement. And I move, swaying into the rhythm of his mouth, as he gets hungrier with each pass.

I realize this position allows me my own modicum of control. He's letting me set the pace and I do. Sitting up, I fist his hair and tip my head back when the vibration of his growl reaches my clitoris and a feverish pulse takes over all thought. My skin lights up, vibrating—every nerve is aware of each flick of his tongue and every sweep of his lips. *I love your mouth, your marvelous, skilled fucking mouth. I love it on me.*

When he laughs, I realize I said it out loud and I don't care—it's the truth. The vibration becomes delicate and the air pricks at each nerve, lighting my skin and opening me to pleasure. My hips rotate on him and with him as he flicks and pushes me higher, oh so high that I'm not sure I'll survive the climb, let alone the fall.

It feels so damn good. Too good, it's too much, too fast.

Just when I'm afraid of it, afraid of the intensity and cry out, "stop, no, please" he takes me in. Sucking, he holds me to him so I have nowhere to go but to fall forward and down, down, down. I scream into the mattress and jerk against him as I crash over and over again. His murmured appreciation chases my orgasm and reheats it, lapping against my sensitivity until I'm tensed for another one. He follows me with a groan when my body naturally wrenches away from the white-hot bliss, yet my hand is fisted so tight in his hair I drag him with me at the same time. It's a duel with only one possible ending and he beats it from me with the flattened edge of his wicked tongue.

Slow, bleating whimpers are pushed into the bed as he shows no mercy and demands every ounce of my pleasure. "Oh, God," I whisper more than once as I find myself somewhere amongst the ruin and crawl back down to lie on top of him.

I press kisses along his forehead, cheek and jaw, murmuring *so good* and *I love your mouth* until mine takes his. I find myself there, my sweet musk mixing with his, and I drown in it. Snaking my hand between our bodies, I find him. Silk and steel melt into my hand as I stroke up and down, swallowing his groans as I want to swallow him. He breaks away, pushing until I'm flat on my back.

"Open for me," he grounds out between his teeth. The storm is back, raging behind his intense gaze. I don't dare deny him and slide further up on the bed, spreading my legs as I go. He's on his knees in a heartbeat, savage and stalking forward, pinning me down with his eyes. I'd give him anything and everything and he knows it. He plans on taking it.

"Please."

"Please what?" he runs his hand along my brand and bends to deepen the outline with his teeth. Looking at me through his lashes he says, "Please touch you or please make you come again?"

"Both."

He grins and straightens, finding the perfect position between my thighs. His wild, undone smirk falls away when he throws his head back and lunges inside of me in one, deep thrust. I lose my breath when he fills me up and stills for the shortest moment, the moment when I feel replete and want for nothing until the second it all changes and I need him to move. I need to fear his withdrawal only to feel the fullness once more. He holds me open with his hand digging into my leg; I wrap the other around his ass and hold on for dear life. Sweet Jesus, I've forgotten what it's like when he's wild and loses himself so thoroughly inside of me. It feels so, so good—he feels good. His body takes over, pounding into a punishing tempo. He's punishing me for the week that came between us and for making him wait so long to feel this free and good and mine.

Bending down, he braces his elbow next to my ear so he can find my mouth and destroy that too. My breath comes in panting waves, a mirror of his, and our eyes lock. I watch his lips part and his head tip back as he slides in and out in long, deep strokes. My hips meet his as we come together until I need more. Faster and deeper, and then my nails rake down his back and he bucks into me with a hiss and stills.

"No," I cry out, on the edge of something far too good to lose.

"Nurse Carter," he says with the utmost constraint, a sassy-ass smirk lifting the corner of his mouth. My heart pounds in time with the now missing beat of his hips.

"Don't stop." I dig my fingers into his backside.

"No?" His lids fall to half-mast and his voice goes with it, sexy as hell. No longer just commanding, but playful, and my skin tingles, as if he's touched me everywhere. "My naughty nurse, tell me what your examination concluded. Am I strong enough to continue?"

"Please, don't play with me." I can't say any more, but if I could I'd tell him how good he feels in me, around me, rubbing all over me. My nipples spike into taut beads as they rise up and into his chest. "Please."

He smiles, a full-blown I-will-rock-your-world-and-you'll-beg-for-more grin. "Don't play with you? Isn't that what you were doing with me earlier? Playing?" Pushing in deeper, he dips to my ear and whispers, "Shall my paybacks start now or later?"

As if testing my resolve, he leans on his injured shoulder, his face remaining hot as hell, no sign of weakness, and reaches with his other to lift my leg around his hip so I'm cradling him in a vice grip.

Holding very still, he says, "I'm waiting."

I'm so distracted. "Huh? What?" I say, breathless, and not at all ashamed to admit how bad I need him to move.

"Strong enough, Nurse Carter? Your patient satisfaction scores depend on your answer."

I try to smile and play along, but it disappears when he bites my neck. My body starts pulsing around him, uncaring he's chosen not to move.

He groans, all sass wiped away and he rocks into me. Slow and sweet, the friction rubs in the most delicious way. I wrap myself around him, licking and sucking his neck and the dip above his collarbone as my fingers explore. I revel in the taut lines of his back and ass that flex as his strokes become more powerful. He is mine. Always and forever mine. With that thought the pulse turns into a tremor and the rhythm of an orgasm taps an ambient chill up my spine. It unfurls into a blinding light behind my eyes and I give in, letting it roll through me and around him.

"Feel me, Colin. Feel me come for you," I groan, at first clamoring to crawl closer and then arching away when the waves of sensation threaten to break me in two. He feeds on my breasts, taking my nipple into his mouth and then clamping down as his breath punches around it. He cries out and slides into the hollow of my neck where I take in the scream of his release as his thrusts become long and sharp a moment before he relaxes against me.

I kiss him everywhere, tasting the two of us on his skin, his face and neck and along his injury, and then I stop to whimper "your shoulder" and roll over with him still held between my thighs.

He chuckles and holds my hip when I sit up to straddle him, my eyes never leaving the white bandage that forever announces he's hurt. My chest rises and falls in time with his as I search for any sign we may have broken open his wound or re-injured what has had little time to heal. "It will take more than loving you to break me, baby."

I can't help but roll my eyes, "You may think you're made of steel . . ." Pursing my lips, I look at the ceiling and rethink that thought. "Okay, a part of you is made from steel, but not that part," I say, and point to his bum appendage.

His smirk is back and he fists my hair to drag me down for a kiss. A sweet and sassy, shallow and deep, lip and tongue kiss. When I pull away, I'm dizzy. Bending his knees behind me, he makes a comfortable rise for me to fall back on. Lights blaze in the suite, the sun shines outside, and here I sit naked with Mr. McPerfect underneath me. Perfect except for . . . I shake my head, refusing to let sad thoughts pull me under.

"What were you and Evan talking about when I interrupted your day?"

"It was a fantastic interruption," he says and tweaks my nipple. "I had no idea you were inclined to enter the medical profession. By the way, where did the outfit come from?"

I look away to find what's left of it on the floor. "Just a store. Tell me about your day. I want to hear it."

The rise of his brow indicates he's on to my plan for deflection, so I confess. "Kyle took me to the mall." He's speechless—mouth-open, eyes-wide, hand-raking-through-hair speechless. "Breathe." I rub his chest. "Ali called ahead and purchased everything over the phone. Nothing was in my name. Kyle ran in and picked it up while I waited in the car."

"By yourself."

I roll my eyes again, sliding off his waist to fall on the bed. "Yes, alone. For two minutes, Colin. You got the bad guy, remember?" I try, I really try to keep the hostility out of my voice but it's there and heavy and pissy. Closing my eyes, I block it all out: Colin, his injury, Drake, the whirlwind of the last week, Shane Roberts and his goddamn gun. I roll to my back and hide under my arms, caging myself beneath them.

"Hey, what's going on in there?" It's a soft question, but I'm feeling hard and for whatever reason I'm ready to fight. To prevent that from happening, I remain silent.

"Talk to me, Charlie."

"Nothing is going on. I'm fine."

"You don't sound fine."

"Well, I am okay? I'm just tired and I want to go to bed."

A long pause—no sound, no movement, no nothing. This is the first time I've shut him out. I know it and he does too. It doesn't feel good, and my skin prickles with unease and the itch to make it better.

I'm mad, and I'm not sure why. That's not true. If I think about it, the simple question has a great big answer—I'm fucking raging-at-the-world mad about everything. Take your pick: security and having to be protected because the threat may not be gone, Shane and his gun, and the red room for bringing the past so close to the present. Drake for getting shot and having complications during recovery, Ali for not confiding in me about Evan because she thinks it'll be too much for me, and Evan for agreeing with her. Charlise Carter and the stranger I've become. And Colin. Goddamn that man for throwing himself in front of a bullet and saving my life. It's eating away at me, every day, every minute—the hole in his chest grows wider in my brain, and he's close to death every time I close my eyes. Fear. Fear like I haven't felt in fifteen years has woven into my heart and is slowly suffocating me. I can't eat. I can't sleep because when I try his glassy eyes stare back and I want to die too.

Now, on the one day I want to have some fun, forget my long list of worries, I'm in trouble for staying in the car for two minutes by myself? Two minutes. Two damn minutes. Before I think better of it, I jump off the bed and dive for my suitcase. I don't look at Colin and I don't wait for him to say anything. Throwing on my one and only Therese Wainwright-approved short-and-tank set, I dig for my tennis shoes.

"What . . .?" He sits in the middle of the bed, his mouth falling open.

I hold my hand out to stop him, stop him from talking or moving. "I'm going for a run."

"A run?"

"Yes, the kind where you put one foot in front of the other and you move them real fast."

His nostrils flare. "Sarcasm doesn't become you, Charlise."

I cringe and look away. "Yeah? Well neither does imprisonment. Don't wait up; maybe I'll run around the world." How's that for sarcasm, Mr. President?

"Charlie . . ."

"I need some time," I say, and fly out the door.

For the first time in six months, I want to run away to the simplicity of my life before meeting Colin McKenna.

NINETEEN

KYLE IS BOUND TO go with me wherever I go, Sawyer is not. Yet both of them are a respective distance behind me as I run down the Virginia Beach Boardwalk. It's not quiet, even at seven o'clock. Die-hard beachgoers, refusing to give up the sun, remain reclined under their umbrellas or wading in the rising evening tide. I'm sure Colin is responsible for the added agent huffing behind me and I'm also certain he's probably beside himself with anger, waiting for me at the hotel. It's not something I can contemplate right this minute.

All I can hear is the rush of my breath, stunted and labored, as I push myself hard and harder still, until the only thing I can think of is putting one foot in front of the other. That's a good thing. What I want is for all of the bullshit to stay shelved, but it won't. It keeps tumbling down in a mess of jumbled thoughts that I can't let go. At this moment, breathing is the only concept I can gather.

"You going to tell me what drove you out of that hotel like a thoroughbred at the Kentucky Derby?" Kyle sneaks up beside me and I shoot him a glare that should wither his otherwise unaffected good looks, but he just smiles. "No? Well, let me tell you something. I've been with you for a week now and we've yet to run. Today you bolt like a bat outta hell, and keep up the pace for forty minutes. I'm not carrying you back to the big guy in a body bag, so let's slow it down, okay?"

I stumble, too tired to listen and place my feet at the same time. "Whoa, okay. We're done here." Holding onto my shoulder as we stagger to a stop, he presses the funny ear thing always stuck there and calls for a car.

"Thirty-first and Atlantic Avenue . . . by the looks of it you have a minute before she collapses." He hands me a water bottle, and says, "Drink."

I'm too busy gasping for air; water is the least of my worries. Asphyxiation will kill me before dehydration, that or the growing cramp in my side. Whichever comes first.

"So, I'm guessing no accommodation papers are in the works as you so promised this afternoon?" His smirk is contagious and I smile in return, only to bend over to retch in the bushes next to me.

Nothing comes out because I haven't eaten in God knows how long and I've yet to drink the water he so casually shoved in my face.

"Thanks," I say, this time taking a drink and swirling it around my mouth. Dear lord, I hope the paparazzi aren't following me now.

"So?"

"So, what?"

"So, you gonna tell me what's going on with you?"

"Now you sound like Colin. Everyone trying to get into Charlie Carter's brain today, is that it?"

"It's an interesting brain."

"You may think so. It's not been so fun for me lately." I kick a rock, but wish I could smash it in my hand like the Hulk. *Smash.*

"Too much stuff?"

"Yeah, you could say that." Turning around to the direction we came from, I start to walk toward the hotel.

"You know what my granddad says to that?"

"You have a granddad?"

His brow falls and he looks at me as if I've sprouted wings before saying, "Well yeah, I wasn't fertilized in a pod and grown amongst alien beings. Although my mother sometimes believes I was beamed down to earth in place of her rightful son, but that's another story altogether."

I burst out laughing. "Sorry, so what does your granddad say?"

"Life is simple—it's that simple."

Shaking my head, I take in his serious expression. "That's it?"

"Yeah, that's it. He'd say it's people who make it complicated and if you get down to basics you'll be just fine."

"Back to basics?"

"Simplify, boss lady. Position, status, stuff—none of it matters. Get back to the foundation that works and go from there." A black sedan pulls up alongside of us. Kyle grabs the door and holds it open. "Your chariot, my lady." He waves me in.

I stop and catch the silver waterfall that is the color of his eyes, and my reflection shines back at me. They're so unique, as is he. "Thanks, Kyle. Thank your granddad, too."

His normally jovial smirk dips for the shortest second. "Next time I talk to him I'll be sure to do that."

ooo

The suite is silent when I return. A low lamp lights the way, casting a glow around the living room. Closing my eyes, I listen and hear the faint hint of running water. Bee-lining to the bedroom, I hesitate and then stop when Colin appears in the bathroom door, naked except for his boxers. The expressionless expression masks his features, but his eyes are filled with worry and compassion. Without a second thought I throw myself across the room, my legs screaming at the exertion, and into his arms. Hitting his chest with an audible thud, he takes a step back from the force I use to reach him.

"Charlie, baby." His hands nest in my hair and hold me close. Mine are already wrapped around to dig into his backside, kneading and grappling to hold every taut muscle.

I'm panting, not from the run, but because emotion is running high and I don't know what else to do or say. I'm sorry seems too little, because I couldn't have overacted more than I did in that moment. I tilt my head up, meaning to say something, anything to make this better between us, but his finger presses to my lips.

"I know. You don't have to say anything. Too much has happened and I haven't taken care of you."

"No, this is not your faul—"

"Tonight is mine. Let me do this and then we'll talk. Wash, dinner, sleep—you need all three and I want to give them to you."

Back to basics. I nod and as soon as I do, he's stripping me. The water I heard running was for a bath and steam is rising from it, filling the room with a calming hint of sandalwood. *Colin.* Wrapping my arms around his neck, I tuck into my favorite place and breathe him in. He chuckles when I won't let go, making it difficult to get my shorts and panties and his briefs off, but with my help and some interesting antics we do just fine.

Stepping in first, he sinks down into the water and takes my hand as I follow. Cradled between his legs, I moan as both the heat from his chest and the water becomes a haven for my ravaged body. Closing my eyes, this time my vision is filled with pictures of naked Colin. His beautiful face and sculpted chest, his arms and rippled abs, the fine lines of his thighs. It's a welcome scene and it helps me relax against him—that and his breath against my ear. Steady, deep and reassuring. *We made it through*. I keep telling myself this, but the fear lingers on and I try to shelve it as I do everything else. *Just give me this night*. Instead of talking to myself, I refocus on the growing bulge taunting my backside.

Wrapping his arms around me—both of them—I turn to admonish his use of number two, which should be held snug against him. Before I can verbalize anything, his mouth captures mine. Soft, yet insistent, we play and tease and he begins to knead my stomach and lower abdomen. He's heaven and I want to live in this place with him for eternity.

"I don't want to lose you."

His response is to nip my bottom lip, sucking it into his mouth he flicks it with his tongue. An instant bolt strikes my clitoris and I'm aching for him again. His teeth follow my racing pulse down my neck to the sensitive point just above my collarbone. Stopping, he rests his head there and takes a deep breath, murmuring into my skin, "I don't know how to ease your fear. I'm here. I will always be here for you, Charlie." He finds my eyes and says, "Always. I will give you whatever you need."

"I need you, whole and healthy."

"And I am. We'll stumble every once in a while, but I promise you we'll never fall." He kisses me and licks my lips. "We will never be broken."

"I hate fighting with you."

The devil returns to his blues and he fists my hair to pull and expose my neck. "We're not fighting; we're finding our way," he grounds out and then feasts on my flesh, biting and sucking and licking until I'm writhing and the water is rolling in undulating waves. I've found his hair, pulling in a silent demand for him to never stop, *never stop loving me*.

"That's impossible. I will love you through this life and into the next. Let me show you." And he does. There's nothing gentle about this joining. It's a lesson of negligence. We'd both gotten lost in the extracurricular activities life had thrown our way, drifting from what we needed the most. This. Us. Individually we're stubborn, together we're downright bullheaded, but we're also passionate and loyal and irrevocably in love.

With his taste on my tongue, I whisper, "I want to be your everything. Your confidant and lover, everything you need."

In a surreal moment where time seems suspended, he lifts his head and his hips to pierce me in every way possible—with his eyes, his tongue that lashes into my mouth and with his body, so deep I perch on the precipice of coming.

"You already are." He holds on so tight, and we come together.

It's in this mindless, numbing moment that I realize this is exactly what I'm afraid of. If he's my everything, how will I ever live without him?

ooo

"Full?"

"Mmhmm." How could I not be when he hovered over me until every bite left my plate?

"Exhausted?"

I groan. Everything hurts. I'm wrung out like a sheet hanging on a laundry line in the sun on a summer day: used, soft and ready for bed. "Very."

"Want more?"

More what? Food? Hell no. I'm about to explode. Colin? I sink down next to him, my hand snaking below the waistband of his briefs. "Maybe."

He laughs. "You want me in you when you fall asleep?" Nuzzling my hair, he slides down further and turns us so my back is to his chest.

"I wouldn't say no to that."

"Wicked, wicked woman," he murmurs in my ear.

We've already rehashed my angst from earlier. He was very patient with me over dinner. I tried to explain everything without sounding pathetic, but it still felt that way. Weak. I've worked hard to be strong and resilient over the last fourteen years. To find myself sinking into a place I left long ago frightens me. I have to move forward and let it go, but for some reason these past weeks are haunting my thoughts. So, I change the subject.

"You never told me what you and Evan were working on this afternoon. Anything interesting?"

"The Democratic vice-presidential candidate. Bryce, announced his man this afternoon. Stephens is a bad choice for him and a good decision for us." Colin's arm snakes between my breasts and my heart rate accelerates as his touch feathers over my collarbone. I'm on Colin McKenna overload.

Ignoring the lusty pangs, I peak over my shoulder. "Why'd he pick him, then?"

He kisses my nose and forces my head back to the pillow with his cheek to mine. "He's young. Bryce is vying for women. He's trying to break the hold I have on that population, but he's going about it in the wrong way."

"Why's that?"

"Stephens has a fidelity issue most of Washington knows about. It won't take much for one of his girlfriends to turn on him. That's what we were discussing when Nurse Carter's house call interrupted our conversation."

I huff and think about the trouble she caused. "I'll make sure she's transferred to another hospital without access to you."

"Hey." His impassioned plea is not lost in the simple word, so I look to him again. "I love your sense of adventure and I don't want it to change. I'll loosen up eventually, Charlie. Give me a minute to get used to our new surroundings, one without someone stalking around every corner."

I can't help but cringe. "Kyle will be around. Does that make you feel better?"

It's his turn to huff and my smile is back, expecting his reaction. "It's like having an infant watch over you. If not for his extensive resume, I'd think he was just discharged from the birthing unit." I bark out a laugh and close my eyes. A night of ups and downs has ended on a high note, and I think I may be able to sleep after all.

"He's good for you." Colin surprises me from a thoughtful stupor.

"I'm comfortable around him, which doesn't happen very often, especially with men. That and his humor make him a good fit for me."

"Kyle's one of their best. I never would have guessed it by the way he presents himself, but he's a fine agent."

Colin's easy acceptance of another male figure in my life, with only a hint of jealously, is so welcome yet unexpected at the same time. I thought he'd go nuts with a charming, handsome man hanging out with me every day, but there's something else, and then it hits me. "You're proud of him."

"Yes. He fought hard for his country in Afghanistan. I trust him and that's why he's a good fit for you." He squeezes in, so there's no mistaking the thickness growing along my backside. "Enough about the infant."

"You're insatiable." I sigh, and stifle my own naughty smile.

He groans. “Nurse Carter? I hurt all over.”

I giggle and it turns into a full out belly laugh when he rolls me onto my stomach, his weight pressing me into the mattress. “Do you think you can put the dress back on?”

I know every night won’t be this easy, but tonight we’re perfect so I tell him exactly, in great detail, what I can do to cure his ailment.

TWENTY

"WERE YOU DREAMING OF me or blueberry pancakes last night?" Colin's warm breath fans over my ear. The sweet slide of syrup sticks in my throat and I turn to find his eyes. He's sassy this morning. I guess a sexed-up night like the one we had will do that to a man. "Should I be jealous over your love for them?"

His hand finds my knee under the table and sneaks up the side of my skirt. I gape at him. Father Cedric and three hundred members of the Virginia Beach chapter of the Knights of Columbus and their families are staring while his fingers snake up my leg.

"Are you out of your mind?" I whisper, and hope my smile is as sweet as the syrup. We're on display and he's going to add to the show. "They're all watching."

He chuckles. "I had to get your attention. The way you're reacting to those pancakes had me worried."

"Hmmm . . ." He wants to play? I'll play. Taking another bite, I leave the fork in my mouth for a moment longer than necessary. Dragging it through my lips and humming, I look up through my lashes and bat them a little too. "They're warm and moist, and when my tongue touches them they melt in my mouth. So, so, good." The words come out light and the breathlessness is not at all feigned because his hand clamps down, as do his teeth on his bottom lip when he sucks it in. "Delicious." And I'm not talking about the food.

Wrapping his bum arm around the back of my chair so he can really lean in to find my ear, he lets me hear his groan. I glance at the crowd. Many are enjoying their food, unfazed by Mr. McPerfect at the head table of their monthly family breakfast. Others are not so immune. One of the curious is Father Cedric himself, sitting two seats down. His rosy cheeks and hint of a smile are telling and I have to look away.

"I want you, Charlie. I always want you. But when you look at me like that . . ." His breath rushes against my cheek and my eyes drop to his open collar. No tie today. His pulse is visible, as are the cords of muscle that wind up the sides of his neck. "When your voice drops like you've had me in your throat all night long, I want to throw you on this table and strip you bare. I want your taste on my tongue and to feel you melt in my mouth."

Oh, wow. I drop my fork and then find his leg. Muscles bunch under my fingers, the rippling strength sending shivers down my spine. But he can't do this. Not here. Not with an audience watching. So I smack that thigh, hoping the sting on my hand is the same pain that resonates through him. Pulling away so he can see the set determination in my eyes, I whisper, "I don't know if I should punish you for embarrassing me or take you in the back room to have my way with you."

He doesn't look apologetic; in fact his smirk is hungry, as are his eyes. "I'll take either option. Now or later, Ms. Carter?"

"You're ridiculous," I say, straightening my shoulders. "Smile to your faithful followers and leave my panties alone."

"I haven't touched your panties, although . . ."

"Stop," I hiss, "or you'll have to take me back to the hotel to change them before the garden party."

Throwing his head back, he laughs and the tension is released. Thank God. This man can make me gush like the fountains at the Bellagio: stimulating and synchronized to music. The music of his voice. *Oh, dear lord.*

"I need the rest room. Excuse me, please." I stand so abruptly he has to catch my chair as it teeters backward. He flattens his grin down when my laser beams make an appearance and I hurry away. Conscious of the many sets of eyes following me, I hold my head high, keep my back straight and weave through the banquet tables. Windows on one wall let the bright sun in and hint at the heat rising outside.

We were up early this morning. Colin's first appearance was scheduled at seven—a Habitat for Humanity housewarming event, where he handed the new homeowners' their key. A brief speech and breakfast with the K.O.C. will take us to mid-morning when we leave for a garden party hosted by the Virginia Woman's Association, and then an evening cocktail party on the beach thrown in honor of Colin. It's a busy day with no room in the schedule for an emergency underwear swap.

"Charlie," Evan's breathless call stops me outside of the bathroom door. He must have jogged clear across the room, loosening a heavy piece of hair onto his forehead. Quick to shove it back, he runs his hands through what I'd now call a disaster and then grips it so it stands on end.

I tilt my head at an Evan Daugherty I don't recognize. He's normally Mr. Suave—today he's out of sorts. "Did you seek out Father Cedric for absolution or something? If you need assistance with the number of Our Fathers I would offer to help, but I think they—"

"Charlie." He holds out his hand. "Do you have your phone with you?"

I glance at my clutch and squeeze. "Yes, why?"

"Ali's trying to get a hold of you and can't get through. Give her a call, okay?"

"Are one of you going to tell me what's going on, because—"

"Not now. Call her, would you, and I'll tell you whatever you want to know later. Alright?"

Backing up, one step at a time, he slows until he confirms I'm reaching for my phone. Only when I have it out does he turn and stalk toward Colin.

Geez, all right already. The ladies room is small, but quiet—a perfectly private place to harass Ali. I got a new phone after Shane Roberts discovered my number and although few people have this one, I'd gotten into a habit of turning it off. When I power it up I'm surprised to see ten missed calls: Ali, my mom, Ali again . . . I jump when it vibrates in my hand, my sister's name popping up once more.

"Hi . . ."

"Where have you been?" she asks, breathless in her own right.

"Sorry. What's going on? Mom called a million times too."

"Who are you with?" An overhead page sounds out in the background, calling Frank Jordon back to the terminal gate.

"Are you at the airport?" Hair stands up on my neck. "What's happening, Ali?"

"Is Colin with you? Where are you?"

"Yes, he's here. Why . . . What . . . just tell me," I push out of the bathroom door to find air. Suddenly it's stifling.

"It's Gram," she says, and her voice cracks.

Tears spring to my eyes, but I blink them away. "What?"

"She had a heart attack last night—"

"Alive? Is she alive, Ali?" I clench my teeth so hard my jaw cracks and a ringing sounds in my ears.

"Yes. God, Charlie, yes. Sorry, I should have said that first. She's fine."

I stumble out to the lobby and press my forehead against a heated window. There's no relief there, no release from the tentacles of fear gripping my chest.

"But you're going home. What are you not telling me?"

"I only have a minute before I have to stow my phone. They put a temporary stent in, but she needs a bypass. They've scheduled it for tomorrow morning and I want to be there."

"I'll come too." I swing around to find Colin. Evan's in his ear, and just when I find his eyes, they divert to mine. He's on his feet in a second and his brow tightens into three lines, then the expressionless expression falls in place as he says something to the group at the table, even though he's already on his way to me.

"No, there's no need for you to modify your schedule. I'll keep you updated with every change, good or bad. Stay with Colin."

"But Gramps. Mom and Dad . . . they've got to be out of their mind."

"I'll be there, and so are Ian and Sammy. We'll take care of them. Gram's going to be fine. Rushing in and rushing back out is going to be stressful for you, and you've already got a lot on your plate. Let me handle this and keep you in the loop. I have to go. Call Mom. I'll talk to you when I get to the hospital. Okay?"

I'm suspended in time. I don't want to let Ali go—she's a lifeline and losing the connection will set me adrift.

"Is Colin with you?"

She knew I'd need him. He's my anchor. The intensity of his gaze warms my skin like the sun on a budding flower. "Yes, okay."

"Chin up, Charlie girl. Everything's going to be just fine." And then she's gone and Colin's here, but my heart is stuck in Michigan with Gram.

ooo

The Virginia Beach Wyngate hotel has a cobbled veranda the size of a football field overlooking the ocean. Plush padded wicker chairs are pulled into granite-topped tables for the luxury of the more than affluent guests. Waiters wind in and out of the standing-room-only crowd with drinks and appetizers. Wendy Jameson, heiress to the Wyngate fortune, spared nothing. She's apparently worth billions and willing to spend some of it on Colin. I can see why. He's stunning in a tan linen suit, molded to the lines of his body. A light blue shirt is open at his neck, sans tie again tonight. His hair, which has grown longer and needs a cut, is slicked back, as if he just walked out of the water. He's the picture of relaxed sex appeal, and Ms. Jameson is taking advantage of his natural grace.

Looking away from her hand on his arm, I watch the sky blend into a cacophony of blues and pinks. It's as discordant as I feel. By my standards, I've had too many gin and tonics. I'm on my third. Without eating since breakfast, my head is flying with the seagulls over the ocean and it's a nice place to be. My mind is not. Suiting up in a Charlise Carter special, cap-sleeved navy taffeta party dress suitable for Jackie O herself, pearls and all, hasn't helped me feel better.

I'd been lost after Ali's call. Colin had offered to fly me home, but Mom had convinced me to stay. Well, not just Mom—it was really Gram. Even in her weakened state, she'd overpowered everyone with her sass and finagled the phone out of my dad's hands.

"Charlie girl, you listen here." She'd been out of breath after one sentence and my heart had fallen to the floor. "I won't stand for anything but you staying out there with that fine fella of yours. Nothing you can do here. And besides that, I'm fine."

"Gram . . ." Again with the damn tears filling my eyes. That time it had taken a minute to bat them away.

"Don't *Gram* me, young lady. Your sister's already disregarded everything I've asked of her, not you too."

"I'm so worried."

"Sweet girl, I'm asking you not to be. The doctors have nothing but encouraging words. The bypass tomorrow is routine nowadays. This isn't something you need to worry about."

"This isn't just something—it's you, Gram." Colin's arm had tightened around me then and I'd needed it. My legs had weakened beneath me.

In the end, she won and I stayed, although I don't know how much good I'm doing for Colin right now either. At the next event, I sat perched on the end of my chair with a plastered smile on my face and what I'm sure was a blank stare. The garden party was lovely, I think.

"You're not planning on bolting for a run in the sand, are you? I didn't even think to bring my Nikes." Kyle nods out to the beach and sighs.

I crack a smile, my first since Ms. Jameson pulled Colin away. She had some surprise to share with Colin. I'm hoping it's the official support from a local politician he was counting on. "Not tonight. Taffeta doesn't breathe well; I prefer cotton for exercise."

"Good call. Can you do me a favor?" he asks, while sticking his finger in his ear.

"Sure, what do you need?"

"Stay right here. Don't disappear on me like you have a knack for doing."

"What?" I find a nice octave to relay indignation. "I don't—"

"Yes, you do." Taking my elbow, he leads me to a more secluded area of the patio and waves to Sawyer. We're alone in the shadowed corner, backed into the wall and surrounding stone rail.

My heart starts to race as Fitz moves closer to Colin. He's always five feet away from him, never attached to his hip as he is now. Leaning in to his ear, he says something that has Colin's head snap up, his eyes searching to find mine. When he spots me, he lurches in my direction with Fitz on his tail.

"What's going on, Kyle?" I look from him to Colin and back again.

His eyes have iced over. No longer a free-falling waterfall, they're sharp and tactile. Even though he's looking at me, I sense he's looking around me too, watching everything and everyone within eyeshot. Kyle's gone from infant to James Bond in the matter of a minute.

"Nothing to worry about, boss lady. Everything's under control." With one last look around, he turns his back to me and crosses his arms. "Sit tight. Everything's just fine."

I giggle and hold my glass up to my mouth to hide behind it. Totally inappropriate I know, but when James Bond and everyone else in my life are telling me not to worry—I worry. Behind the tasteless laughter, bile rises in my throat.

BOOM! I jump back when the explosion registers, my head cracking against the wall. Freddie and a gun. *BOOM!* Colin pushes me out of the way and all I see is red. *BOOM!* Breathless, glassy eyes fall away into darkness. Dropping to my knees, I press my hands against my ears and hum. I tunnel away, until the outer rim of my sight is fuzzy and a numbing blur eases my raged nerves.

"Charlie?" Colin tips my chin, his arm circling my back. When he does, the horizon comes into focus, as do the sparkles. *Fireworks.* Just after each shot, the sky brightens by a burst of light, the simmering tails snuffed out by the darkening night.

"Baby, come here," he whispers.

I stay tucked away in my mind just as Colin tucks me into his arms and holds me against his chest. Standing, as if I weigh nothing, he turns to find an escape into the hotel. As he does, my gaze falls to more than one horrified pairs of eyes. They're all watching—watching Colin McKenna carry his crazy to the car. I'd laugh again but I don't have the strength. Kyle's leading the pack, not so subtly directing people out of the way and if need be, using his hands to open a path. I gasp on our way through the lobby. It's filled with red roses. They're on every table, on the counter and in the lapel of the concierge.

The sickening floral stench gives way to each rose left for me before, and Shane Roberts is in my ear whispering sweet-face. I'm on the verge of screaming when the fresh seaside breeze sweeps the image away. Colin steps outside and slides into the waiting car, somehow without displacing me from his arms. I ease around the faraway place and realize it's a lot like being drunk, but more potent. Right now, I can't be anywhere else.

In a few minutes we're at our hotel. Kyle must have coordinated a special arrangement during the short ride, because we pull around back to use the staff entrance and elevator. It's unusually quiet. Either everyone was pulled away from this area of the building for an assignment or they were pulled away because of me.

No one speaks—for that I'm grateful. I don't know what happened and haven't a clue on how to explain it. In the quiet confines of the industrial car, details start to become clear. My dress is soaked. The sweet blend of lemon and pine needles roll my stomach. Gin and tonic coat not only me but Colin too. I've made a mess of things.

We follow Kyle out and down the hall, where he swipes us into our suite.

"Good night Senator, Ms. Carter. Call me if you need anything." Our eyes lock for just a second and the side of his mouth raises just a smidge. For some reason I take it as a reassurance, a been-there-done-that, everything-will-be-okay kind of smidge.

Colin heads directly to the shower, and doesn't release me even while turning the water on. Only after the streams are flowing does he set me down on the counter. I let my head fall and it pounds. Remembering the smack against the wall, it makes sense. I'll need ibuprofen before bed.

"Charlie?" he whispers, running his fingers along my cheeks and neck, into my hair. "Talk to me."

I nibble my lips, top and then bottom. "I don't know what to say."

"Tell me what happened," he says, massaging my shoulders.

I push against his chest and hop down when he gives me just enough space. "Help me with this?" I turn around so he can release me from my navy prison. Alcohol ruined the dress, but I'm not at all sad to see it go. I hate taffeta.

Left standing in bra and panties, I find us in the mirror. Colin's hands are spread along my stomach, the expanse of them covering my midsection—so strong. I close my eyes and lean back—he's hard and warm and comforting. "I got scared."

Turning me toward him, he nudges my chin up and I'm forced to find his eyes. "Scared of what?"

"Kyle, Fitz, something was happening. Then you . . . and the boom . . ." I hang my head, dejected. *So stupid.*

"It's not stupid. Security was tightened because there was an unexpected delivery. It's protocol. Part of Wendy's surprise was the firework display, celebration of Finkle's support of my campaign. I wouldn't have left you had I known this would happen."

I'm so ridiculous. I'd bury my head in the sand if I could. As it is, the only thing I can do is burrow into my favorite place and let him wash the memories away. And hope he forgives me for making them.

TWENTY-ONE

IT WAS ANOTHER LONG night. I stayed wrapped in Colin's arms for hours, comforted by his breath on my neck. At two I got up to watch television. When *Nick at Nite* reruns failed to keep my attention, I tried reading. Even *Cosmo* couldn't make it all go away. By four I was on the computer, tweeting, messaging, updating articles and writing new ones. At seven, Colin was in the shower and Ali called to let me know Gram was in surgery. When I was reassured she'd call back every hour or if something happened, I joined Colin so he could make it all go away. And he did, in a wicked, wet way.

Inside the shower, not even the steam could come between us. With my body coiled and tight, his erection sliding long and deep, the worries of the world slipped away. I let myself go, getting lost in his scent and the rough pads of his fingers as they touched me everywhere and made me feel everything. My legs clamped around his hips, as he pushed me against the tile and held my hands above my head so I was forced to accept all of him deep, deeper, proving he was my anchor and all I needed to survive was this, us, him. We moved fast, faster, until our breath became so labored his mouth fell away to my neck and all I could hear were the slick sounds we created together.

When I came the first time he released my hands and they fell into his hair, pulling, just as he pulled the scream from my lungs. The second time, I tugged his head back to touch my open mouth to his. I was speechless and could barely breathe, but I let him take me. I gave him all of me. And when he collapsed against me, spent and gasping for air, I knew whatever happened I'd make it through. I had him. My Colin.

By nine, Gram's surgery is well underway and she's doing fine. No complications so far and if that stays the truth, she'll be in recovery by eleven. I want to see her, but I'm not sure how that can happen with our current schedule and Ireland days away.

Colin's first speech went off without a hitch and we just arrived at the venue for his second. I've been hanging on by adrenaline alone until now. Exhaustion is setting in and I know he can see it under my eyes.

Taking my hand, he lifts it to kiss my palm and then my wrist. The warmth of his lips radiates into a shiver down my spine. I tilt my head and smile.

"You're tired."

I nod. "I'm tired."

"Go to the hotel and sleep. I'll be there by six, earlier if I talk really fast." He smiles his sweet, shy smile I don't get from him very often. The second it settles on his face and reaches his eyes, I see the gentle boy that grew up into a strong man. "I'll wake you up and put you back to bed when I get home."

"That"—I lean in and kiss him, my tongue feathering against his lips—"is a great idea. I'm not going to argue this time."

"Good." He reaches around and pulls me onto his lap. "I always know what's best for you."

"Hmpf," I grunt and then kiss him again. I won't admit it, but most of the time he does. "Come back to me soon."

"You know I will, baby." He brushes his lips against mine once more before sliding out from under me.

Stepping from the car, he approaches Kyle and after thirty seconds James Bond is behind the steering wheel and I feel like Miss Daisy in the back. I can tell by his smirk the joke is not lost on him.

"Where to . . .?"

"Don't say it."

"Boss lady." He laughs. "Sleepy-time it is."

I recline into the leather seat and close my eyes. I try, I really do, but I can't get my mind to relax. Last night brought everything front and center. The stupid fireworks began a rapid-fire montage of our ill-fated 4th of July celebration, and all of the events that followed. Add to it Gram's health and I'm a bundle of nerves.

Sleep is elusive and by the time we arrive and then enter the lobby, I'm wide awake. "Can you give me a minute to grab a magazine?" I point to the rather robust shop nestled in the corner.

"Sure. I'll be right outside if you need me."

He smiles when I roll my eyes. "I think I can make it down aisle two without assistance," I say before heading in. Glancing up once I'm through the door, I second-guess my statement when Alex Miller walks over to the cold-and-flu remedies. Stopping to hide behind a display of children's beachwear, I shiver and reach for my phone.

Then I call myself foolish when Alex is really a look-alike customer with the sniffles. Lord, I am losing my mind.

Heart pounding a mile a minute, I admonish myself under my breath with "get a grip, Carter", and then swing around to wave at James Bond for the reassurance that he's there. His brow quirks up and he flips a salute my way. Just as his mouth opens, his cell phone rings. I head straight for the checkout and wait behind three customers. I'm bummed the only *Cosmo* available is the copy I already have. *Glamour*'s a possibility, so I grab it to read the headlines. As I flip through the pages, I feel the stares, something I'm getting used to, but this is different. They're heavy and heated and many. Looking up through my lashes, I'm taken aback by the woman in front of me. Pure animosity lifts her lip as she mumbles under her breath "You should be ashamed of yourself" and steps out of line.

My mouth falls open and then another catches my gaze, this time not as menacing but it's still a wide-eyed stare. By now my skin tingles. A flush sweeps across my forehead as if I have a sudden fever and I drop my eyes back to the magazines. Then my world crumbles. I glance at the incessant phone buzzing in my hand. *Colin*. When I let it go to voicemail, it starts again.

"Charlie?" Kyle's voice is soft, but I hear it as if it's magnified through a bull-horn shouted in my ear. Even with that I can't move. I'm glued to the *Nation Enquires* headline, and then *Hollywood Hotspot*, then a flick to the left and it's confirmed that *Celeb News* is running something too. There, for the entire world to see is my most hidden secret, spelled out in block letters. *McKenna a Fraud:*

Finances Abortion and *Dumped: McKenna cuts Carter After Abortion* and *McKenna Scam: Campaign Built on Lies.*

All I can think of are Joan's words. "*We work on margins in this business. There's no room for error.*"

The vibration in my hand continues and seems to spread like a virus throughout my entire body until I'm shaking. My knees give out under the strain, but I'm caught around my shoulders. "Let's get you out of here."

The images of the headlines and the angry pictures that accompanied them are frozen behind my lids. When Kyle's phone rings again, he steers me out to the car and shoves me in the backseat. I stare straight ahead. If I could cry I would. This is just too much. But I can't, so I watch life fly by out the window and pay halfhearted attention to the dialogue coming from the front. Kyle's phone to his ear, he says, "On our way, sir. I'll have her to you in less than five."

Every minute or so, he glances in the rearview mirror. He bangs his fist on the steering wheel when we get caught at a light and then pulls at his hair like he's mad at it.

He should be mad at me. I'm sure everyone else is. My worst fear has been realized. Scandal, of any kind, true or fabricated, could cost Colin the race. Voters latch onto the smallest rumor, run with it and have a hard time forgiving it. *"There's no room for error."* Joan's words work on repeat in my mind. The past I fought to keep hidden, has been found and used to try and hurt Colin. He doesn't deserve this.

In the next minute, Kyle is hauling me out by the arm and half carrying me into the back entrance of the Carlton Hotel, where Colin is speaking. Sawyer is waiting to show us to a conference room where Evan and John Montgomery are pacing. I'd like to blend into the paisley carpet and disappear, but before I can try for camouflage Evan's gripping my shoulders. His eyes are dark, his brow heavy, far from his usual, carefree self. The Carter girls are doing a number on him. Poor guy.

"Colin will be done shortly. I'm sorry this happened. We tried, Charlie. I tried to get them to pull the stories back. In fact, I was assured they did." He rakes a hand down his face and looks away. "I'm sorry."

"You knew about this?"

He flinches and nods. "Last night. I got a call from a friend. She gave me a heads up the story was leaked and multiple rags were running with it. You were . . . indisposed. This wasn't something I wanted to add to your plate."

Ah, of course. I was huddled in a corner because fireworks apparently induce nervous breakdowns.

"It's not your fault, Evan. We should have all known better. There's really no such thing as a secret. If one person knows, the world will too. Everyone likes to talk and make it a better story than the one who told it before. It was destined to happen and I'm a fool for ever thinking otherwise." I try for a smile, to provide some kind of reassurance, but it's dead before it's even born. *How ironic*.

"No one blames you . . ."

My eyes swing to John, who's unusually silent, and now so is Evan. I've avoided contact with any Montgomery, and I'm disappointed he's here for this intimate discussion.

"I appreciate that, Evan, but this is my past, my decision and my responsibility." My shoulders straighten as another brick is added onto the pack of them I've been carrying lately. "I'll figure out how to make this right," I mumble more to myself than him, but he's quick to respond.

"You don't have to. Damage control is my job."

Turning toward the window, I wrap my arms around myself and wait and think. How do I help Colin recover from this, or can he? Some of his supporters will despise me just for the simple fact I had an abortion—others will believe he'd lied to them, and hid my past so he wouldn't be perceived as indecisive or playing the line. How do I help them understand he did it to protect me?

There's only one way.

Swinging around to find Evan, I ask, "How quickly can you coordinate a television interview?"

ooo

Colin nods once to Kathryn Hess, host of cable's highest-rated news magazine for five years running, his face completely impassive. If laser beams are my superpower, the expressionless expression is his, granting him cool composure in the most intense moments. Glancing up as he heads in my direction, I feel the full weight of his mood and his fear for me. Superman himself would have a hard time lifting this burden.

Fully suited in navy with a red tie at his neck, he's dazzling, all-American goodness, like apple pie and fried chicken. And he's mine. Even though I've crushed his campaign with one secret and twenty-four hours, he still loves me. He made sure I knew it, too.

After I convinced him telling my story was the only way, and it took a long time—all afternoon in fact—he gave in and then came into me. His passion last night was unmatched. It's as if he didn't want me to think about anything but him and I didn't. I couldn't. Overwhelmed with all things McKenna, I passed out in the early morning hours. When I woke, he was staring at me from the chair next to the bed. Brooding and quiet, his mood carried through the entire day. I know he's worried about me, but this is the right thing to do—for him and for me.

Telling my family has been the hardest part. Other than my parents and Ali, no one knew. I'm sorry they found out about it by reading sordid half-truths in line at the grocery store. This whole fiasco couldn't have come at a worse time. Adding to their stress while Gram remains in the hospital is painful, but can't be helped. I must speak now if I'm to assist Colin in the battle to reclaim his standing in the polls.

While he kept his speaking engagements this morning, I spent two hours with Joan, who flew in to assist me with preparation for the interview. Of course Therese was there, along with a campaign advisor. The three of them worked me over until I was robotic perfection. I can spew out answers to the script the moderator and I will follow in my sleep. Colin will join me halfway through the interview. I'm trying to match his superpower by exuding calm confidence, but inside I'm a mess of nerves.

I smooth my hand over the plain, red three-quarter-sleeve dress hugging my frame from collarbone to just above the knees. My fingers shake as I twist them through the double-strand of pearls and tug them away from my throat. They're too tight, suffocating, just like this studio.

On TV, guests appear to be interviewed in a luxurious, but comfortable home. In reality it's all a pretense. The plush surroundings are centered in a warehouse. Every surface is painted black, lights hang from exposed beams and huge cameras surround a relatively small sitting area. A fake backdrop anchors a fifteen-by-fifteen square foot set filled with two chairs sitting face to face. They'll bring a second one in when Colin enters.

As I whittle away at the pearls, staring into the façade of comfort, Colin's arms surround my waist.

"You don't have to do this."

Tears spring to my eyes. Turning, I squeeze him close and find my favorite place, taking two deep breaths. "I do. I won't let my past hurt you anymore. If I don't speak out, those vultures will make up their own story: I need to tell mine."

His chin rests on top of my head. Therese will kill him and me if he messes the bouffant she petitioned for. It was my only freak-out of the day. When I looked in the mirror I'd never seen anything like it before. It almost reduced me to tears. After all the shit that's happened over the last month, my hair nearly brought me to my knees. I wasn't going on national television reminiscent of Marion Cunningham. After a great many tweaks and a lot of smoothing, my heart beat at a normal pace when I could evoke a tamed down version of Brigitte Bardot. It wasn't exactly me, but I could see Charlie in there somewhere.

"Watch the hair or the bulldog will come after you. And just so you know . . ." I slide out from under him and touch his nose with the tip of my finger, ". . . I can't protect you from her. She's vicious."

He chuckles, but the levity doesn't reach his eyes. A sorrow I haven't seen in a long time fills them. "I'll fire her on the spot if it'll ease this for you."

"No worries about me today and I can see that you are. If you don't watch it, you're going to get a wrinkle right here," I say and smooth out the lines between his eyes.

"Charlie . . ." He sighs. "I'm . . . God, I'm sorry. I did everything in my power to keep this from exploding. I haven't a clue on how it was exposed. I buried it; I fucking dug the hole myself." His fingers dig into my hip and I know I'll feel them there all night long. "I'm so sorry I failed you."

I cradle his cheeks and run my thumb along his full bottom lip. "This is not your fault." After an excruciating moment of self-recrimination plays out in the rigid set of his jaw, he nods and bends to press his lips against mine.

"Okay ladies and gentleman." Kathryn clears her throat when she walks by, "Let's get the show started. Literally people, let's move."

If Therese Wainwright is a bulldog, Kathryn Hess is a great white shark dressed in a kitten costume. She purrs at the right time and then snaps and takes off a limb. She's the best and is so highly rated, John Montgomery called and she jumped at the chance to add me to her list of prey.

Kathryn's all business. Swift directions and points of her finger have staff bustling to adjust the lighting, move my chair by a fraction of inch and tweak the picture hanging on the wall behind it. She gives one last glance at my dress, hair and accessories and she flicks her wrist, a silent demand to take a seat.

My heart races and it's impossible to catch. Panic strikes in an unexpected invasion—nerves I was prepared for. Blinding fear I was not. Fifteen years has boiled down to this moment. I can no longer hide behind it, but must face it head on and accept it as a part of me. Colin takes both of my hands and squeezes, hard. I know he can see my fear, but I'm more afraid Kathryn can smell it. "I'll be right here," he murmurs.

I nod once and adopt his superpower. On my way, I glance back for one last look at him, but Ella stifles my quest for reassurance. She's always waiting in the wings to take my spot. I hate that she's here, but when Mommy dearest arrived she was with her. Colin steps out of Ella's reach and with his move away from her, Joan corners me.

Closing my eyes, I take a deep breath.

Rubbing my shoulders, she says, "Charlise, dear, don't be nervous." Her eyes roam over my hair and they narrow. I imagine she would like to click her tongue, but she just shakes her head. “Follow the plan and all will be well.”

I glance at the empty chair waiting for me. What she means is *put on the performance of my life*.

“Look at me.” When I do, she says, “Do not deviate from the script. Think of the television audience. They don’t want details; they want a sweet, untainted good girl. If you can deliver, you’ll salvage this for Colin.”

My heart thumps harder than before. “I understand.” Pulling away from her grip, I find my chair. It’s comfortable and I think it’s done on purpose. I’m not foolish enough to think Kathryn Hess is the best because she plays with her food. She’s going in for the kill and I have to be ready for her when she does. No details.

As soon as she sits, two staffers, one for her and one for me, retouch makeup and ensure the microphones are adjusted. She doesn’t wait for them to clear out to begin instructions.

“We’ll jump right in with the questions. Ready?” She nods and the lights spring on. Their glare is intrusive, as if splaying me open. Kathryn throws a half–hearted smile in my direction before turning it on for the camera. Her grin grows and her shoulders relax transforming her from hunting shark to playful kitten. “America’s dying to know who stole the heart of our most eligible bachelor and presidential candidate, Senator Colin McKenna. Tonight you’ll get the chance to meet Charlise Carter . . .”

For the next few minutes we adhere to the choreographed questions about the beginning of my relationship with Colin. The dance is seamless—she asks, I answer.

"The crowds embrace Colin McKenna, some have even called it a united front with Senator McKenna as their voice. Do you feel that same welcoming embrace?"

"Touring with Colin is a fantastic experience…

"So, you've dreamt of being in the White House?"

What? I shake my head. "That's not something I've thought about. I . . . I've only ever wanted to be with Colin . . ."

"If the White House is your goal, how will you help him get there?"

I stumble. The dance hits a stride I've not practiced. What would Joan have me say? What would Charlise say? My temper flares for the briefest second and dies out just as quick. Their foundation is not mine, so I respond from a place I'm comfortable with. I answer as Charlie. "I'll stand by Colin's side, wherever he is. If the White House is his future, I'll support him and this country everyway I know how."

"Let's get to the elephant in the room, shall we?" I swear her teeth sharpen and her smile stretches farther than I've seen before. Looking down her straight nose, she goes in for the kill. "Senator McKenna's platform is built on honesty and trust. Americans feel betrayed by his hypocrisy."

Anger flares and my eyes sink a fraction. "Colin's never lied. The McKenna campaign is built on truth—his truth. I've never met a man with more passion for this country and the people who call it their home. He's worked his entire life to make it stronger and healthier—that hasn't changed, nor has his belief in the right to life."

"But you've admitted to having an abortion and he protected you or some would say the Senator hid it from public scrutiny because of the implications it could have to his campaign, a lie by omission. How do you explain this?"

My brow falls and my hand goes to the bracelet I wear every day, the weight like gravity, pulling and centering my thoughts. I can do this. Tears coat my eyes and I blink them away but my throat remains thick. *It's do or die, Charlie.* I won't let my world crumble and take him with it.

"Colin . . ." I clear my throat and look down for a short moment before starting again, "Colin is a gift. When he learned of my choice, he didn't judge me for it. He looked beyond it and opened himself to know me and love the person I've become. No one should hold that against him—if anything, it confirms his integrity."

I hesitate, knowing this is not part of the scripted plan. No one wants me to go into details. Yet in the moment it seems right. I want everyone to know what happened: the events that shaped the woman I am today.

"For anyone to understand, you would have to experience what I did. I hope that no one will ever know this pain, but I will share with you mine." A sharp inhale comes from the shadows. Out of my peripheral vision, I see Colin step forward. To hold him off, I lift my hand to my heart. I'm resigned to this. I never wanted to hurt him or his future and sharing my story may right the wrong that's already occurred.

At first I keep it superficial, reminiscing about my biological parents and the foster-care system, which placed me with the Kerrs. Kathryn remains passive, kind, yet unaffected. She can't feel my pain and I need her to. I need her to be in the moment with me, so I call upon the memories I've held at bay for so long. Diving in, I let them take over and roll freely into my mind. I wrap my arms around myself to ward off a chill and prepare myself to revisit a place I rarely think of.

"The first time, he snuck into my room and placed a pillow over my head. It was suffocating. It smothered my breath and screams as he ripped away my clothes." I gasp, remembering the claw of my nails against his shoulder and face. "I hit and scratched him but he . . . was so . . . strong." I look at her, and my chin trembles. "I'm twenty-nine years old and I still hear him every day. I wake up in the middle of the night and wonder if it will ever go away. His voice, you know? When I met Colin . . ." My eyes flick to the darkened corner. I can't see him but I know he's there. "The voice grew weaker and I thought I could . . . that I might not have to hear it anymore."

I shudder and tighten my arms. "When someone says they'll kill you if you tell anyone and then play it out in detail while doing heinous things, it sticks with you. If I let myself think about it . . ." If I do, I can feel the shadow of his hands, what his body did to mine, and the pain. I tell her and all of America so they experience it with me. My fingers crawl up to my neck and work on the pearls as I do, plucking at them one at a time. And then they're tangled in a chokehold, mimicking hands that squeezed the life out of me.

"He stole my innocence that first night and a little piece of my soul died when he did. Night after night I prayed he wouldn't come back, but the pillow became his fist shoved so far in my mouth it cracked my lips until I gagged on my blood. I wished . . ." I stop for a breath. "I began to pray he would use the pillow again. If he pressed hard enough it would take me away and I could find a peace that fled the moment he entered my room. I wanted to die."

The room is silent; a pin could fall and be heard as if it were a siren. "Every night I'd plead with God to take me and let this be the last time. Then I was saved. My new family found me, took me away from hell and brought me a little piece of heaven. Do you know what it's like to go from wanting to die, to finding a sliver of light?" I lean forward in my seat. "The Carters were my beacon of hope and I clung to them. In their home I believed I could survive what was done to me—maybe even overcome it. They gave me hope. And one morning I woke up and the glimmer of hope died. I was left with a permanent reminder . . . I can't explain to you the devastation." Kathryn's wide-eyed, but I don't know if she comprehends my explanation.

"Will you close your eyes? Please. Bear with me and close them." When she does, I continue, "Imagine the one thing that has brought you more joy than anything else. When you wake up in the morning it's the first thing you think of, when you go to bed at night it's the last thing you pray for." I pause to give her time to imagine it. "Do you see it? Can you feel it?" When she nods, I say, "Now it's gone." Her lids snap open and her lips part. "This was my new home, the comfort of living without fear, the hope of having a future. When I found out I was pregnant, the light I clung to diminished and another piece of me died with it. This, compounded with the emotional devastation of being repeatedly raped, was too much to deal with." Kathryn's no longer the implacable woman who sat down with me earlier. *She can feel me*.

"I wanted to die again . . . and then my new family did something no one had done in six years. They loved me." My armor cracks when I think of them. "For the first time since I was eight years old, someone put me first and they loved me. My parents supported me, allowed me to make the decision to live, because if there was any other decision made for me I wouldn't have survived it."

Kathryn shakes her head before saying, "Do you think your mother had a responsibility to . . .?"

"No, this is not about my mother. Please don't bring her into this. She's the best woman I know." A tear wells, and teeters on the edge of my lashes. I squeeze my eyes shut to catch my breath and it falls. When I open them, I watch the small puddle seep into the fabric of my dress. The well of the stain grows, as does my heart when I think of the great expanse of love she has for her children. I will not let Kathryn Hess bring Anna Carter down with my sinking ship.

"My mother saved me," I respond through clenched teeth. "She chose to love me when she didn't have to. I was a foster child. When she found out I was raped and pregnant my parents could have thrown me back as so many did before without the added problems, but they brought me into their home and loved me as if I were their own.

"I wasn't naïve to the fact my parents wanted to adopt a baby, not a teenager. They wanted a baby and they settled for a fourteen-year-old rape victim who wouldn't engage in living. When inside of me . . . I had what they wanted." I choke on the words as I remember the hollow feelings of disgust and fear. "Every minute I lived with what he did to me and then I thought, oh my God, he's going to be with me every minute of every day for the rest of my life. I will never escape him. Do you understand?"

The back of my fist is against my mouth and I swallow a lump. *Almost done*. I can do this. "It came down to life and death. I knew in my heart I wouldn't survive having the baby, not at fourteen, and not after what Sha . . . that boy did to me." Tears threaten against the brim again and I shake my head to clear the emotions. "I had no control—everything in my life up until that point was taken from me. My birth parents, my home, my innocence, and now the future I had barely dreamt of having. I was going to lose it all if I didn't fight to keep it." My chest rises and falls too fast to rein it in and my face crumbles. Time seems to stop and a deafening silence fills the room. Kathryn leans forward an inch, as if readying herself for attack. *It's now or never*. "I made the decision to have an abortion." There, I said it out loud. "It was my choice. Please don't hold it against the people who loved me through it and despite of it."

"Is that why you've come forward to talk about this today?" Kathryn asks, her eyes narrowing.

I nod. “No one should be held accountable for my actions. Not my parents and certainly not Colin.” I bite my lip and pause. One breath, two . . . “Colin told me this was for me to share when and if I wanted to. He didn’t purposefully keep it from anyone, because it wasn’t his to give away. I’ve lived my life with this secret held tight to my heart, because I was ashamed and because it . . . hurts. I’m sharing it now so you know the truth, because Colin believes in honesty and because I want people to know me. I don’t want to be afraid anymore.

“Please don’t persecute Colin for a decision I made fifteen years ago. He’s an amazing man, whose only crime is loving me.”

TWENTY-TWO

THE DRIVE TO THE hotel is quiet. Evan's riding shotgun with Kyle, and Colin and I are in the back. The entire line of my body, from my shoulder to the foot I slipped from my heel, is pressed against him, but he's a million miles away. My hand is gripped in his and has been from the moment he barged his way onto the set and snatched me out of the chair. Based on the storm in his eyes and the fact he can no longer look into mine, the interview was harder for him than either of us expected. Now he's staring out at the fading day as it passes by the window, pulling on his bottom lip.

I'm not sure how I feel. A part of me is relieved. For so long I've been afraid my secrets would be found and even more so, that I'd be judged for them. Through the strange course of events, whoever leaked my greatest fear actually unlocked the prison gates. Colin's acceptance was liberating, like an infant learning to crawl and then walk and play with the miracle of life, yet there was always something holding me back from full exploration.

Now I'm free to move beyond the walls he built for my safety. I've learned the past can only hurt me if I let it. Yes, I still wake with Shane Roberts in my ear, but he's not as loud and I'm not as afraid. Maybe that has to do with the six foot three, two hundred and ten pound of gorgeous I lie with every night. More so, it's from the power he's instilled within me. The courage and self-confidence I scraped together for fifteen years has doubled under his watchful eye. Maybe now that the world knows, I won't have to pretend anymore. Charlise can go into hiding and take her pearls with her.

The last test is how America will respond to the interview tomorrow night. They'll accept my reasoning and forgive Colin or not. Let the judging begin. This drives my current angst. A wait-and-see game with the answer coming in twenty-four hours. In the meantime, I need to keep it together.

"What are you thinking?" I ask, resting my free hand on the tense line of Colin's thigh. The muscles ripple beneath me.

His eyes are hooded when they find mine, so full of emotions I can't read. His mouth parts, and he sucks in a breath. In a voice barely audible over the sounds of traffic, he says, "You live with that every day."

My stomach clenches. "It's a part of me. Everyone has something they wish hadn't happened. You have Sara. I have Shane."

"Mine is full of light and it hurts because she's not here. Yours is . . . unspeakable, and I made you speak of it to the entire world." He draws me in. Releasing my hand, he wraps both of his in my hair, pulling the pins out so it falls down my back. "Please forgive me," he whispers against my ear.

"Colin." I try to pry away, but he's too strong.

"Just let me hold you."

I do. The rest of the way to the hotel and up to our room he's fastened to me. When we step inside the suite he heads straight to the bar and pours a heavy drink for both of us.

Our fingers brush when he transitions a glass to me, and he stares at the connection for too long. My heart is a wild drum, a mirror of the storm raging in his eyes. “You’re scaring me.”

His hand clenches into a fist and drops to his side. “Charlie . . .”

“You’ve had something to say all day. What is it?” Each vertebra in my spine snaps in line and I’m at attention, shoulders back and head held high.

Loosening his tie, he wrenches it away and flicks at the first two buttons of his shirt, as if he can’t breathe. When he’s done, he drags his hand down his face and then up through his hair. “I’m sending you home to Michigan to spend some time with your family.”

Not what I was expecting. “Come again?”

Forced by my incredulous tone, his eyes connect with mine. “You need time away . . . from all of this. The fallout from the articles and the media attention after the interview will be incessant. This is a good time to get away.”

“Are you . . . breaking up with me?”

He shakes his head, nostrils flaring when he speaks again. “I think it’s best if we take a break.”

“A break. What? I don’t understand this. Not one fucking bit. I . . .” I stare open-mouthed and then at my stupid drink, and at the goddamn robot-red dress I’m wearing. “This isn’t happening.”

“I’ve pushed you too far. It was never my intention to cause you harm—”

“Pushed me too far? What are you talking about? I’m fine!”

"You're not fine." He slams his now empty glass on the bar. "You haven't slept in weeks, you barely eat. I want to lock you up in a goddamn cage to keep the crazies at bay and you run away. A fireworks display has you cowering in the corner. We are not okay. You are not okay."

Oh, well, when you put it like that. "So that's it." My throat closes on the words and I fight the tears that rush to my eyes. "Just like that you're throwing me away because I'm not perfect." *Not good enough.*

Shaking his head, he says, "No, of course not. I love you."

"You love me so you're sending me back to Michigan. This logic makes absolutely no sense."

"It's exactly right." He takes two steps forward and stops. We may be within touching distance, but we might as well be in different time zones, we're so far apart. "I've hurt you. My position has hurt you. It's kept you from your family when you've needed to be with them. I'm giving you that chance. Go where your heart is, Charlie."

It freezes over and stops. My lip curls because if I don't get angry I'm going to wail to the world. I find my fingers wrapped around the strand of pearls at my neck. "You're supposed to fight for me."

"This is me fighting for you. I've been so goddamn selfish." Both of his hands drag through his hair and land clenched at his sides. "Everything I've done is to keep you with me, when what you need is time away. This is the hardest thing I've ever done in my life. I'm breaking you in two—can you see that?"

“I don’t see anything but you giving up on me like everyone else did.” My shoulders betray me, rounding in with two long, heaving cries. “Of all people, I never thought . . . you promised me always. Don’t you remember? Together always? You said it, Colin. You said it and now you’re taking it back!”

“Baby . . . no.”

I jump back from his reaching arm, afraid if I let him touch me I really will break in two. Tipping my head to the ceiling I count to three, but it doesn’t help. I still want to howl at the moon.

“I’m not saying never—I’m saying not right now. Take some time to relax and find yourself again. Time I can’t give you because of my schedule. Stay home and be with Gram. Help her recover. I’ll come for you after the European tour.”

I nod and stare. When I can speak, it’s full of spite. “Is this because you think I need time away or because you can’t look at me knowing what he did to me?”

Anger flares like a torch in his eyes. “That’s not fair.”

“And this is? You get to decide what’s right for me, again. I don’t want to leave you; I don’t need a break.”

“My intention is not to lose you.” The fist at his side clenches and unclenches in time with his jaw. “Your parents and I agree . . .”

“My parents? What do they have to do with any of this?”

“Please—”

“Forget it. You want a break? You got it.” The necklace pinches my skin as I pull and before I can stop myself, because the pain feels right, I tear them free. The jewels fly and scatter around us as they fall, in mimicry of my life. "I shouldn't have expected anything different." I give up and walk to the door. Dropping my head on it, I rest for a minute, but it's really because I don't know how to leave him. I feel his heat before his arms, and I can't help myself. I sink into the warmth.

"Why are you doing this?" I whisper, turning my head until his nose is at my ear. His breath washes over me and for a second I pretend this conversation didn't happen.

"Because I've broken you and I swore I never would. It's the first promise I haven't kept, and this is the only way I know how to fix it. You're my life, Charlie. More important than anything. I will quit the campaign and walk away with you, but you'd resent it. Place blame on yourself for my decision. Am I right?"

I don't want him to be, because then we could be together. "Yes."

Turning in his arms, I stare up into beautiful torment. "What choice do I have?" His forehead falls to mine. "Tell me what I can do so you won't wake up screaming on the few occasions you do sleep? How can I ease your stomach so you can eat? I'll do anything. Sending you home is the only option I can come up with. You need rest and family and time away from all of this bullshit."

"I need you." I pound my fist into his chest. For all that's holy, why can't I have Colin? Haven't I lost enough in my life? *I shouldn't have to lose him, too.*

"You haven't lost me," he says into my hair, holding me tight.

I don't know how long we stand there. Minutes, an hour, long enough our bodies speak to each other and a spark ignites. "Don't send me home like this. Please . . ." I pull away to find his mouth. "Please.

"Will it be easier to go in the morning?" he breathes the question into me, hovering against my lips.

"No," I say and bite his. "But I'll have one more night to love you."

ooo

I don't know if Colin is right in sending me home. Time will tell. Neither one of us slept last night, using each other so thoroughly that when we said goodbye, the promise to be together again seemed plausible. Like this separation isn't permanent. Now, walking through the halls of Munson Medical Center in Traverse City, he feels a million miles away.

Kyle's footsteps echo against the walls behind mine. His presence keeps the link between Colin and me real. Only hours have passed since I left him, but with each moment the details of his face dim. I'm willing to admit I'm fragile. The interview has had a lasting impression. My past roared right into the present and I'm not only sad, I'm tired. The last few months caught up with me during the flight and the diagnostic beat of the hospital is opening still-fresh wounds. Through each door I see Colin in bed hooked up to tubes and machines.

The sounds of life and death are inescapable. I've experienced loss so often I thought I'd become immune to it, packed it away on a shelf labeled the past and moved on. It's how I've lived my life. Deal with it later, Carter: a philosophy that's worked up until Colin. The last six months brought rapid change and obstacles, so many, so fast I couldn't keep them shelved. I'm drowning because I haven't dealt with any of them. This is why I can't sleep or eat.

Maybe it's why I gave up so easily when Colin asked me to take some time with my family. I knew deep down his is a world I'm not strong enough for and pretending to be isn't working anymore. Even Charlise Carter can't keep the demons away. When the façade broke, I imploded. Maybe being with him was a fantasy I wanted to be strong enough to live in and now I know I'm not. Maybe he realized it too and sending me away is the easiest break for both of us—a smooth transition into permanent.

My chest tightens at the thought and I clutch my stomach, forcing myself upright as pain slices through me.

Thirty-three, twenty-six. Gram. "I'll be a few minutes," I say absently to Kyle before pushing through the door.

I stand just inside the room. She's sleeping, so small against a big bed. I can't imagine losing Gram. Not my gram who held my hand when I didn't know I needed it done. Not my sweet gram who sat with me in silence because I had nothing to say, my voice lost in sorrow. Not my loving gram who held me when I was too broken to cry, but needed some connection to humanity. Not my gram, not now when I need her wisdom and her heart and her strength more than ever before. I'm afraid if I lose her, I'll drift astray, because she is one of my anchors and I'm already separated from another one. I don't know how to lose her and not lose a part of myself.

But that's what death does. It takes a little bit of you away each time it visits and memories are what remain. My eyes fill until Gram's face swims before me, and the tears begin to fall. Large drops slide into the hollows beneath my cheekbones and I feel the second they're suspended in limbo, perched on the edge of my skin, readying for their release and the flight to the floor below. The sob in my throat surprises me. I've kept my emotions and memories bottled up nice and tight. Coming home has shaken them up, and I'm exploding with everything I should have let myself feel long ago. Falling to my knees, I let them come and I cry. Silently and out loud, hunched over and head back.

I let it go. All of the anger bottled inside me for years explodes from my chest in a ball of white-hot fury. It comes in a mournful rush. All of the loss sweeps through me. My birth parents, and the countless faces that crossed my path after their death and the death of Charlise Hilton, the little girl lost to the system. The baby I once thought of as a monster, but now see as a victim of circumstance and age, and an inability on my part to see beyond the immediate need to survive.

The Carters—my saving grace, Ali—my rock, Gram and her unconditional love—my entire family, I bleed for them until it runs clean and there's nothing left. I'm empty, a spring garden waiting for the sun. I feel the warmth of the rays as it finds its way into my soul and forgiveness lightens my limbs.

The tears subside and I struggle to my feet. I want Colin. I want his arms around me, and the soothing words he'd whisper in my ear. I want the life that was dangled like a carrot in front of a bunny to entice her out of hiding.

When I look up, Gram is staring with a sad half-smile. In two steps, I take the hand she offers. "I don't want to be afraid to live anymore."

Her fingers curl around mine, stronger than they have any right to be. "Charlie girl, you have more life than most. You've risen above hurdles that would bury the strongest man. You are living. Free yourself to enjoy it and believe you deserve it."

TWENTY-THREE

"SURE YOU DON'T WANT one? I make daiquiris better than chocolate cake."

The sun is bright, so much so Kyle has sunglasses on and I can't read his eyes. If I had to guess by the smirk lifting the right side of his mouth, I'd say he's following my train of thought.

"Is that right?" He lowers his shades and inspects the drink in my hand as if he's been stationed in the desert for a thousand years.

"Yup, and another thing? There aren't many terrorists in the Traverse Bay area, so I think you can take a break."

His gaze narrows and he stares for a moment, but then he smiles and leans back in the lounger, bare feet digging in the sand. "First of all, you never know where a threat may be hiding. So stick with me."

He looks around, as if peering behind the trees, and I mock a salute to acknowledge my agreement. "Second, with or without your home cooking, this is the closet I've had to a vacation in years. I can't drink on the job, and even though you're living at the beach I have work to do—although I usually work for people who wear clothes." Always acting like a big brother, he wasn't pleased when I first sported one of Ali's bikinis. His frustration was apparent when he threatened to pull his gun on the next-door neighbor, as he got a bit frisky. I giggle, remembering Gabe's hug that was a little too long and the hand that strayed a bit too low.

The lake is split when a boat flies by just like it has the last two weeks. Fast and before you know it, nothing but the wake remains and waves are rolling in.

Gram's home, and she's doing better than anyone expected. I've cooked so much the freezer is exploding, as is Kyle's belly. I have a plate of baked goods around at all times to bribe him. I usually get my way when he's well fed and in a food coma. Colin would be proud—a bit of my appetite returned and I settled down to regular meals and good conversations with my parents. The time with my family was more cathartic than I expected. I've had nothing to do but think and work things out in my head. It's not so bad to be inside of it anymore. I feel good.

Unbeknownst to me, my parents have been in contact with Colin for weeks. At first I was mad, but now I know it's because they all care and I wasn't responding well at the time. Colin did what he had to do. Somehow my childhood counselor is in the area and I've met with her every day. I'm sure Sylvia's availability has more to do with Colin than her relocated retirement. He makes everything possible and as always, meeting with Sylvia is exactly what I need. She knows my history and after explaining everything in great detail, along with the flashbacks to the night Colin was shot, my fear he will die and the use of the faraway place to numb everything, she was comfortable treating me for the beginning of post-traumatic stress disorder. Apparently people with a history of assault are more likely to experience PTSD after a traumatic event and the stalking, red room and the shooting certainly qualify as that. Treatment is basic:

understand my feelings and talk about them versus bottling everything up inside.

The media quell calmed down after the Kathryn Hess interview aired. It's been well received—America's fondness for Charlie Carter returned and I've received an enormous amount of support. More than that, it brought Colin's campaign right back to where it was before the story leaked. He left for Ireland yesterday. My heart twinges at the thought of him there without me, but I'm committed to giving us both the time to decide if being together is healthy and what we need. I know what I want, but each time we've spoken he hasn't alluded to a reunion, so I stay silent.

The days in Traverse City have been peaceful and I've lived in relative anonymity while the world thinks I'm still by Colin's side, a place I long to be.

"Do you have a girlfriend, Kyle?" I ask, embarrassed by my self-absorption and that I haven't asked before now.

"Nope, I'm more of a connoisseur of fine wines, you know what I mean?" His smirk lifts the right side of his mouth.

"I thought you didn't drink?"

"Funny, boss lady. I consume when the time's right, and if the vintage is a particularly good year."

"You're gross," I say, tossing a chocolate-chip cookie at him.

He's quick to snatch it and take a bite. "I'm glad you think so. But there are many women who find my charms irresistible."

"Do you want to find someone and settle down?"

He shrugs. “If the right lady comes along I’m all for it. My granddad told me I’d know when she walked through the door. Said the world would stand still and I’d do anything to keep her in mine. I haven’t had that happen yet. Have you?”

My eyes fall to the water rolling into shore and my heart falls with them. “Yeah, I did, and I miss him.”

“Then go get him. There’s no mandate stating you can’t go after what you want. No need to wait for an invitation.”

My pulse picks up, thundering in my ears. “What if he’s better off without me?”

“You’ll never know unless you give him a chance.”

“I guess that’s true . . .”

“What’d Gram tell you?”

I roll my eyes at his easy endearment. My gram is his gram is everyone’s gram. She’s adopted Kyle into the family too, and it makes me smile.

“Charlie . . .” Mom calls from the cottage door. “Phone call, honey.”

“Bet I know who that is.”

I ignore him and hop up, taking a quick jog to grab my cell. “Hi.” I’m all breathy from the run.

“Charlise? John Montgomery.”

“Oh . . . hi,” I stumble on my reply. He’ll always be the principle of fear, the one I’d rather not cross. “What can I do for you?”

"With Evan on the other side of the world, he's left me to oversee the media campaign."

"Ah, I thought I left everything laid out. Pre-scheduled posts for at least another week. Is there a problem with them?" The hair at the nape of my neck bristles and a chill rolls down my spine despite the heat.

"Not exactly."

"Then why are you calling?"

"I want you to resign."

I fall against the wall, my head sagging into my waiting hand. "Is this what you want or what Colin wants?"

"I'm vocalizing what he never will. It's the perfect time. You're gone now, it'll be a simple transition to never come back." After a minute of silence he adds, "Ella's traveled with him all week. She can take over the blog campaign and the social media sites. I'll provide you with a healthy severance."

Ella and a buyout. I know exactly what he means. A Charlie Carter replacement in every way. "How much?"

"Name your price."

"No, you tell me what it's worth to you." I slip my phone from my ear and hit record. Better to have it all documented to ensure I'm not screwed in the end. I may have had a breakdown, but I'm not stupid.

"A million dollars. It'll be in your bank account before closing time this afternoon."

Holy cow. Emotion clogs my throat and fills my chest close to exploding. Swallowing it down, I say, "Not enough."

His harsh breath comes through loud and clear. "Two million. Submit your resignation to me now and it's done."

I bite my lip to hold in a cry, but the tears begin to stream in rivulets. My heart clenches into a knot. "Not enough," I grind out in the most difficult negotiation of my life. I know what I want. "It will never be enough, do you understand? There's not enough money in the world to keep me away from Colin. You can take my job, fire me—I don't care. What I do care about is him. And if you had any kind of compassion, you'd stop interfering."

"Stupid girl."

I laugh. It's a cathartic half cry, half giggle. "You've called me that before." *Sticks and stones won't break my bones and words will never hurt me*. "Thank you, John. This conversation has helped me figure things out. I know exactly what I want. Don't call me again."

I'm quick to end the call, but dial another number just as quick. I need to hear Colin's voice. I need to know we're going to be okay.

"Hi."

"Hi, yourself."

I smile and picture him in my mind. I spoke to him six hours ago, but it seems like forever. "Are you having fun?"

"Fun?" He chuckles and my spirits tumble. "Uncle Niall just drove a golf cart into the fishing pond. We're going to limit the amount of whisky on tap at the wedding. Someone's going to have to watch him."

"Oh, he's okay, I hope?"

"Everyone's doing great. Ryanne's only had two meltdowns so far. Better than I thought. Mom's handling her so we can take Brett out to the pub after the rehearsal."

"Sounds . . . nice."

Unusual silence stretches between us, and then he huffs on an exhale. "I miss you, Charlie."

"Do you?"

"You've stolen my heart. I won't be whole until we're together again."

"When will that be?"

"I don't know."

My knuckles clench around the phone until the tendons twitch. "Not knowing isn't working for me."

He sighs. "I won't make another promise I can't keep. I vowed to protect you, baby, and I did a shitty job at best. You'll only get hurt again if I bring you right back onto the front line."

"But . . ."

"I have to go. The rehearsal is starting."

"Colin?"

He doesn't answer. The only indication he remains on the line is the faint hint of his breath. "Good bye, Charlie."

Tears well and fall as the phone tumbles from my hand. I've had enough time away, damn it. I feel as if I've lost him, that the miles aren't the only thing separating us. Goose-bumps spark on my arms, even though it's eighty-nine degrees.

Love doesn't have an ending. You don't turn it off or redirect it. You'll forever love and suffer with it if it's lost. Time will dull the pain into an ache, but the hole it leaves behind is an open wound. I feel the beginning of a breach.

I can't let that happen.

Colin told me yesterday that Evan's angry with us. Maybe angry is the wrong word. He thinks we're imbecilic for taking time apart, and I happen to agree. Grabbing my phone I call him and he answers after the second ring.

"Charlie Carter, nice to hear from you."

"I know you're pissed."

"I'm not pissed, I'm disappointed."

"Great. Should I expect a guilt trip extraordinaire?"

"When have I ever done that to you? No, I'm just going to give it to you straight."

"Good, that's what I'm hoping for. How is he?"

"Shitty."

"He doesn't sound shitty."

"Well he is."

"What should I do?"

"Listen, Colin's been alone for a long time. He's a different man since he met you. I'm not willing to face the devastation his life will become if you're not in it. Figure your shit out and get back here. I know you love him, and you know it too. So, I'm confused about this whole 'time apart' thing you've got going on."

"It's complicated."

"No, Charlie. It's really not. You're an expert at un-complicating complex issues, but for someone so smart, you're really messing this up."

"Don't hold back." I can't help but laugh. "And you're forgetting this was his idea."

"Yeah, but he's a self-righteous ass. He'll always believe he knows best when it comes to you."

"Kind of like you with Ali?" She finally confided to me he'd broken it off with her just before we got to Virginia Beach.

"Don't go there."

"Why? We're digging deep into my relationship. I think I owe you the same."

He pauses for a second too long to make me think he doesn't care. "It just isn't the right time."

I smile. It might not be the right time, but I think she might be the right girl. "Maybe that's something that'll be worked out when you settle into Washington come November?"

"Let's get back to you, shall we? Colin would sacrifice anything to keep you happy, and right now he's convinced you're better off without him. He's wrong. I've always been honest with you and I'm not stopping now. This isn't a hard concept. The two of you got caught up in a mess, but the chaos is cleared and if you're healthy then nothing is standing in your way. He's got a big life, but that never stopped you before. Don't be afraid to be a part of it and love him."

I swallow my tears. "I do . . . love him, but love isn't the issue."

"What is? Your worth? Your fit in the White House? How you could harm his chances at getting there?"

"It was." I sigh. "Now I don't know."

"What are you afraid of?"

My stomach pitches. "That maybe *he is* better off without *me*."

"What?" he chokes. "Okay. You're not living in Michigan; you're living in another universe. Listen to me. He can't think straight. For the love of all that's holy, he ran a golf cart into the fishing pond this afternoon and Uncle Niall had to save him. He needs you." Evan sighs and I imagine he might be pulling on his hair. "You don't have to listen to me, I'm just saying it like I see it."

"I've always appreciated that about you."

"Thank me later and get your ass here. I'll call the airport and hook up the flights."

"I need to think."

"No you don't—you're thinking too much."

Maybe he's right. Maybe it's time to stop analyzing and let the towline drag me in. Maybe it's time I take back what's mine. "Maybe."

"I'll have you on the next flight out of the States. The itinerary will be e–mailed to you in ten minutes. Get your passport."

"Evan?" I say his name with a growing smile.

"Yeah?"

"Get me a window seat."

ooo

Seven hours to London. The following seventy minutes was barely enough time to catch our breath from the sprint to make the connecting flight to County Cork, Ireland. All of which was easier than navigating away from the airport to the McKenna's estate on the southernmost tip of the Island. Without Ali's help we'd be in Dublin, rather than nearing the wrought-iron gate on the edge of the property. It was the middle of the night in D.C., yet she stayed in contact for moral support and driving directions when we feared the GPS was sending us in circles.

I found myself straying to the right side of the road on more than one occasion and frankly, driving on the right side of a car is just wrong—very, very wrong. Ireland is a safer place without Charlie Carter on the road, but I'm on a mission, and nothing will stop me from getting to him.

"Christ Charlie, slow down. You drive like a mad woman. If you kill us, the big guy will kill me a second time—dead as in not breathing, buried in the ground. Now slowly remove your foot from the accelerator."

"This is me rolling my eyes. Can you see them from there, or do you need me to—"

"Hell no, eyes on the road and pull over. I'm driving."

"Not today, my friend. You drive slower than Gram by about twenty miles per hour, or RPMs, or whatever the hell they are over here. I'm trying to make it there before the wedding's over, not when the DJ's packing it up for the night."

"I'm insane. There is no way you should be behind the wheel."

"If you recall, I didn't give you an option when I stole the keys and hopped in before you."

"Watch the road," Kyle screams just as I swerve over to the left lane, the wrong, but right side of the road. He's clutching his chest with one hand and gripping the dash with the other, panting as he mumbles an apology to the passing car I almost nailed.

I laugh and it feels good, loosening the tight grip holding my chest. "God, you're such a baby. I missed him by a mile." I glance in his direction and giggle again. His hair is disheveled, more so than usual, as his fingers run through it for the twentieth time in the same number of minutes. "I told you to go home for a couple of days. I've totally got this."

"No, you don't. You don't get it at all. I'm stuck on you like a fly in a spider's web, like a moth to a flame, like white on rice . . ."

"I got it! You're stuck to me like glue on paper." I roll my eyes again, this time turning so he can see them for dramatic effect. The long blare of a car horn pulls me from my fun, and Kyle's brash expletive sharpens my hearing. "Okay, okay, I'm paying attention, promise. Do you think these roads are smaller than those in the States?"

"I'm so getting early retirement after this assignment, or maybe the Medal of Honor." He groans, leaning his head against the window.

My smile grows. "That's probably true." I'm silent for a moment, letting the country air calm the confines of the compact car. The hills roll on around us, a green so rich I've never seen it before.

Kyle's shoulders relax, as do his fingers, releasing the death grip from the door handle. "I'm sorry to be such a pain all the time, Kyle. It can't be fun to get stuck with the girlfriend when you want to be with Colin."

Our eyes meet across the seat before he points to the road and my gaze follows his finger. "I won't lie, Charlie. I was bummed when they assigned me to you, but now I realize you get into way more trouble than he ever will. I may even get to use my gun one day."

He has the audacity to laugh when my jaw falls open. "Now, just a minute. I don't get into trouble . . ."

"What?" He laughs harder, slapping his thigh. "I've been with you for a month—let's recap the events."

"No, how about we don't. I get it. It's my life, and I've lived it for twenty-nine years."

"Okay, but you know, boss lady . . . I couldn't have asked for a better gig." He smiles and I return it.

"You're just saying that because you got some home cookin' this week."

"That was only taken into the slightest of consideration. Hey, you're going to pass the gate!" He grabs the dash at the same time as I veer heavily to the left.

A long winding drive greets us, the gravel kicking up under the speed of my tires. I'm going too fast, but not fast enough at the same time. The wedding started ten minutes ago and although we're on the property, the family farm is gigantic. I'll be lucky to find the party by nightfall.

We pass a golf course on the right and a river on the left. Dirt puffs up behind the compact car as I speed past them both. Kyle and I changed into our wedding finery at the airport when we realized time wasn't on our side. I smoothed my hair into a classic French twist after scrubbing my face and washing up from the long flights as best I could. I evened out the flush of my complexion with light foundation and then concentrated on accenting my eyes with a touch of shadow, liner and a heavy coat of mascara. It's enough to change my look from tired traveler to nervous wedding guest, or maybe an unwanted one.

Just over the next hill the gravel turns to cobble stone and a sprawling manor, nestled in a valley, spreads out before my eyes. Moss covers a large portion of the flat façade. A grand entry is surrounded by window after window on the first and second floors. The drive rounds to the front where a man in a black tux is waiting to assist with my door.

I have it open before he's able to do it himself. Breathless with anticipation and the fear that Colin may be lost to me, I ask, "Can you point me in the direction of the wedding, please?"

"It's in the back; I'll have Peter escort you . . ." His words fade as I take off, Kyle left to follow at his own pace. The emerald-green silk of my gown flares out behind me as I run. When my heels stick in the grass I hop on each foot to rip the stilettos from my feet. Tossing them aside, I race toward the white tent rising in the distance. Everything about this property is big: the grounds, the house, the trees, and the wedding pavilion are all equally impressive. Ryanne McKenna has coordinated a fairytale.

I slow to a walk when coming upon a small out-building covered in the same moss as the manor. Staff burst in and out of the doors with various items, hustling to the tables set up for the reception, and back again for more last-minute preparation. Just beyond that is a path covered with arched arbors of floating flowers. The bustle of the staff falls silent as the peaceful serenity of the ceremony unfolds before me. Row after row of white chairs line either side of the long aisle. A larger frame of vines and flowers is the backdrop of the altar, the center filled with the beauty of a bride and groom.

Hiding behind the final trellis it's not hard to find what I came here to claim.

Colin.

He's standing next to the groom, a tux stretching across his broad shoulders. The hint of a smile lifts his lips as he watches his sister say her vows. I can't tear my gaze away from him, not even for a second. Stupid tears sprint to my eyes because he got a haircut and he looks so, so good. At one point he glances in my direction, squinting in the sun. It feels as if the air around me shimmers, or maybe it's my skin humming in anticipation of his touch. An overwhelming need to throw myself down the aisle and into his arms is only subdued by the chorus of awe as Ryanne and Brett say their I dos. Colin frowns and shakes his head, returning his gaze to the couple before him.

I'm glued in place, time stands still, and before I know it the crowd cheers. Every guest stands as the newly-weds turn and head directly for me. Oh, shit.

Backtracking down the aisle, I sidestep behind a row of flowers until I'm clear off the path, leaving it open for the small wedding party. Ryanne and Brett have eyes only for each other, but mine are drawn to Colin once again. He tilts his head down to listen to the woman on his arm and while straightening he catches my gaze. Mouth parting, his chest rises with a sharp inhaled breath. My skin tingles as the gap between us closes and I wait for a further reaction. It doesn't come. His face takes on the expressionless expression, impassive and somewhat severe. Eyes diverted, he marches straight ahead, without any more of an acknowledgement. My hearts drops, as does my stomach.

I'm too late.

Colin McKenna doesn't want me.

TWENTY-FOUR

SLINKING INTO THE SHADOWS of the trellis, I stare wide-eyed as guests proceed to the reception. For a minute I forget how to breathe. My body demands the missing oxygen and I gasp, sucking in air until I'm on the verge of hyperventilation. What have I done? I let my chin fall to my chest, hiding the tears coating my eyes. I can't let this be the end. I won't let it be. But what should I do? I've just crashed his sister's wedding, for the love of God.

"What are you doing here?" The familiar timbre of his voice washes through me and my nipples rise in response. *Oh, my.* I've missed him ten thousand times over the last two weeks, and just as many memories spin around my useless brain—a snowy winter day, pizza in bed, the warmth of his fingers tracing a path down my stomach, lazy showers, racing in a pool, the stubborn set of his jaw, but most of all, the brilliant smile that touches me like a bright star in the darkest part of a midnight sky.

"Colin . . ."

When his arms wrap around me from behind, I fall helpless against his chest and revel in the heat of his hands as they splay open on my abdomen. I'm afraid, petrified my future doesn't have him in it, but I've come this far. It's time to decide our fate.

Taking a deep breath, I turn and smile. It's small, as is his, but it's all we need. I find his cheeks to cradle them. The subtle texture of his barely-there beard and the soft skin underneath are a welcome touch to my palms. I've missed this, missed him. His expression loosens and he presses his forehead against mine. The miles between us slip away and time stands still as we breathe each other in. *So good.* I lift up on my toes to press my lips to his and he breaks away.

"Not here. Come with me." He's got my hand in his faster than I can say "no" and pulls me behind him at a quick pace. Kyle, off to the side of the tent nods and offers a salute with one of my discarded stilettos. I barely have time to acknowledge him with a smile. We fly through the ceremony site and I blush when Colleen spots us. Fanning her eyes, as if to spare her makeup from tears, she tugs on Michael's arm and I wave while Colin hauls me along.

"I'll have him back in time for pictures," I say, loud enough that they can hear me above the growing distance, and skip to catch up with Colin's long stride. We race past a row of five cottages, moss growing around them in mimicry of the other buildings on the property. We stop just past them when the green grass falls away to a rocky cliff and the ocean crashes into it from below.

Colin swings me around so we're face to face and tips my head back.

"You're here," he whispers so low it's taken away in a gust of wind and lost to the brilliant cloudless sky. And then I'm in his arms. His nose is buried in the crook of my neck, and he breathes in deep drags of air as if he just ran a marathon. When my fingers nest in his hair, he lifts me from the ground and holds on tight, so tight breathing is compromised. But I don't mind. I want him everywhere—in my heart, touching every part of me, inside and out, until there's no distinction between him and me.

Over the last couple of weeks I've learned I must express emotion, as tough as it may be. Now is no exception, so I allow the tears to well. Not from pain, but at the joy of having him hold me again. Minutes pass, enough so that our breathing takes on the pattern of the rolling waves. In time his grip loosens and I kiss his neck and then bite it, loving the sharp inhale that follows.

"Don't start what we can't finish, baby," he says, and then I shiver as he brushes his lips up to my ear.

I pull back just far enough to find his eyes. "Who said I wasn't going to steal you away and take advantage of you?"

My heart stumbles from his smile, broad and gorgeous. "You just promised my mother you'd return me for wedding festivities that are about to begin. I plan to take more than five minutes when I get you in bed."

My grin matches his. "Who said anything about a bed?"

His eyes widen when I grind my hips into him. "God, I've missed you," he grounds out, just before his mouth crashes into mine. It's not sweet and it's not loving—it's hard and passionate, deep and long. Every missed minute is poured into this intense connection. And it happens. Where he ends, I begin. It doesn't matter where we are, what we're doing, how far apart we may be—we are *us*. Colin and Charlie. It *is* that simple.

I put my hands on his chest to garner some distance. His hair has fallen over his forehead, imperfect yet perfect at the same time. I push it back so I have a clear path to his eyes.

"So . . ."

"So?"

"I have some things to say."

"And apparently you couldn't do that with three thousand miles separating us."

I shake my head. "No. I couldn't, because I don't ever want distance to come between us. I don't want anything between us ever again."

He closes his eyes for a brief moment and nods. "Charlie . . . I will always want what's best for you. Your well-being, your happiness is more important to me than my own."

"Then you've got it all wrong." I smooth out the lines burrowing in his brow. "Here's my truth. I'm strong, and sometimes I'm weak. During the good times I want to bask with you in the freedom that comes along with them. And when I'm struggling, I need to know I can wrap up in your support and you'll carry me through." I grab his lapels and draw him close to dispel the sadness in his eyes. "I'm going to trust myself, Colin, and I need to know you can do the same. I love you. It's that simple."

I push away and twirl, arms lifted in a dance playing out to his laughter. I'm full, so full of happiness and love. I'm with the only man who will ever allow me to feel . . . everything. I don't have to hold anything back—fear, pain, sorrow or love, so much love, I have it all with Colin McKenna. Mr. McPerfect is perfect for me.

I stop, breathless, an arm's length away. "I can't forget my past, but I can move beyond it. It doesn't define me, yet it's a part of who I am. I'm proud to be Charlie Carter and I'm not afraid of the future. Not anymore. It's an unknown, it always will be. But I can do more than survive it—I can live it. I want to, more than anything; I want to live my future with you."

He drags me in for a kiss, a slight sweep of his lips and then his tongue. "I'm sorry . . ." he whispers into my mouth.

"Why?"

He kisses me again, this time with a bit more zest, and when he breaks away I would have stumbled backward if his hands weren't wrapped around my waist. "I'm sorry I wasn't enough to get you through . . ."

"You *are* enough," I grind it between my teeth and shake him. "So much more than enough. You're my everything. Everything I've dreamed of and never knew I needed all in one big, handsome, stubborn package."

He grunts, but smiles, and cradles my face between his palms, thumbs brushing my mouth. "Here's my truth. I never thought I would love again. Not like this. You've conquered my demons and made me believe in a future that I thought was buried long ago. You are my life, my reason and purpose for each day. You're my heart, Charlie. And now . . ." He flinches as if scared, ". . . I'm going to trust you to keep it safe. Please don't lose faith in me."

Tears that I tried to keep at bay fall over my lids, and I smile through them. "Never. We're a team because . . . guess what?"

"What?"

"Colin loves Charlie."

He bites his bottom lip, and if he wasn't blurry from my sudden waterworks I might suspect he suffered from the same condition. But I can't confirm it because he kisses my eyes closed, and then his mouth is on mine. This time he's sweet and loving, soft and intense. I let my head fall back when his lips trail a path to my ear.

"Yes. I do," he whispers. Days of longing and separation flood through me. Colin wraps me up, holding me close, and takes in my tears. I take in his whispered words. *I love you* and *thank you for coming to me*.

We untangle our limbs and he wipes my face when our names are called from afar. Evan, smirking in front of the last cottage, waves us over to begin pictures. His shit-eating grin is enough to bring about mine, and I gladly hold Colin's hand as we walk to reach him.

"Good flight?" he asks, hands stuffed in his pants pockets.

I don't know what comes over me. The freedom I've given myself to express how I feel? Maybe. The need to thank him for his continued honesty? Could be. The fact that he's a good man who wants the best for his friends? Definitely. I throw myself at him. He grunts when I squeeze him in the biggest bear hug I can manage. I just giggle and say "thank you" over and over again in his ear.

Colin pulls me away, laughing and tucking me into his side. "So I have you to thank for this surprise?"

Evan shakes his head and starts walking. "I was just saving you the trip to the States tomorrow. I shaved a day off your European tour, all in the name of business."

I get whiplash swinging around to find Colin's eyes. "You were coming to get me?"

He nods. "I can't live without you, baby."

Then we're swallowed up by family and friends. Colleen and Michael, Ryanne and Brett, and so many others their names escape me. Uncle Niall is an elder version of Colin, and when I'm folded in his hug he thanks me profusely for rescuing his great-nephew from further depression. Blake and Carla promise to catch me later, as do Aiden and the rest of the Kellys, too.

Pictures follow the introductions. I don't want to be included, but the entire family insists, and Ryanne patches my makeup so I'm presentable.

The whole day feels good. Surrounded by laughter and happiness and Colin, it passes in a blur. After dinner, whiskey is poured. It's no wonder Colin crashed into the pond yesterday if this was what they were drinking.

Dancing is gregarious and silly. I get to know Colin's cousins and friends, Brett and Ryanne, and all of us are giddy until the sun falls below the cliff. Lights sparkle to life and candles flick to flame around us. As the reception winds down and guests say their farewells, Aiden takes my hand for a subdued dance. He's on better behavior than I've seen from him thus far, with hands draped on either of my hips. Mine lie on his shoulders.

The best we can do is sway to the Eric Clapton song. I half listen to his story of Brett's bachelor party and half watch what remains of the crowd. We're one of a few couples taking a break from the fast-paced dancing that ended only moments ago, the floor big enough to allow us room to move.

I smile when Aiden says, "Ah, Charlie. You should have seen him. He could barely hold down the last shot . . ." but then Colin catches my eye. He's talking with Brett and Ryanne. They're animated in a good way, waving their hands toward me and then she shoves against his shoulder. I can read the word *go* as it falls from her lips.

Colin turns, straightens his shoulders and nods at the D. J. while making his way across the floor. His tie is loose and hanging beside his opened collar, sleeves rolled to his elbows. My heart thrums and Aiden is set aside with an "excuse me" for the god coming to collect me. Our eyes never part, and my arms are free and ready when he steps near. "May I have this dance?" He bows, catching my eye, and then kisses my hand before pulling me in.

"You can have all of them if you wish, Mr. McKenna," I say, punch-drunk on love and all things Colin.

His smile is disarming and I lose myself in the dance, letting him swing me around so I feel elegant like Ginger Rogers. The swirl of silk around my legs is luxurious, as is the man holding me.

"You take my breath away," he whispers in my ear.

At the end of the song, his mood transforms and he settles into the expressionless expression, but his eyes are flickering with emotion. The atmosphere changes, voices become hushed, and the only sound to accompany my heighted breath are the first notes to "At Last" when they pipe through the speakers. Our steps slow, but my heart does not. I'm caught in his spell and the rest of the party falls away, so there is only us. Leaning in, he kisses my cheek and then whispers, "Please love me enough."

In one second I'm in his arms—in the next he sinks to his knee.

"Colin." *Oh, God.* All at once the world stands still and I wonder, is it possible to have everything I've ever dreamed of and more? To have this moment, with Colin at my feet, even with a nervous sheen on his brow, more gorgeous than I've ever seen before? Am I greedy for wanting this, for wanting him?

"Charlie." He licks his bottom lip. "I'm so in love with you."

One of my hands is held in his, the other is pressed to my mouth to hold in the ugly-cry I'm afraid might interrupt this moment. He digs behind the lapel of his vest and produces a ring, but the only thing I can see is him.

"Love brings with it a great responsibility—sacrifice and growth and the most incredible experiences. You've opened me up to all of them. I promise to give you all of me, and everything I'm capable of giving. I will live in the shadow of your joy if you'll have me. Please, baby. Give me your forever. Marry me?"

I want to close my eyes and savor him and his words, let them sink into every crevice of my heart, but then I realize they're already there. So instead I drop to my knees and hold the hand that's lifted between us.

"You are my forever." I lean in to kiss him, but he pulls away before I make contact.

"Is that a yes?"

TWENTY-FIVE

COLIN

CHARLIE IS NOT THREE feet away when she catches my eye and grins but it feels like a thousand miles due north. Her answer, *it's a million times a yes,* still rings in my ears. Even now I can feel the kiss that followed along the bruised lines of my lips. As soon as we'd made it to our feet, the wolves descended, namely the dozen or so women who wanted a look at her ring and the men offering a slap on the back and a booming congratulations to me. Including Kyle and Fitz. Everyone, along with a phone call to Charlie's family, has kept her attention centered elsewhere. That's about to change.

The energy between us is palpable and wreaking havoc on my ability to concentrate on anything but my fiancée and what I want to do to her.

Alone.

Charlie's smile lights her whole face, and the blush creeping up her chest is sexier than the Nurse Carter get-up. She can seduce me in an instant. In fact, I was caught by her spell the moment our eyes met. The fall was fast and hard. This time when her eyes find mine and screw into a comical crossed roll, I slam back the last of my scotch and hand the glass to Sean, a third cousin on my mom's side.

"Excuse me, ladies," I say, and slide through the bodies to get to the one I want. The tilt of her head and slow sinking of her lids to half-mast is enough to increase my hunger and my desperation. When my nose is pressed into her ear, I bite it, and then whisper, "I need you so badly I can't think straight. If you're not under me in three minutes I may not fully recover."

I take in her shiver. Muffling her cry with my mouth, I sweep up her legs. This leaves few options, and I'm pleased when she doesn't protest, but opts to hang onto my neck. A cheer from the remaining crown vibrates behind us as I carry her away from the waning reception.

Her laugh tugs at my heart. It's something I will long to hear for the rest of my life, and I'll do anything to ensure I do.

"Shouldn't we say goodnight to your parents?" She asks, her fingers tugging at my open collar.

"Hmmm," I murmur, but it's more like a growl. "I'd take you seriously if you didn't have my shirt half off."

She giggles and kisses down my neck. When she's done biting a trail along my clavicle, she looks up through her lashes. "I love you."

The whispered words hit me in the chest hard enough to take my breath away. When she says it again, my stride lengthens along the cobbled path lit only by the full moon. I'm at our cottage door in seconds. It only takes another three to get her inside the small one-room guesthouse and tossed onto the bed, tucked in the far corner.

"Charlie." I choke on her name. It's thick and heavy in my throat, just like my love for her. I can't look away. The dusting of freckles on her nose is new from the summer sun—my sweet girl. Her tilted head and narrowed eyes hint at the trouble that's never too far behind. When she juts her hip out and her body curves in a feline arch, she speaks of silent seduction. Every man wants her, yet she's mine.

My hope for the future. My second chance.

"Baby."

The hum resounding through her chest is more like a purr, and it's followed by the crook of her finger as she beckons for me to join her. "What are you waiting for?"

Finishing what she started, I slip the shirt from my shoulders. "Would you like to know what I'm going to do to my fiancée?"

"Fiancée . . ." She blushes. "We're getting married."

A smile tugs at my lips. I don't know if I should laugh at her rather dumbfounded expression or jump on her to reinforce the notion. It'd be easy to lose myself in her and the thought of our unknown and mystifying future. But now is not the time to grapple with the enormity of what lies before us. She's here. Here for me, before I could go back and right the wrong I set in place when I sent her home.

I did it for her. To give her time to heal without the incessant pleas from reporters to steal more of her life's story.

Despite this, I struggled the moment her plane took off. Every day was harder than the one before it until I couldn't think straight. I can't live without her. I knew it and my mother did too. After the rehearsal was complete, she pulled me aside and slipped my grandmother's engagement ring into my hand without a word. I immediately called Captain Green to schedule a flight plan to Michigan. If Charlie hadn't shown up in Ireland, I'd be over the Atlantic by now.

Her selflessness knows no bounds. The world she'll live in, as potentially one of the most influential women in modern history, could destroy her. She's strong in so many ways. Yet there's a fragileness woven throughout the very passion that drove her back to me.

I'll probably never admit to Charlie the effect she had on me the day I met her. The thundering beat of my heart hurt my chest. I was alive again—no longer moving through one day only to find myself in the next. I was present and unsatisfied, starving. A hunger I hadn't felt in years warred on in my stomach and in the energy consuming every part of me. I had to have her.

And have her I do.

"Mine," I say it for the hundredth time and now it's true.

The sharp intake of her breath stilts my own. "I'm ready to belong to you."

I squeeze my eyes shut against the onslaught of emotion. It's more than love and possessive pride or intense physical need. My faith is restored. It's hope that our separately troubled histories will not affect our future and if it does, we'll make it through. My life is now more than opinion polls and fundraising and garnering votes. It's not about public perception, or a microcosm viewed through narrow minds. It's limitless, and much more important than the career I've meticulously planned for twenty years.

When I find Charlie again, her arms are open to welcome me home. But before I go anywhere, I slip free from the remainder of my clothes and fall in love again because of her reaction.

All of it intensifies: her widened eyes, the dilated pupils, the spiked breathing and parted lips when I stroke over my length. My name falls from her lips in a whisper, her gaze frantic as it flicks from my hand to my face and back again. I'm stretched in multiple directions. I want to bury myself inside of her, yet kiss and bite my way over her entire body at the same time—worship every inch of skin that now belongs to me. Slide into her slow and easy, yet possess her hard and fast.

"I've wanted you since the moment I heard your voice. It spoke to me on a level I didn't understand. Now I hear it during my easiest moments, and it calls to me at my darkest hour. You're the beginning of my end, Charlie. I'll spend the rest of my life ensuring each day brings you a happier tomorrow."

Her chin trembles when she whispers, "Colin, please . . ."

I kiss a path from ankle to hipbone, pushing her gown aside as I go. I catch my growl and then let it loose when I skim over the dampened silk between her thighs. Nudging at her clitoris with my nose, I groan and harden to the point of pain from her scent and the gasp that fills the silence. Teasing her with my tongue, I draw out a cry and then kiss her before sliding to the mattress.

Taking my time, I rid her of everything that's in my way, along with the pins holding her hair in place. Pure ivory, her skin glows in the moonlight, shining through the window above the bed. It's as if she's a beacon to straighten my course. *I need this woman.*

"Beautiful." Soft curves, full breasts with tight pink tips and legs I want wrapped around my waist.

Her thighs easily part for me and we come together. Hovering over her mouth, our eyes lock, and I breathe her in. *This is living.* I rock into the soft heat of her sex, running my length over her clitoris until she's squirming beneath me. Charlie's gasp is loud when I dip to take her nipple in my mouth, sucking as if I haven't tasted her in months versus weeks. Christ, I've missed her tough grip as she kneads and pulls my hair.

"Colin."

Each time she calls my name it spurs my need to drown in her softness and bring about the insistent pleas that follow. Leaving her breast wet from my tongue and ruddy from my teeth, I murmur into her neck, "I love you."

I take her groan as reciprocation and continue vibrating words into her flushed skin. *I love your laugh. I love your smile and what it does to me.*

Everything speeds up—my pulse, my hand as it skims down her stomach and thigh, sliding up to dip into her wetness. I muffle her cry with my mouth. She's hungry. Stroking deep lashes with her tongue, she claws my back and lifts into me.

I can't help but pull away to watch and feel her tremble around my fingers. "Come on, baby," I hiss into the crook of her shoulder, looking at where we're joined. Our once sweet reunion is replaced with pure need. I know I'm the only one she trusts to make her come. To let loose, and feel. I never doubt it, not like this. Not when she's in her most raw, primal state. Her skin is flushed with sweat, her head thrown back as she arches into me, only until she opens her eyes to find mine and whisper my name. Every time, goddamn, every time I hear it, I fall harder than the moment before.

And there she is. Her gaze pulls me in and we both whisper "yes" when her orgasm hits hard. I pull out of her only to replace my fingers with my cock, in one long glide. *Oh, fuck*. She's soft and tight and rippling around me.

"Charlie . . . baby." I'm panting already. It's like the first time every time.

Her legs round my ass for leverage. I groan as she claws up my back and then down my arms, only to grip the sheets.

"If you don't move, I'll scream. What will your family say to that?"

"Hmm," I murmur into the hair just below her ear. "That I'm taking care of my fiancée, giving it to her nice and slow." I smile at her growl and then laugh when she bucks up beneath me. Giving in, I pull out and then bury myself until our hips meet. "You feel too good." So good, I almost can't go slow and love her as I should.

To distract myself, I take advantage of her neck when she throws her head back into the mattress and I feast on her flesh, licking, biting and kissing a path to her mouth to claim that too. When I do, we both moan and feed on each other for long moments. Finding a rhythm, we rock, easing back and forth. She breaks free to gulp in a breath and I say, "This is me loving you. Do you feel it?"

Her eyes widen as I hike her leg over my shoulder so I can go deeper and deeper again. Biting her bottom lip, she sucks on it until a gasp pulls it free. "Yes, I feel you. Colin . . ." She groans again and grabs my ass to push me faster. "Please."

It's so intense, as I start to move I fear I won't last long. Not like this, with her wrapped around me in every possible way. "I want to savor every minute with you."

She shakes her head. "Next time."

I nudge her nose with mine and then kiss her long and hard. "Every time," I ground out while pushing and pulling into her again and again. And she drags everything from inside of me. All of the feelings I'd hidden for so long. The exhaustion of living alone and the long-standing fear it would always be that way. Most of all, the love I couldn't feel for anyone. I give it all to Charlie.

"I want to come with you. Take me there."

I jerk against the words and her. Letting go of her leg, I sink down, chest to chest, and rest my elbows on either side of her head. I'm so far gone, so desperate to feel every inch of her that I press her legs farther apart with my hips so I can fully seat myself inside. Taking in her cry, I start moving, long, deep thrusts that push her up the mattress each time. Her arms find the headboard, even as it bounces on the wall. The creak of ancient wrought-iron groans into the slapping rhythm as our bodies meet. My name falls from her lips in a rapid-fire pant.

All of it is too much—Charlie, her voice, the breath rushing along my neck and the reality that she really belongs to me. I will never let her go.

Holding tight, I focus on her and the low mewls now bleating in her throat. In return I tell her how good she feels, how much I need her, and that I will work hard every day of my life just to come back home to be with her. "Christ, baby. I'm so close."

I know she's there too when she tries to get away. She always does, it's her tell, and I know it better than my own. It's as if she's trying to escape the pleasure, as if she doesn't deserve it. But she does. And I'll always be the one to give it to her.

Trembling beneath me, she starts crying out.

Colin . . .

So good

I . . . oh, God . . . yes

Please . . . please

I groan at her first spasm and it starts the burning sensation in my lower spine. Clamping my teeth on the soft skin that connects her neck to shoulder, I spiral into oblivion. The best kind, the only kind I ever give in to.

"Charlie." Groaning out her name, I spiral down, pressing deeper, harder, faster and when I fall over the edge, the only thing I care about is her coming apart around me and my certainty that wherever life's journey will take us, she will always be the center of my world.

I'll make sure of it.

○

Thank you for taking time to read *Midnight Sky*! If you enjoyed it, please consider telling your friends about it or leaving a short review. Word of mouth is an author's best friend and is much appreciated.

-EM

Midnight Sky is the second book in the *McKenna Chronicles*. Charlie and Colin's story will conclude with, Midnight Sun.

Look for these titles by Elizabeth Miller:

Midnight, A McKenna Chronicle

Only Tonight, a short story

AUTHOR ELIZABETH MILLER resides in Rochester, MI with her very sarcastic husband and two young boys. In 2013 she decided to flex her writing muscles and began her debut novel: *Midnight*. Published in 2014, she continues writing the McKenna Chronicles with the second and third installments due for release in 2015. Elizabeth loves to chat with readers.

Contact Elizabeth - emillerauthor@gmail.com

**Follow Elizabeth on Facebook at:
https://www.facebook.com/midnightelizabethmiller?ref=hl

**Follow Elizabeth on Twitter at:
https://twitter.com/EMillerMidnight

61869464R00190

Made in the USA
Charleston, SC
29 September 2016